A One-Handed Novel

Caitlin Press Inc.
8100 Alderwood Road,
Halfmoon Bay, BC V0N 1Y1
www.caitlin-press.com

Text design by Vici Johnstone
Cover design by Gerilee McBride Design
Printed in Canada

Caitlin Press Inc. acknowledges financial support from the Government of Canada and the Canada Council for the Arts, and the Province of British Columbia through the British Columbia Arts Council and the Book Publisher's Tax Credit.

Library and Archives Canada Cataloguing in Publication

Clark, Kim, 1954-, author
        A one-handed novel / Kim Clark.

ISBN 978-1-987915-62-4 (softcover)
        I. Title.
PS8605.L36229O54 2018 C813'.6 C2017-906521-1

A One-Handed Novel

Kim Clark

CAITLIN PRESS ·

A One-Handed Novel is dedicated to all of you—whether disabled or temporarily abled—who can still locate your funny bone, even through these interesting times.

Contents

1
The Twelve Days of Xmas

On the first day of Xmas, I try to get into the spirit of the season. I clear a small space on my desk, shovelling aside piles of bills, papers and books, and start a to-do list. My newly dominant right hand is still awkward, so I do random warm-up doodles—your basic boxes, circles and spirals. I practise my signature, trying to capture previously familiar strokes. Melanie Farrell. Melanie Farrell. Melanie Farrell. Then I write Nanaimo Nanaimo Nanaimo, because it's a tricky word to pen as beautifully as it deserves.

Time is of the essence, says a voice from the past. I increase pressure on the paper, expanding the list while considering the relationship between time and waste. I cross off Ornaments and replace it with Photos, opting to decorate the tree with old travel photos. I won't have far to look for the photos. They're in boxes stacked at the foot of my bed. It's been a mere six months since the latest move—another breakup.

But going through old photos means coming face to face with better times—before the emotionally backward Bastardo, before my multiple sclerosis got seriously progressive, before the unwieldy convergence of both under the same roof, which led to my present solo status. Rifling through my past requires a surge of positivity or objectivity or, at least, humour. Best to delay the photo project until one of those moods surfaces. Meanwhile, Xmas looms. There's just so much to do, to think about doing, that my resolve makes a run for it.

1. *Presents*
2. *Xmas dinner?*
3. *Cards*
4. *Tree?*
5. *~~Ornaments~~ Photos*
6. *Liquor*

I hit the stores with my list, starting at the bottom with Liquor—something to counteract the news that my best galpals, Jackie and Char, are currently enjoying a trip to Hawaii without me. In fact, if I was a better—able-bodied—traveller and could afford to be anywhere else, anywhere without Xmas celebrations, I would "X" the whole extended jollification from my calendar.

And I'm not alone in this. A snowballing underground movement aims to abolish the whole mess. I overhear proclamations, both hushed and brash, in the rum aisle. People are actually giving away Xmas heirlooms. Burning glittery thirty-year-old cards. Refusing to buy three pounds of butter for shortbread. The manager of the liquor store admits that he sent the store decorations to the local thrift store. I want to join in the subversion.

When I get home, I see that my Xmas-obsessed next-door neighbour has strung a six-foot rope of twinkling red and green over my front door. I get why he did it. It's my cane and the fact that I can barely bend over to pick up the newspaper without losing my visual connection and landing on my ass. It's the fact that I'm new in the 'hood and live alone. It's the assumption that I need help and want cheering up. All I want to do is rip down those lights, but I just wave and mouth a thank-you.

As soon as I manage to take off my damp coat and hat and scarf and mitts, I modify my list, crossing out *Cards*. It's too late anyway. Be realistic.

1. *Presents*
2. *Xmas dinner?*
3. ~~*Cards*~~
4. *Tree?*
5. ~~*Ornaments*~~ *Photos*
6. *Liquor*

I'm not a total humbug. There's one seasonal tradition I have serious respect for. It's an all-natural event, an elemental backlash. This great rush of wind blows down from the north the very first night the lights are strung and lit so that they swing and dip. They clatter and burst against the vinyl siding with every gust, and coloured shards rain down through leafless branches. Something out there must be pissed off, disgusted by our yearly bombastic swag. Guaranteed, there will be a flurry of ladder activity tomorrow.

〜〜

On the second day of Xmas, I get a voice message on my cellphone while I'm in the shower. Unknown name. Unknown number. I listen to the message three times.

"Hey, Nicky. It's me, man. You shouldn't come home for a while. I'll explain later. When I phone you back." Wrong number, and he doesn't call back. I wonder how much worse things can possibly be for this Nicky guy than for me. I keep imagining him in an old gangster movie, something starring Jimmy Cagney. I can't help but play the Maybe Game. Maybe there's a bloody crime scene and Nicky is guilty. Or maybe a deal's gone bad.

Clearly I need to get out more. Get social. Just phone calls to start with. I'll start tomorrow. Meanwhile, I raise my glass to Nicky, wish him well and delete the mystery voice message. I also cross *Tree* off my list. Environmentally suspect any way you look at it. This leads to the *Photos* strikeout as well. They can stay in their boxes, right where they belong at this time of year, along with any and all associated feelings of guilt. I add *Guilt* to the list just so I can cross it off.

Considering the rate of my fluid intake while wrestling with the pen and the sudden inclination to cry buckets, I decide to buy more wine and put *Liquor* back on the list.

1.   *Presents*
2.   *Xmas dinner?*
3.   ~~*Cards*~~
4.   ~~*Tree?*~~
5.   ~~*Ornaments Photos*~~
6.   ~~*Liquor*~~ *Liquor*
7.   ~~*Guilt*~~

m⁓

On the third day of Xmas, I escape a hangover by the skin of my teeth. As I'm reaching for more ibuprofen, I see my half-brother's number on my phone display. Time for our annual yawp. "Hello?"

"Ho, ho, ho and it's twenty below!"

"Yeah, I saw that on the news, Dave. Winterpeg's living up to its charming reputation?"

"Still got your sense of humour, I see."

"You're staying put for the holidays, I take it."

"Not a lot a choice, Mel."

Thank you, Prairies, for holding Dave hostage for another year.

"You won't believe what the girlfriend did last week," he says.

I can't picture her. "What's her name again?"

"Crystal. Yeah, well, she had some trouble with the fuckin' axe."

"Ice fishing?"

"Nah, just listen. She took the axe, eh..."

"You're okay, though?"

"It happened at the peeler bar down the—"

"Is she okay?"

"Who?"

"The girlfriend. Crystal."

"Yeah, yeah. You shoulda seen her. She lay a lickin' right on their goddam doors."

"So nobody got hurt?"

"Well, I had to stand behind her. It was a protest!"

"A protest?"

"It's what people do now. Where you been? So this dive—well, not really a dive, they've got free pool on Mondays—but the thing is they don't have male strippers, and Crystal says it's not fair to the women."

Dave carries on. "Woulda been okay, but somebody had to go 'n throw more logs into the fireplace. Did I mention it was minus twenty all week? That wind was just whistling through the new window Crystal punched in the door. And the smoke backed right the fuck up. So the alarm went and the fire department showed up. Then things got ugly."

"Dave," I say, while he catches his breath, "you're not in—"

"Not yet, no. And I'm not asking for help. Not that kind of help. I just wanted to reach out to you, you know, at this time of year. Send you a hug or something. See how you're doing. Haven't won the lottery, I guess, eh?"

"Not yet, no. Listen, I have to go, Dave. A doctor's appointment and—"

"You doin' all right? You sound good."

"Yup, but look, I'm already late so..."

"Don't worry about us. We'll manage. You have a good one, Mel."

"You, too—"

Dave gets the last word, wrapping things up with his signature send-off: "Next year for sure, eh?"

Not a snowball's chance in hell, I think, knocking on wood. And so ends my kinship duty, Dave being the sole remaining member of what was never much of a family to begin with.

⌒

I had no idea, until the TV news tells me on the fourth day of Xmas, that fruitcake, like the ones I considered sending to the Syrian refugees, is the same density as plastic explosives, causing havoc with airline security and CSIS. I can see it so clearly now, the suspiciously pristine marzipan with the fuse of holly on top.

⌒

On the fifth day of Xmas, I feel better about everything so I drive out to the big mall—one-stop shopping—determined to make some kind of progress. The lot outside is a wasp nest of cranky, aggressive activity. There's nowhere convenient to park for a cane-swinging leg-dragger like me. I circle on high alert, ready to dart. The designated handicap spots are full. Funny, that. Every other cripple must have left their blue parking tag at home today.

I give up and drive downtown, parking in front of the Boy Scout Xmas trees. I lurch and tap right past the greenery and into the Kink Spot next door.

This is one of the most fascinating places on the planet. I'd like to take my time perusing the thousands of products, but I'm on a mission. I try to find something for Jackie and Char but, honestly, I'm still miffed about the whole Maui thing. I hate being left out in the cold, resent being the odd man out, loathe feeling like the weakest link. Fuck it. Neither of them really needs a damn thing.

But 'tis the season and all that, so I'm compelled to do something heartfelt for *somebody*. I remember a somebody who's actually in need—a fellow MSer who no longer drives and hates shopping more than I do. Sharon's age and her MS are so much further along than mine that she makes me feel nimble. Her wheelchair-bound body mirrors my future, but her warm gaze softens the effect with an enviable grace.

I can't afford to give her a fancy hundred-dollar-plus, seven-speed, sync-your-own-tunes vibrator, so I lower my sights dramatically. Accessible toys don't come cheap. The affordable stocking-stuffer Buzzers are too small for her uncooperative hands to manage. Then I find the perfect gift at the bottom of the discount bin. It's half-price. It's a medium-size, three-speed Magic Santa vibrator. His face isn't perfect, but his hat, suit and sack are cute as anything. And bonus—batteries are included. She'll love it.

I'm so tickled with my find that I pick out a present for myself—the discreet keychain Silver Bullet that *fits anywhere*. The novelty of my phone vibrating unexpectedly in my underwear was wearing off anyway. Especially if the train-whistle ring tone went off.

I pay for the goods and totter out. I'm kind of excited, thinking maybe I'll just jump the gun and give the Bullet a test run after I drop off Santa.

An Xmas tree delivery truck is parked across the sidewalk outside the Kink Spot, and it's blocking the way to my vehicle. My legs are getting tired, and my choices are limited: limp out into traffic to skirt the nose of the truck or wade through the brigade of Boy Scouts unloading the trees. I opt for the latter—shorter and safer.

I almost make it through the line of Scouts when one darts out in front of me, bumping my cane and throwing me off balance. "For fuck's sake!" I blurt out, struggling to regain my balance while watching my bag skid across the sidewalk and dump its contents under the branches of a blue spruce.

"Sorry, ma'am, sorry!" the kid keeps saying, as he scrambles to retrieve my things.

I'm surrounded by half a dozen beige boys of various sizes. They want to do good deeds and I'm a perfect candidate. They ask me if I'm okay, try to take my arm, pass me the bag and the Bullet, realize I don't have enough hands to put one inside the other, take back the bag, take back the Bullet, then discover the Santa. All progress stops.

"Hey, cool!" the little one says, examining Sharon's gift. "What does it do?" Now they're all in a cluster, checking it out.

I gesture for it. "Do you mind?"

He's trying to take in as much package information as he can before he hands it over. I have to admit this learning experience may not present itself every day, but patience isn't one of my virtues. I make a grab for the stuff. "Give me that!" I don't mean to poke him with my cane.

He slowly drops Santa into the bag. "You going to buy a tree?" he asks.

I snatch the bag away, turning to leave. "Do I look like I want to buy a tree?"

"You're mean!"

"And you're not even old enough to be a Scout."

"I'm a Beaver!" he says, showing off the badges under his coat.

"Perfect!" I yell back.

As I pull in to Sharon's driveway to drop off the Santa, I notice the menorah in her window. Oh, shit. I remember now. I reverse out of there like a sleigh on fire. Now Santa has nowhere to go but home with me.

᛭

On the sixth day of Xmas, I wake up with a hug and not the good kind. It's the infamous MS hug, that uncomfortable corset-like band of pressure around the torso. It's anything but erotic. When the hug finally dissipates, I check the mailbox and find kisses on a postcard from Maui that says *Mele Kalikimaka* and a whopper of an electric bill. I turn down the heat, pull on a sweater and practise my cursive. *Mele Kalikimaka Mele Kalikimaka.*

There's no one left to buy for, so I cross *Presents* off my list.

1. ~~Presents~~
2. Xmas dinner?
3. ~~Cards~~
4. ~~Tree?~~
5. ~~Ornaments Photos~~
6. ~~Liquor Liquor~~
7. ~~Guilt~~

On the seventh day of Xmas I force myself to reconnect with my old neighbours, well, one anyway—Carol—because, to tell you the truth, I've avoided getting to know the new ones. After a few minutes on the phone with her, I'm reminded that Carol never really liked me. She finds me useful as a sounding board, but that's about it. Right now she's trying to decide if the tall dark erection pressed against her slow-dancing belly at the Xmas office party was a gentlemanly hard-on since he left his hand on her lower back rather than sliding it down over her ass. I'm wondering what difference it makes when our conversation is cut off. By my finger twitch.

I'll buy more liquor, right now while I have the cash. A bottle or two to accompany me to festivities. To toast the "gentlemanly" hard-on. To toast my twitchy finger. To toast trade-offs. To toast crossing *Xmas dinner* off my list because I didn't get around to inviting Carol, and Carol showed no intention of inviting me.

I'm hungry enough to eat toast, and I never touch wheat. It's one of the foods I've developed an aversion to. I heard that a farmer with MS made a strange discovery. When he spread bird repellent on his fields, it gave him a burst of energy, so he started asking questions. Now there's a study, but I was ineligible because I don't have relapsing-remitting MS, the popular type for pharmaceutical studies. I'd have probably ended up in the placebo group anyway. Now where was I?

1. ~~Presents~~
2. ~~Xmas dinner?~~
3. ~~Cards~~
4. ~~Tree?~~
5. ~~Ornaments~~ Photos
6. ~~Liquor~~ Liquor
7. ~~Guilt~~

Before she left town, Jackie invited me to a party in the condos across town. On the eighth day of Xmas I decide to head over there on my own. Looking in from the street, I see enough interesting possibilities to enter. The room's packed. There's a pile of shoes by the door and scarves and coats have been thrown over the railing. I add mine to the festive jumble and slip past the kitchen. Jackie was supposed to bring shrimp dip, but I'd made no such promise.

Fitting in is a challenge. Disability has an insidious way of inflating a person's social inelegance. And I don't see a soul I know. Everybody here is a J, it seems: June, Jim, Jasmine, Jared, Julia, Janet and a couple of Johns. Apparently, Joe, a local lounge crooner, was here earlier. No wonder Jackie was invited.

I sidle behind a loose knot of men, laying claim to minimal territory. I find a table just the right height for leaning and an arrangement of gingerbread-scented candles to temper general anxiety.

The men are animated, one with wavy hair, a particularly attractive voice and an easy and most agreeable laugh. I catch his name—Justin—and a few attention-worthy phrases: "Magic Hour," "clean or dirty," "wants it cowboy."

My temperature rises.

He's jokingly accused of having DP brain, and my head filters through a disjointed range of possibilities: Domestic Partner, Displaced, Detained or Depraved Person...Dew Point.

His eyes slide over me as he steps away from his buddies into the throng. I almost follow, think better of attempting it, and remain frozen, smiling purposefully at the air just above their heads. I should either go home or find a drink.

Boom. It's Justin, slipping a wineglass into my hand. Gawd, but he's lovely. And witty. And flirty. And a DP.

"What is that exactly?" I finally ask, between gulps.

"Director of photography," he tells me. "A glorified cameraman."

"Oh. Nice."

"In film."

"Must be interesting!"

He gives a perfect laugh. "At times, very."

"You know you should really be in politics or something."

His smile is sparkly. "I'm ready for anything but that. How'd you hurt your leg?"

I weigh my options, whether to play this from the inside or the outside of the disability closet. I laugh it away. "Skiing."

"Cross-country?"

"No. Whistler." I look away like it's too painful to talk about. "It's a long story."

"Uh-oh, you're almost out of wine," he says, touching my arm. "Hold that story. I'll find a walking bottle. Be right back."

I watch him go, wearing my desire like a skin I can't shed. Unfortunately, everything inside that skin is getting too tired to keep leaning. I need to sit down. I spot an empty chair, a small wooden one, but it's halfway across the room. I'm not alone in wanting it. She's brunette, low-cut gorgeous in toasty pink. We eye each other through the minglers, litigate with smiling eyes and cheekily share the seat. Jeannie's a lawyer. "In family law," she says, "the friendly settlements."

I like the fact that she doesn't question me about my cane. And that she's not hard-ass. Sweet, smart, a little older than I am but won't say how much. We argue with each other about who looks younger.

She gives a wry laugh. "Thirty-nine and holding."

"You can't be a day over thirty-eight! Your hair, it's gorgeous."

"You can fool some of the people some of the time."

"So how *do* you manage it?"

"Just try and hang on. Daily."

"You wouldn't know it. I should be so lucky."

"What do you mean? Just look at you. Your complexion—"

"It's just the lighting." I can feel myself glowing.

"Well, I have to say," Jeannie admits, "I noticed you when you came in."

"I noticed you too. You were radiant."

"I was hot," we both say, laughing, and it's true. And of course there had been the heat from all the candles. And from wavy-haired Justin. And that smouldering internal combustion that could be generated by a combination of Xmas cheer, hormones and group chemistry.

I want to find an excuse to hire Jeannie on the spot—legalize this minute, entwine her dark shoulder-length hair in mine. So I kind of lie, hinting that my latest breakup is really a separation moving in the divorce direction. She turns to me, suddenly serious, and says, "It might not be better, you know. Different isn't always better." The chair we share is getting smaller.

I tell her I think I need to see her.

"In the office?" she asks.

Without answering her question, I kind of blurt, "Sometimes any difference is better than none." That comes out all wrong. I'm worried I'll start to stutter soon. I try to relax.

She reaches across my back with one arm and passes me a business card with the other as a hush spreads through the crowded room. Jeannie whispers, "Just in case, yes?"

People are shuffling toward the walls and three kids fill the void. They start singing carols. They're dressed up like kings, beards and all, except one king looks too sweet, more like Cindy Lou Who. She's the star, and she leads her backup well for her age. Eleven, she says. Somebody passes around a hat, and it's filling up nicely. Then they disappear into the frosty night intent on their mission.

"This is my date," says Jeannie, looking up. It's Justin. He pulls up a seat to my right, and she shifts to a chair on my left. Justin sets a full bottle of wine next to my cane. His hand moves to my thigh to emphasize the punchlines of some pretty clever jokes that I'll never remember. Jeannie's not laughing.

I want to punish somebody, slough off my awkwardness onto someone. If Justin brings up my ski injury, I'll correct him and bring up my MS. That will make everyone equally uncomfortable. But he doesn't bring it up. Jeannie yawns. They exchange glances.

"You're tired," he says to her. They both avoid the mistletoe when they leave.

The party's still raging into the ninth day of Xmas. At precisely 2:00 a.m. I find a platonic soulmate, another redhead, a smoking buddy. This is not only a woman to smoke with. She's also willing to carry Justin's deserted bottle of wine as well as an orphan Shiraz as she shuffles and I cautiously tap across the icy patio to two wrought-iron chairs frozen to the cement.

"I've been wanting to find you all night," she says. "John told me all about you."

"John?"

"So, we have good friends in common. And you write *too*, eh? What is it *you* write?"

I get it. Like a bazillion others, she's a writer with a story and wants to talk shop—her shop. I can't bear to deny that I'm a writer, so I go along just for the hell of it but attempt to distract her.

"Puff?" I ask, offering the slender joint from my cigarette package.

She doesn't hesitate, offering up notes on herself between deep inhalations. Judy...grew up in Ontario...moved to the Okanagan...for a few years...then farther west to the Island...as west as you can get in Canada...and as wet...but it's home now—

"Do you mind?" I ask, taking the joint before it's toast.

My smoking buddy looks into my face with one eye squeezed shut and passes me the bottle. "We could be family, you know. It's the freckles."

It's true. We could be closely related, both our noses finely sprayed with the rust colour of dried blood on a white bathroom mat. We could be shaded and dotted with the same cinnamon crayon.

"I'm writing a memoir, but there's a problem," she continues, quickly losing interest in genetic connection.

A short man with frothy dark brows slides the patio door open. "There's John now," says Judy. I don't know John. I don't care if I ever know John. He seems to want to join us, steps outside but then retreats, slides the door shut behind him.

Judy shrugs. "This is so hard to talk about...there's a curse." She's tearing up now, wiping at her eyes with the back of her hand. "My boy-friends keep dying, even my ex-husbands, three in the last year." She fights off sobs. Collects herself. Drinks from the bottle. Takes an extend-ed drag on her cigarette.

"With you or without you?" I ask, forced into speech, heartless. Well into our second bottle of wine, I'm wondering if I'm safe out here with my new sister on the frozen patio.

"Without," she says, staring without expression. Maybe I'm safe and should just keep quiet.

"One husband, the second, had a bad liver. They found him in his house with two hundred, no, not quite, one hundred and ninety-two empty vodka bottles. It was Stoli. We used to drink it together, toast each other, but not so much, you know. His third wife and all our kids—there are five of them—are fighting over his company. He died without a will.

"My last boyfriend, Zane, had a heart attack. And the love of my life, Kenny, his car hit a pole. About halfway up. He thought he was fly-ing. Now there was a fucking angel."

This reminds me, for some reason, of a sex-toy party I went to a few years ago. For the icebreaker, I was paired up with a woman in her early sixties. I drew a question out of a brown paper bag: "Where is the funniest place you ever had sex?" and she answered so honestly it was painful. "I've never had sex, funny or otherwise." Now, that's a shock. Nothing funny about it. I'd tell my freckled friend but she's still spilling her story. I should be more compassionate. A better listener. But by the third bottle of wine I have no heart. And no beat if I don't go in and warm up.

I'm surprised and relieved that Judy hasn't mentioned her soon-to-be book in at least four minutes when she says, "Wait till you read it! Gonna be like five, six, seven hundred pages. It'll be a real page burner."

I don't question the fire reference. "I bet. But time to say good night, Judy."

Judy ties my scarf in a Paris knot while I try to kiss away a too-drunk-to-drive-versus-taxi argument between two strangers. She walks me out to wait for my cab, sharing my last cigarette. Judy tells me I have great legs, which is pretty hysterical because by this time they're working even less than usual. Plus the fact that I'm layered up like a snowman now.

We laugh and some curly-haired woman hollers at us from the second storey of the condos across the way, "Keep it down out there!" She stands firm at the open window, her hands on her hips.

"Or what?" I yell, emboldened by Judy's presence. I shake my cane in Curly's direction.

Judy tries to get control of my air-jabbing cane, raising her voice just a little too much. "Never mind, Mel!"

Curly leans out her window. "Hey, you're Mel! That friend of Jackie's!"

"What the—" Annoyed and confused, I look from Curly's building to the J-Party building, then back to Curly's.

"Yeah," she yells. "Thanks for the no-show! You were down for shrimp dip! Thanks for letting us know!"

Oh, shit! I see what's happened here. Wrong party. I limp farther down the street, out of Curly's sight, with Judy at my heels. I quicken my lopsided pace when I see the approaching taxi. As soon as it pulls over, I yank the door open and catapult myself in. I leave Judy in the dark. The only thing more annoying than a social misstep is having a witness.

◊⎯⎯

On the tenth day of Xmas, I watch three episodes of *Game of Thrones* back to back. A diet Pepsi and a non-medicinal joint accompany me and my buttered popcorn. I flip through the newspaper with greasy fingers and come across my horoscope. It says spend some time with my main squeeze. I love that term and, right now, my "main squeeze" is me. It's date time and I don't want a quickie.

Despite the mood-setters—fresh sheets, dim lighting, scented candles, sultry blues tunes and an array of colourful gadgets—I can't quite get there. I'm this close, this close to release, but for some reason this particular orgasm is eluding me.

Every body failure, even a genital one, is a niggling concern when you have a progressive disease. I can't help but play the Maybe Game. Maybe the numbness is spreading up my leg. Maybe it's spreading down from my arm. Maybe it's spreading to my right side. Maybe this orgasm didn't happen because I'm too tired or I'm dehydrated or I'm too hot or everything's getting worse really fast and I'll wake up in the morning totally paralyzed. Maybe I won't.

What a capricious rabbit hole of a game Maybe is. I mentally print "For two or more players" on its imaginary box. I add "Warning: Do not play the solitaire version, especially in December."

I blow out the candles, put away my toys and aim for the positive effects of sleep but I do it in a roundabout way through a book, any book. It usually only takes a couple of pages but tonight I read three chapters. I may have to count sheep.

I get up for one last late pee so I don't have to get up for a ridiculously early pee.

My body comes back to me through the mirror when I step into the pale column of light pouring through the bathroom skylight. This body is not thin. Not beautiful. Not free of scars or flaws. But truly familiar. Not reliable in the least, but in the mirror, a hopeful friend.

A mirror, a moon and a solitary pulsating star. What more could one ask for?

I step into shadow, lean against the counter, my back to the mirror, admire the heavens, the starlight, and take pleasure in the clear definition of the chipped Arborite, the horizontal pressure, the cool sharpness. My instinctive fingers' gentle flutter of encouragement reminds me to be patient. The stroke of chimes from the old clock in the cupboard spells "Be kind." This is pure me being kind to my friendly body. Straight up. Honest. Standing has always been the best, anyway. Just to see if I can bring myself to my knees. It's a revelation. An epiphany. And before I know it, before I know it I'm absolutely—absolutely—

there.
It is a

fucking
(well
almost)-
miracle.
The best.
The best.
The best.

I stand my ground. Hold on to the coming until the moon has crept almost out of sight. Knees buckle but I stay on my feet. Turn and kiss my face in the mirror. These may not be lips to dream about, but for now they'll do just fine. Subtle lips. A little thin but sensitive. Kiss my cool mirror lips. As chill and sweet as a West Coast spring rain. Merry sweet Xmas.

I feel energetic, sexy, clear-headed. Creatively optimistic enough to visualize a bright shiny new year.

2
Chicken in Mourning

It's time to kick last year to the curb and officially welcome the new one. February may seem a little late, but it takes time for me to muster enough energy to organize a celebration that includes my best buddies. Not pizza or takeout or a pity potluck. This dinner party is going to be special. And civilized. And fun. I'm excited!

I'm also nervous. I want to prove that I still have some abilities, that I can be independent, and that's harder to do with friends who've known me as a fully functional person than it is with strangers who haven't. It takes work to appear capable, never mind making it look effortless. I have a lot to do.

The kitchen—just a corner of my suite—is still a mess. Luckily, my Tombstone Tiramisu has been chilling all night. Chillin' like me until I notice the reminder card on the fridge door. My yearly MS checkup is this afternoon, not next week like I'd thought. These appointments are so hard to come by that I wouldn't even consider cancelling. Nor do I want to. My neurologist might have some novel brand of hope to offer.

Measuring out my energy, I do enough dishes to clear a workspace on the only counter and start prepping the main course, Chicken in Mourning. This is a recipe for new beginnings. I can feel it in the act of emptying the body cavity, rinsing it and patting it dry, inside and out. I can feel it in the blast of Bif Naked's old *Purge* track.

The phone rings like it always does when you're up to your elbows. What now? I wash my hands. "Hello?"

"Hi, Mel," says the familiar voice.

"John. What's up?" I'm suspicious of rejection, ready to argue, cajole, arm-twist through the phone line.

"How goes it?"

"It goes fine. Why?"

There's the briefest hesitation.

"Don't tell me you're not coming."

"Uh, I'm not coming."

"Why the hell not? I've planned everything! You said this was a good day! Seriously. You do this every—"

"Hang on. Let me finish. I can't make it for dinner. But I can get there by about nine. Is that too late to bother? Should I just skip it?"

"No, just come. Come for dessert. Char and the hubby are coming and—"

"Glen's now 'the hubby'?"

"I meant Glen. Dave rubs off on me. I talked to him at Xmas."

"Your brother's coming?"

"Gawd, no. But Jackie's bringing her new boyfriend—the one from the internet dating thing. I think Cameron's his name. So they're all coupled up, and I'll be the odd man out. I need another odd man... plus, I've missed you. You're so busy these days. You know, right?"

"Uh-huh."

"And, inevitably, Jackie will come up with some anecdote from Maui."

"Still a sore point?"

"No, I'm over it, totally. But you know what they brought me? One of those stupid T-shirts that says 'Get Leid.' Leid like the flowers. And it's extra extra extra large! You know the—"

"Mel, Mel!" John laughs. "I'll see you at nine. Wear the shirt."

"Not in this lifetime. Nine at the latest, yes?"

"At the latest." Click.

I wonder how we've been friends for so long without spoiling it with sex in one of those sloppy-drunk desperate moments.

〰️�``

Back to my recipe. I used to love to cook. Ah, maybe I still do. This recipe is written in such a sensuous way that I don't know whether to be famished or aroused. Slide your fingers under the breast skin, it says. Overlap paper-thin layers of black truffles under the skin. My mouth is watering. This recipe should really be reserved for lovers.

I tenderly place the dark aromatic slices under the skin, across the breasts, along the leg. It actually says to tuck a couple of slices along the inside of the thigh. Then I turn the bird and slip in more along the shoulders below the neck.

Charlene's coming tonight and she has a beautiful neck, a few springy ringlets always evading capture, sassy blond bun enhancing her height. A tall attitude, that woman. She always brings veggies, long lean carrots, string beans, English cucumber. Freudian pods and peels. She'll give my poultry a pass at dinner—too meaty, too avian.

I mustn't let slip the fact that I blew my budget on the truffles. She'll jingle her bangles and crystals and remind me about her New Age, clairvoyant monetary successes. She'll tell me to find my passion, that people will buy if you just believe. Tut-tut me as if I'm irredeemable. Like an outdated coupon. She'd tell me how to live hopefully so I can enjoy life later, but what about now?

Looking down at the bird, my Chicken in Mourning, I envision the finished product, the dark veil of truffles under its golden, crisp, translucent skin—a beautiful chicken widow with a dusky mantilla trailing to her footless ankles. A delectable bird. I can almost taste her.

The fine art of trussing is next. I follow the detailed instructions carefully. Slip the string under the bird above the legs, pull the ends along the breasts, the tail, the wing tips, pull snugly to the body, wrap three times. It feels so ritualistic, maybe I should write the word SEX in caps on a piece of paper and insert it in the widow's body before baking—a steamy dispatch sent up through the stove vent to a literate spirit. Tying up the loose ends makes me shiver. Perfect timing. I have to get across town to the clinic.

I put my chicken in the fridge, slap some colour on my cheeks and grab my coat. So far, so good, Mel. I'm barely frazzled, and I can even rest my legs on the drive.

$\sim$

As I wheel into the parking lot, my first visit to the clinic comes back to me in all its embarrassing glory. Suddenly I can see myself standing in the doorway of the waiting room, not only anxious but bewildered. Patients were parked with caregivers and mobility devices. No one looked like me. I thought *good*, no young ones here struggling to be able. Then I thought *bad,* how many fucking years can you survive with a disabling disease like MS?

When I headed over to the receptionist, I felt all those waiting faces swing in curious unison to watch me negotiate the room with my cane. I wanted to give them stink eye or moon them or wave a wreath of garlic.

"Can I help you?" name-tagged Mary had asked.

"I have an appointment with Dr. Sharni for two o'clock."

Mary was one big old frown. "Dr. Sharni? For the MS Clinic?"

I've dealt with Marys before. It was time somebody assertive straightened this Mary out. "That's right," I'd said. "And don't tell me I'm already lost in the system. And do not tell me he's not here!"

"He's not here." Mary had picked up her phone. "Hello, hello," then, "Hold, please." She'd cradled the ergonomically correct beige receiver into the hollow of her blue turtleneck and turned her attention back to me. "I *mean* this isn't the MS Clinic."

"What do you mean, it *isn't*? This is where they told me to come." There's something wrong here, I thought. Why should I trust this Mary, anyway? I'd felt a flush. I was pinking up like Mary's lipstick. The eyes on my back were becoming downright intrusive.

"No. It's *usually* here," she'd said, "but it's *Friday.* Today is the Alzheimer's Clinic. We share the space on alternate days. Are you sure it's not the Alzheimer's you wanted?"

I suddenly identified as disorganized, stupid, forgetful. Were these the cognitive issues I'd been warned to watch out for? Wait a minute, no. No! I knew exactly what had happened and I was annoyed, pissed right off. Somebody screwed up—probably Mary!

"There must be some mistake, Mary." I'd dug in my purse for my reminder card, something we could both trust a hundred percent. We'd tussled with the card, finally examining it together.

The mistake...it was mine. "Oh," I'd said, waving Mary off and backing toward the exit. A sandwich board outside the door read Alzheimer Clinic Today in big purple letters.

I remember how lucky I felt that day to have only the MS mess.

m—

Today, when I see Dr. Sharni approaching the waiting room, I feel lucky all over again.

He scans the room. "Melanie. Melanie Farrell."

He's tall, angular and lovely as ever—crinkly blue eyes that perfectly match his conservative blue shirt and navy tie. He's not my type at all but I like to imagine slipping off his glasses, loosening that tie and tearing the buttons off that blue shirt with my teeth. He always makes me feel like I'm a special part of his medical club. Like I'm not just a folder full of notes or a medical puzzle.

I follow him down the hall to his office.

"So, Melanie, how are things? Still taking classes?" he asks, settling back in his swivel chair for a comfy chat. I want to hug him, squeeze him in his swivel chair, climb into his lap while he pats my back.

"I'm pretty good. It was just one class at the college."

"English, wasn't it?"

"Writing. Nothing serious. It's all done now." I don't tell him that I quit after a month, that I couldn't keep up or that the hillside campus was a challenge. "I've needed the cane more." But I'm quick to reassure him. "Actually some things are better." I don't mention that I'm living on my own. I try to retain information control and to keep my adrenaline up so I can show him, prove to him that I am no worse, that I'm not a dysfunctional person.

"Well, good. Let's take a walk then," says Dr. Sharni. This is the cue for my performance.

He holds my cane, observes my ambulation, the way I swing my left leg out so that my drooping foot clears the waxed floor. I lurch to the end of the hall, trying to overpower my progressive disease. I only cheat twice, reaching out for the wall, but stumble before I'm halfway back.

He swoops in, taking me in his arms. "Do you surf, Melanie?"

I look into his eyes, get a whiff of his aftershave. This is it. This is rom-com but in real life. He's asking me out on a date—a hot, albeit odd, wet adventure. "Surfing? I think storm watching might be more, you know..."

He pats my shoulder, offers my cane. "You do have a sense of humour. I mean couch to wall, counter to table. Surely, at home you must—"

The idiot that can only be me blushes raspberry, leg-swings and wall-cheats straight back to his office ahead of him, nattering over my shoulder. "Oh. Oh, *furniture* surfing. Um, sure, I guess I do, but only sometimes. Like a baby learning to walk, isn't it, but at the opposite end of the curve, *un*learning it?"

He doesn't comment.

My cane is set aside when I stand next to the exam table, facing Dr. Sharni. I brace myself for the next test. It's a lot like those team exercises where you let yourself fall back into the arms of your waiting teammates. Only this time I don't have to consciously fall back. I just close my eyes. The falling happens without my knowing. I can't tell I'm tilting through air until my only teammate, Dr. Sharni, grips my arms to stop me and my eyes fly open. It's too scary for inappropriate thoughts. I survive, get control, slow my heart, not from the feeling of falling but from the lack of it. Without my visual connection, I am incapable of erection, not *an* erection but the uprightness kind of erection.

"Mm-hmm," my teammate doctor acknowledges, and motions me onto the table. I slip off my shoes, climb up and swing my legs while he records his findings.

We move on. He strokes my cheeks. His fingers are silky, the effect, titillating. Oblivious, he asks, "How's the sensation here? Here? Anything different?"

I give my head a tiny shake, no. I want to draw his titillating fingers into my mouth with my tongue.

"Trouble swallowing?"

"Swallowing's just fine," I assure him.

"Cover one eye. Follow my finger," he says, and my eyes both follow pretty well, I think. Then taking my right hand, he places it near his shoulder, but instead of asking me to dance, he lets go of my hand, saying, "Okay, touch your nose." This is easy until I switch hands. My left hand forgets how to find its way to my nose. It falters, searches my memory bank for directions, lands closer to my mouth. It's a bad connection. My proprioception is faulty.

Reflexes are next. The "bad" side is always a fascination. It seems logical that there would be little response along with the numbness and tingling, but the left knee flings up the lower leg with such ferocity it could be detrimental to Dr. Sharni's private parts if he were less wary. He also does the Babinski reflex test, running his key up the bottom of each foot, heel to toe, like I'm a newborn. My feet curl and splay in opposite directions.

We go through all the strength tests. In various positions I pull and he pushes or he pulls and I push. I play hard to prove I still can.

Now come the sharpie challenges. He pokes my extremities repeatedly with a long pin. I respond with "sharp" or "pressure" unless I can't feel it at all, in which case I remain mute wondering what the hell is taking him so long.

"There is a bit of improvement, actually," he says, adding notes to my file.

I have succeeded in pleasing him. "Enough to slide me down the scale?" I ask. I'm talking about the Kurtzke Expanded Disability Status Scale. I resent the very existence of this scale but always ask, need to know. Am I changed? By these numbers less is more.

"No. Sorry, Melanie. Your upper strength, your resistance, is improved but your reliance on the cane bumps you up to a six. You need to be able to walk one hundred metres without assistance."

I move to get off the table. "I can try it again."

He pats my shoulder. "You've likely done more than enough for today."

"But that puts me closer to ten than zero. Closer to death by MS than symptom-free."

"Death by MS is a very rare occurrence. Have you felt depressed lately? It's common with MS."

"I'm not some sad chicken."

"I wasn't implying—"

"I'm not afraid of dying," I jump in. "And I'm not scared of living either. It's the chunk in between."

"Yes, well..."

"It's the complications..."

"Let's not jump the gun, now."

"Oh, I won't be needing a gun. But I am planning a Wild West theme. A hero with a hypodermic holster and a couple of pill-bottle bandoliers slung across their chest. A big old stetson. And—"

"Melanie..."

"Chaps! Chaps are a must. You can do chaps, right? The hero, I mean. Oh, and a bottle of whiskey, Canadian of course, hanging from the IV pole and maybe—"

"Listen, Melanie..." He's slightly less attractive when he's serious.

"Oh, c'mon, Doc," I say, smiling. "It's a long way off. Let a girl dream."

"The legalities are still far from clear. In the meantime, there's research and you're nowhere near—"

"I know. I know. And if the research doesn't pan out in time, maybe my Wild West theme will become a clear legal option."

We both sigh.

I tone down my voice. "Five just felt better. You know?"

"I do know," he says, "but six is a huge area on the scale. And the scale isn't perfect. It's just, well, no one's come up with a better way of measuring disability. It's difficult to knit together eight neurosystems."

Thoughts of the future are overwhelming, so I vow to stay in the present. But the present is rather complicated. While Dr. Sharni scribbles in my chart, I just concentrate on formulating a mental list of those eight neurosystems. *Cerebral. Visual. Cerebellar,* which reminds me of a Jellicle cat. *Brain stem,* which reminds me of gardening. I wanted to grow Graceful, row after row of it in my garden, an abundance of brain flowers on fragile stems against the porch steps at my feet. Damn. What are the others? *Pyramidal. Bowel and bladder*—how could I forget that one? *Sensory.*

"Things aren't bad overall." He has that ever-optimistic tone of voice, so I'll follow his lead, relieved, and put an up look on my face. "There is one other thing we should talk about," he goes on.

"Something new to try, you mean?" I've been pretty game so far. Tried the steroids, a few different drugs, a few hundred injections, having all my amalgam fillings replaced. Hell, I even tried rubbing ostrich oil into my skin, but I got tired of smelling like turkey dinner. The neighbourhood cats sure loved me though. I'm grasping at straws. "What about scorpion venom? I heard it was hot in Hong Kong. And it might be more fun than the bee sting therapy."

"Scorpions aren't that far along in the research yet."

"What about fecal implants? You know, that gut-brain connection. Sharing good bacteria through—"

"There's really nothing new, Melanie, nothing that's proven, but I'll make sure and let you know if anything promising comes up. There are always studies."

But I'm already at six.

Dr. Sharni goes on, "Speaking of studies, we got the results back from the Sexual Neuro-Response study. Do you still want to know how the study went?"

"Sure," I say, shrugging. Then I panic. "Is there something I should know?"

"Nothing life-threatening or anything like that. But the data collected from you does show that you have a diminished number of orgasms before your sensory nerves will stop responding. According to your file you've had a pretty inactive or lost libido for quite some time, since the onset, really. It's common with MS. We've talked about it." He looks a bit concerned.

I keep a straight face while I digest this for all of ten seconds. That lovely libido only reappeared in the last few months. So I'll just turn it off again, shut it down. There are more important things in life. People lose their libidos all the time.

I decide the course I'll take before I respond. "You had me worried for a minute. How can they make a scientific prediction like that?"

"They've been most successful in their estimations."

"So what's my magic number? A hundred? Two hundred?"

"The number they've given you is six. You have six orgasms. The research, the technology...it's amazing really."

"Right. Amazing. Now we just need something equally amazing to get rid of the MS." I put my shoes back on. "Six, you say? Absolutely six?" But every orgasm is so different, an erotic entity with its own personality.

"They've been very accurate."

"Is it treatable?"

"There's nothing to date. Are you sure you don't want to speak with our psychologist, Ruth? I think you've met with her before. We could line up an appointment."

I have two reasons to avoid this. Ruth was witness to my previous meltdown, and Ruth rhymes with truth. "I don't need to see her. I'm fine. Really. It's just weird, two sixes in the same day. Maybe it's a sign."

"Just coincidence," he says with a quiet laugh. My time's almost up. I can feel it. He reassures me, and gets up out of his chair.

"Anyway," I go on, "I'm relieved it's nothing worse. And the cane, well, I'm almost used to it."

"You manage just fine with it. And they are working on the research. Something may come up." Dr. Sharni sees me to the door, resting his hand against my shoulder blade. "Keep in touch, Melanie."

"Thanks." Why do I always say thanks, no matter what? What a weird relationship. Keep in *touch*.

That word *touch* sticks with me as I weave back out through the waiting room and finally to the sanctuary of my old car. Van, really. *Touch.* I repeat the word until it stops making sense. But as I pull into heavy traffic, the word I can't shake is *six*.

n~

By the time I get home, park, pick up the newspaper and get in the door, I'm exhausted. Still trying to think tough instead of touch. Life is too fucking bizarre. I'll have a drink or six. Six! I'll put my feet up, even the good one. I carry the wine bottle under my arm, my favourite glass in hand—the orange one, the biggest—and the corkscrew in my pocket. Settle down, Mel, I think, as I lean back into the couch. I should buy this wine by the case so I don't have to go to the liquor store so often. They're starting to call me by name.

I really can't let all this—especially this orgasm thing—bother me. The latent stress of post-clinic reality strangles me. The thought of people, guests, overwhelms me. I could postpone, call off the dinner. These friends would understand, but stubborn pride demands another performance. I don't really want to be alone anyway. I know myself at least that well. I can always sort my life out in a crowd. It takes the edge off.

Maybe I should have ordered that Swedish wallpaper—the cocktail party in a twenty-foot pre pasted roll. My living room would be papered with life-sized, non-judgmental paper dolls—some solo, others in random groupings. Or maybe a costume party would be better. Oh, man. It reminds me of that goth party. Everything reminds me of something else. Like that girl called Abattoir with the black star nipples or the pale powdered vampire with the ten-inch Zippo. Like the necking Kiss imposters and shadow puppets and me dancing and toasting and holding court at the head of the smoking table, a martinied matriarch with a bottomless bag of tricks. It feels like another life but it's not. It's all greedily mine.

I have an hour. One hour. Why did I think I could do this dinner easily? My chicken widow is still mourning in the fridge. The guests are coming at six. *Six*. "Let it go," I warn myself. "Six is just a number." But it's a minuscule number that feels like the remainder at the end of pages and pages of long division. This should not be a math problem. Especially when my libido had just rebooted itself! Six is so close to sex that even the curlicue numeral becomes a visually erotic tendril. That seductive character is everywhere. Channel 6. Page 6. February 6, open a 26er.

It's time to get occupied instead of preoccupied. Let's see, we need all *six* chairs.

The microwave reads 5:16 when I hear the doorbell, but people are always ringing the doorbell here, so I listen for a voice that I recognize. It's Jackie. Jackie's got a key so I don't have to get up in case I can't. Why is she always early though? It's a personality flaw. And now it's too late to cancel.

"Come on in," I call vaguely toward the door as I move to the kitchen to posture. I'll put on my imaginary host hat, get seriously cheery. It's either buck up or fuck up—both of which I've had considerable experience with. It'll be fine. It'll be great.

"It's just us, Mel." I hear both reassurance and a coded warning in Jackie's voice. She's making sure I'm not doing anything I wouldn't want a stranger to see. It must be her date, Cameron.

"Jackie. You're finally here," I half joke, and she bustles her food and drink out of the arms of her attractive accomplice and into my kitchen, which suddenly feels more like her kitchen. This doesn't sit well. It's *my* dinner.

I find my manners, face the new man. "I guess you've figured out I'm Melanie, Mel if you like. You must be Cameron," I say, smiling, balancing against the counter and reaching out my hand to take his much warmer one.

"Actually, I'm Marvin." He's still holding my hand.

I'm trying to get my head around the switch-up, recover my manners and figure out why that name tickles something in my memory. "Sorry, Marvin. Of course! My mistake."

Jackie gives a little laugh, saying, "Oh, Mel..." as though I need to be humoured, forgiven for one of my endless shortcomings. She tosses her coat, smooths her already tidy hair and rolls up her sleeves.

I'm thinking of pushing Jackie right out of my quasi kitchen when Marvin asks, "Now, what can we do, Mel?"

Suddenly, I'm happy to acquiesce, give up culinary control. "Well, she's still in the fridge. I haven't made it as far as the oven yet. Three seventy-five, if you would, Jackie. And, Marvin, could you pour some wine? The bottle's by the couch. Unless you'd prefer something else. Beer's in the fridge. Glasses are here," I say, pointing in the general direction of the cupboards. You can tell a lot about a person in a new situation, especially in your own territory. Marvin seems smart, relaxed, but curious. As though he expected something worse.

I whisper to Jackie, "Who is this Marvin? And what happened to Cameron?"

She ignores my question. "Why are you calling our dinner 'she'? Charlene won't like that. Too personal." Then to Marvin, off fetching the wine, "Wine for me too, please."

Jackie's bustling around, clearing and reorganizing. I follow her, attempting to explain my special relationship with the widow. "It's the recipe, Jackie. It's called Chicken in Mourning. Charlene won't eat it anyway. I don't mean the chicken's a "she" like a puck—shoot her in—or a truck—park her over there. It's the recipe."

Jackie pulls the veiled main course out of the fridge, mumbling that she gets it. Marvin refills my glass, and I can't help but notice his left hand. There are two thumbs. In opposition.

The knuckle of the shapely outer thumb bends just around the bottom of the glass's tall-stemmed base. The other, the inner thumb, stretches high, almost to the rim, and in between, Marvin's fingers cup my wine.

I'm trying not to stare while imagining the double smudge of round whorls against my skin, stretching from nipple to nipple or sliding down my belly. Too bad he's with Jackie. Marvin and I are inexorably linked by our sinistral flaws and our numerical synchronicity. Six digits. Six orgasms.

He's here with Jackie, but Jackie's obviously all wrong for him. *Six.* I'd never break the friend code but Marvin's wrong for Jackie, too. *Six.* I tell the private little voice in my head, "Shut up!" but my big public voice is what comes out. All eyes are on me so I make a critical split-second decision. Forging ahead, I stand tall, grasp the table and blurt it out, "I'm going to...Climax!"

Jackie snorts, spraying wine out her nose. Marvin freezes like some marble Adonis, his arm still outstretched offering my wine. I want to go into detail about my new goal but figure maybe now's not the right time, seeing as I haven't worked out those details myself yet.

The doorbell rings, bringing Marvin back to life. He strides off toward the sound, holding my wine hostage while Jackie grabs a swath of paper towel for her running mascara.

Charlene—preceded by a waft of fruity essential oils—swooshes in, draped in elegant eco-friendly hemp or bamboo fibres. "Aloha, lovely friends. I would have let myself in but I had my hands full." Her crystals tinkle as she slides a covered tray onto the counter. "Now, who's this fine being with the fiery aura?" she asks.

"Marvin," he replies, returning me my wine to grasp Char's hand. "Aloha."

I weasel my way between the newly acquainted. "Let's drop the luau references, shall we? Marvin, this is Char. Where's your better half, Char? Glen parking the car?"

"He stayed home with the girls. Sorry, Mel. The sitter cancelled. Strep throat or something...and you know how they get when they're left alone, poor babies."

Marvin gives his head a sympathetic shake. "Kids, eh."

Jackie clarifies, still sniffling. "Dogs."

"Schnauzers," I add. So much for planning. Literally gone to the dogs.

When Marvin asks Jackie if she's okay, Char takes a closer look. "You're not sick, too, are you, Jackie? I have some turmeric lozenges in my bag. Hon, you look positively—"

"No need. Not sick, Char. It was a joke. I was laughing at a joke. Mel's joke."

"Oh, do share," Char says.

"That was no joke," I say. "I'm dead serious. What I said was—"

"John's not here," Char interrupts, looking around, counting heads. "Is he coming? I had the strangest dream about him last—"

"Never mind John. Yes, he's coming later. But this is important! I *said* I'm going to Climax. It's suddenly crucial that I do this," I say, looking into their wide eyes, one pair at a time.

"How...enlightened of you," says Char.

Marvin finds his voice. "Do you need a hand with that?"

Jackie pipes up, "Mel, are you losing it or what?"

"That's what I'm trying to do. Not lose it! Climax, it is. Climax, Saskatchewan. I'm going to be a writer!"

I'm bombarded by questions.

"Saskatchewan?"

"A writer? Why Saskatchewan?"

"What would you write about?" Jackie's anything but subtle. "You can't just *be* a writer. You have to be able to—"

"And you did just move into this place, Mel," Char adds.

"Smart man," I say to charming Marvin who is staying the hell out of it. He silently passes Char a glass of white and tops the rest of us up.

"I have a plan. Don't worry. I'll explain. Let's just get dinner on the road here."

"Jeezus, Mel, you can't just...you know it's getting worse, the MS."

"What do you do that for?" I ask. "Of course I know. And I hadn't planned on the disability discussion tonight, but since you brought it up, that's exactly why I have to do something now, before I can't! And I'm not moving there. If you'd give me a chance to explain...it's just one bloody week in Climax, Saskatchewan, at a writers' retreat!"

Marvin maneuvers me around the counter to the table and sits me down. The man is brilliant. He's just what I needed.

"Let's have a toast!" he says. "A toast to..."

"To the end of last year," I say, "because that's the reason I planned this whole dinner thing." We tilt our glasses back and look for more reasons to continue tilting.

"Anything else?" Marvin asks.

"Positivity!" Char hoots, giving Jackie a nudge. "And..."

"Support," Jackie says. "But—"

I cut her off. "How about we drink to friends. And, Marvin, to you. Welcome to our little club."

"You're sure I'm not..."

"Of course not. And let's drink to drink. And drink to fabulous food." So we do.

"The food!" Jackie says. She pops the apron she brought along over Char's head, ties a perfect bow and they get down to high-velocity kitchen business.

Marvin pulls up a chair next to me.

"So, Marvin, how long have you known Jackie?"

"I met her at Cam's video store a couple of months ago. It's the one down on Nichol Street."

"So...you know Cameron?"

"That's how I met Jackie."

"Now I'm confused. Are you both...?"

"Dating Jackie, you mean?" Marvin's soft laughter is charming. "See, Cam couldn't make it. And I just happened to be there so Jackie said, why didn't I come along for dinner then."

"So you're not *with* Jackie?"

Charlene, all ears, leans across the counter.

"What?" I ask.

"Oh, just...where's the butter?"

"Ask Jackie," I tell her, frowning her back to the kitchen.

Marvin doesn't miss a beat. "I'm most definitely not with Jackie. But when she said she had a fascinating friend..."

"Fascinating? Jackie said that?"

Marvin gives a little nod. "She also said this friend didn't appreciate her meddling..."

"Or matchmaking, blind dates, general interference..."

"And that this fascinating friend wouldn't hesitate to kill Jackie for setting something like this up. So..." Marvin opens his hand. It's an invitation.

Jackie moseys in with an empty breadbasket. She can't seem to find the perfect position for it.

"Problem?" I ask her.

"Oh no," she says, brushing at invisible crumbs. "Not really. I just, uh...where's your butter?"

"Ask Char," I tell her, waiting for her leave, then turn back to Marvin. "So, here you are. And I'm very glad. To meet you. To have you. Here, I mean. You know you have the most beautiful, uh, thumbs, er, hands. Hand. You have two thumbs on your left hand, which is really quite... unusual."

Marvin smiles. "I've noticed, Mel."

"I think we need another toast, Marvin. To an optimistic number. To the number six."

I brush my hand against his, then hold it there, mesmerized by the heat of it, the beauty, the curl of the fingers, the glistening hairs on the back of his hand. We touch glasses and sip. Okay, I gulp. "I didn't mean to embarrass you. I just think you have a lovely hand...I mean hands..."

"It's okay. Really. My hand is flattered."

He leaves his hand resting near my glass. I take my eyes off Marvin's thumbs to study his face. Not bad at all. Better by the minute. There's a gloss on his forehead. A burnish like dark wood. Fullish lips. Eyes deep and dark and...

"Excuse me, Marvin, there's something I have to do." I'm on a mission. I've decided two goals are better than one.

I head into the kitchen without my cane and just counter-surf as I go. I scribble "6" on a turquoise Post-it, squeeze past Jackie and Charlene at the sink, open the oven door and shove the crumpled paper between the chicken's curvaceously plump legs. Then I text John: *Don't come. Too late. Sorry. Headache. Early bed.*

Jackie says, over her shoulder and with her hands full of romaine, "Smells delicious. That bird won't be long."

"Thanks, Jack," I say, giving her a quick hug as I head back to the table, to Marvin, to his hands.

~⌒•

The Chicken in Mourning was fantabulous. So were the Tombstone Tiramisu and Char's fresh pineapple and the vino and especially the camaraderie. All that's left are crumbs and snuffed candles, Marvin and me. The radio's still on, FM in the background. Our two chairs are almost facing.

"Well, just you and me, Marvin."

"You seemed to want me to stay."

And there they are, those lips on mine. Six left digits rest hotly on my right thigh.

I can't stay on this chair forever. And I can't possibly stand up and neck. If he moves that fabulous hand up under my shirt...oh, man, here it comes...

"I have to lie down," I say into his lovely neck.

He pulls away, concerned. "Are you okay?"

"I'm fine. But I want to get comfortable, lie down. Come with me."

"To bed?"

"Yeah."

He doesn't make a run for the nearest exit.

"Come on." I get up, grab my cane and wobble into the bedroom. And Marvin's right behind me.

"The cane," he says. "It's pretty sexy."

"You think?" I'd give him a smile, but I have to concentrate, keep my eyes on the prize—in this case, the bed.

I sit on the edge. Marvin is right there beside me, undoing my buttons with his magic hand, his thumbs working as an agile team. Our clothes keep coming off, dropping, to reveal a lot of skin—warm, smooth, tasty.

We somehow crawl in and here we are, eager lips and hands, torsos and legs, together under my flowered quilts. I feel like a perpetual virgin.

I have to ask. "Have you got a condom, Charmin' Marvin?"

"For my thumbs?" He's not joking.

"No. I want everything."

"My special thumb is everything, my everything. It's my tool, my organ, the quintessential me."

"But you do have a cock, right?" I reach down his belly to confirm.

"This thumb," he says, flaunting its now tumid, dusky beauty. "This thumb is the best way, the only way, for me to come."

I'm not averse to something new, but I really want the slide—body to body, the most skin to skin I can get—so I tell him that.

"It won't disappoint. I promise."

The double thumb is impressive. "Okay, the thumb it is! But stay close. I want your whole body. And lips. I want your lips."

"You should take me and my lips and my thumbs to Climax with you."

Breathing hard, moving slow, still that rocking motion. "Slower... slower. What?"

"To Climax."

"Almost...almost there. Wait, make it last. Not yet! I want to stay right here on the periphery until..." Until I totally lose control. But I can't afford to lose sight of my limits: this is a single orgasm deal—Number 6 only. That's where Thumb's magic must end.

"I want to go with you to Climax."

"You keep saying that."

"I mean to Saskatchewan. I'm not working right now, so..."

"What? No. No! I have goals, my own goals. I just met you. And you're not even a writer. It's a writers' retreat!" I have this terrible feeling of dread. I lie stock-still waiting for it to pass. But then a second terrible realization stacks itself on top of the first. I had that Xmas orgasm after the neuro-sexual study and before Dr. Sharni gave me a six. My number is not six. It's five. My fucking number is five, so Marvin and I have no numeral-related synchronicity. We have next to nothing in common.

"Marvin, stop. Stop moving."

Marvin groans, rolling onto his back. "What's the matter?"

I slide away from him, lifting his arm, that sixy sexy hand away. It still looks so damn good but this is all wrong. How could I be so stupid?

I wasn't paying attention. I even messed around with karmic magic.

Marvin is reaching for me. "Hey, come back here."

"I just realized I used up my number six before Xmas."

He's getting nervous. "What are you talking about? Are you into numerology or something? Do you want me to leave? It's the size of my thumb, isn't it?" He's got exit signs in his eyes now, but he'd have to climb over me to make his escape.

"It's complicated," I say. "You see, I have this number. I've sort of been given this number. I know it sounds crazy. You wouldn't believe me anyway if I told you about today and my appointment and how or why or what exactly...but it's important that I commemorate...you know, show this number some appreciation...and I thought...this is kind of embarrassing...that my number was six. I don't want to talk about it anymore but I can tell you I've been responding all wrong...*to* the wrong...tonight, anyway...to the wrong fucking number. What I really needed, need, is a five. It's all wrong, Marvin. This is all wrong."

I keep looking at Marvin's hand poised on the sheet near my thigh. It's become a no-contact zone.

He lies back, thoughtful for a couple of long minutes, then lifts his arm a little and spreads out the thumb and fingers on his other hand. He raises an eyebrow. Marvin is a genius.

"Marvin, that's it! Five. Can you say it for me, Marvin? Give it some, I don't know...cachet?"

He whispers it perfectly into the nape of my neck.

"And no more talk of size or Saskatchewan."

He agrees to that, too, probably relieved.

"Say five again, Marvin. Say it five times. Humour me." And he does until I'm back under the covers, sinking mouth to mouth.

Sink. Cinque. Sunk.

3
Cougar Sighting

Char and I are tucked into a booth at Sam 'n Ella's, a café in Saskatoon. She's on a coast-to-coast tour, and she's looking every bit the New Age life coach that she's made herself into—hair all done up and a flowy moss-green tunic with a gold-embossed fossil pendant at her throat. A trilobite, she'd explained, to enhance her leadership skills. I, at least, remembered to put on my writerly oversized scarf for the hour trip from Climax into the city.

I'm telling her about the drive through the pale April sun and patches of melting snow. How I could see winter receding, even here.

"Yes, but what's it like, this writing retreat?" Char asks me.

"It's good."

"Good? Is it fun? Inspiring?"

"It's...intense," I tell her.

"Intense doesn't necessarily sound good."

"It's intensely...busy. I was so glad you called. I'm supposed to be writing right now and every other minute that I'm not reading or listening or looking for my muse."

"I bet you've met some amazing writers! With dark secret memoirs and noms de plume!"

"It's mostly women, a dozen our age or older. Sincere women. One flaky chick about thirty. Two guys...more like gentlemen. The place is nice. Oh, look, here comes our food." What a relief. I concentrate on my napkin. I can't admit to Char that I've skipped a couple of workshops. That all the others at the retreat are more serious than I am about writing. They've got outlines and manuscripts. A couple have even been published.

Our server delivers my gamey venison burger, a recent craving, and Char's wheatgrass, kale and soy smoothie. She takes a couple of thick green sips, pointing out the benefits of her meal as opposed to the detrimental effects of mine.

I take a big juicy bite and savour it while Char sips. "*You* are looking fabulous," I say to her. "Actually oozing success! The lecture circuit's
a good thing for you, I'm thinking."

Char's excessively modest. "It's been quite a year. I mean I've always believed in myself, but I never imagined there'd be this kind of
hunger..."

"Cultural appetite?"

"Exactly! This need...for *my* knowledge. It's my life path, my passion."

"Is it Glen's passion, too?"

"He's managing everything now—marketing, booking, finances.
He's a natural. We make such a great team! You know, Mel, there are a
lot of people who need this. People right out there..." Char gestures to
the street, "who are ready, even eager, to embrace this."

"Mmm-hmm." It's easier to be vague with a mouth full of burger.

"What about you? I can set you up with a whole life program...
tapping meridians, clearing your blockages. It's the EFT method. I know
it would help."

I give a little laugh. "I'm good, but thanks, Char. I prefer the SIA
method." I don't explain that means Sorry I Asked. "Save the EFT for
your flock of paying customers."

"Clients, Mel. Anyway, enough about me. Tell me about your writing." She dabs her lips, checks her watch and kisses her trilobite before
going on. "What are you working on?"

"Well, it's complicated."

"The plot, you mean? You're writing a novel?"

"I didn't say it was a novel."

"So, what do you mean, complicated?"

"It's, um, the process. It's experimental. But in kind of a classic
way."

"Poetry. That's it, isn't it? Poetry."

"Char..."

"No, no, you're not the poet type. So, what is it, your life story? A
how-to motivational book?"

"Inspiration porn!"

"I didn't mean..."

"Honestly, Char, I can't say too much about it just yet. It's, you know, gelling. Percolating. I actually have pages and pages..."

"So you've really been working at it. Atta girl."

I nearly snap. "Did you just say atta girl? Really, Char? Of course I've been working! I have goals like anybody else."

"I'm impressed. And I totally understand. Your wanting to keep it under wraps. But not even a hint?"

"Nope, not even a hint."

"Hmm. But you like it? The writing? The retreat?"

"Oh, yeah. Totally love it. And it's good for me. Sitting is what I do best and a change of scenery is...invigorating." I don't tell Charlene what I'm thinking, which is a friendly *Screw off!*

"Saskatchewan is invigorating?"

"Hey, don't knock it. Stubble can be sexy."

"So there's someone here with sexy stubble?"

"No, I mean the natural surroundings. I'm a prairie girl, anyway, you know—deep roots."

"You wouldn't stay, would you?"

"Not a chance in hell."

"Hey, speaking of deep, the tarot reading I did for you back in February..."

"That was kind of fun."

"Maybe you were more open, Mel," says Charlene, shifting responsibility to me. "I had a good feeling about that near future of yours, which is actually now."

"You saw me travelling and education being *big*."

"Exactly! Here you are doing both. And don't forget your cat chakra will continue to empower you, but you have to keep talking to the universe about what you need. Ask the great universe for it!"

"Come to think of it, you also said there'd be a stranger. You said he'd be younger. You said he'd want my mind." I notice two men sitting down at the counter. "Hey, when did glasses become sexy, anyway? I never noticed that before."

"So, this guy's got glasses. Tall? Short?"

"I've suddenly started to notice them on everyone. Strange. But anyway, he's taller than I expected."

"Expected? You *are* exuding positivism."

"And he's younger. Maybe mid-twenties."

"Jesus, Mel, that'll take some energy."

"I have no intention of actually doing anything about it."

"Really?" Charlene raises one eyebrow into an exaggerated crescent.

"He's just a pleasure to be around. All you can do is watch and wonder. Every woman in the class wants to chat him up, impress him... or undress him."

"Oh, he's another writer?"

"He's our instructor. Witty...intellectual...subtly gorgeous. But he'd never..."

"Never? Right. So when do you wrap this up?"

"No, I mean *I'd* never..."

Char laughs. "I mean the retreat, Mel."

"Oh, day after tomorrow. Then I'll head home. Back through Calgary, Van, the ferry. You know."

"I'll fly home to the rain in a week or so, too, but from Ottawa. Three more gigs."

"You sound like a rock star."

Charlene shrugs, slips into small talk, which is unusual for her. I'm thankful. I keep nodding, half listening, but really I'm thinking back to my first morning at the retreat. I'd expected introductions, maybe an orientation. What I got was a bad case of teacher crush. A stuttering, blushing zap of attraction far worse than anything in high school. Which is what Charlene seems to be prattling on about—attractions.

I catch up to the conversation. "I know! It's crazy but it's desire that keeps a person going. Makes you want to shave your legs, paint your toenails, buy a new bra, maybe even a black one."

"What happened to Marvin? That guy who..."

"Not my type. But, this young guy. He's just pure pleasure to... observe."

"You make it sound like some kind of surveillance. Aren't you kind of preying?"

I have to laugh. "Down on my knees every night? Not likely."

"No, I mean preying as in predatory. As in cougar."

I claw the air, bare my teeth and snarl, then drop the cat spoof. "No worries," I assure her. "Not enough time to set a trap."

Char checks her watch again. "Uh-oh. Show time. I have to go to the ladies. Grab the bill, will you? Be right back."

I watch her go. She makes me feel unsophisticated, even feral. And the topic of desire keeps feeding my imagination. My hairline beads perspiration just thinking about it. Imagining bodily contact. Stroking. Maybe I *could* learn to purr. I shake off the daydream, call the waitress over. "Do you have beer on tap?"

"No, just bottled."

"That'll do. Just one of those."

"All we have is Wildcat."

"Sounds perfect. Oh, and the bill, thanks."

She nods. "One Cat coming up."

"You bet."

Charlene must be putting on her karmic face. I grab the newspaper from the empty table behind me, flip through it. And there on page four, I'm struck dumb by a headline reading: "Cougars and You: A Safety Guide."

Charlene returns. "You might need this," she says, smirking, tossing a Lynx brand condom onto the open newspaper. I close it quickly, covering up the suggestive evidence, both hers and mine.

"Don't be too good," she says, and we both laugh. We share a goodbye hug, wish each other well, and she's gone.

I sip my Wildcat, slip the Lynx into my purse—the species is close enough—and turn back to page four.

Cougars and You: A Safety Guide

1. Cougars are most active at dusk and dawn. They will, however, roam and hunt at any time of the day and night and in all seasons.

2. Generally, cougars are solitary.

3. Consider getting a dog. Play loud music. If there have been sightings, take an escort. Don't walk alone.

4. Never approach a cougar. Although they normally avoid confrontation, all cougars are unpredictable.

5. Stay calm. Talk to the cougar in a confident manner.

6. Rapid movement may provoke an attack. Do not run. I repeat, do not run. Try to back away from the cougar slowly. Otherwise, their instinct to attack may click in.

7. Do all you can to enlarge your physical presence. Don't crouch down or try to hide. Pick up sticks or branches and wave them around.

8. Cougars are a vital part of our diverse wildlife. Seeing a cougar should be an exciting and rewarding experience, with both you and the cougar coming away unharmed.

> A rewarding experience...
> Coming away unharmed...
> Perfect!

m⌒•

The last class comes to a close and everyone's ready to head home, mostly right here on the prairies, two farther east. I'll be heading back to the West Coast. The youngster in the group, Yvonne, is returning to Nelson.

It's her, of course, who's brought a box of wine for a quick farewell toast. Spirits are high. Yvonne, looking more like fifteen than thirty with her long blond braids and bright Sherpa toque, flutters and flirts her writerly exuberance around the group, pouring wine into paper cups.

Folks are exchanging email addresses and patting each other on the back like they've survived the greatest word war ever. I hold back until I feel the beginnings of a buzz. A touch of courage. A little added heat brings desire to the fore. I really can't concentrate on anything else.

I sidle around the hugs when it's over, prolong the book bag shuffle until they're all finally gone except the instructor, who suddenly looks beat.

I've waited until the last minute to make my move. I like to raise the stakes. Push the possibility of failure to make the success pot a little sweeter. And that way I have only myself to royally blame for a short time.

My time has come to either speak or wave goodbye. "I'll miss this," I tell him, trying to sound as sincere as the serious writers. "We're all on our own again...with the writing, I mean."

He smiles and nods, maintaining his professionalism as he packs papers into his briefcase.

"I kind of hate to go back to my room," I go on. "I won't leave till morning."

"Me, too," he says.

"I guess you wouldn't be up for the pub? I could buy you a real thank-you drink. I've barely had a chance to talk to you, you've been in such demand."

It's out of my hands now, up to the universe.

"I won't be very good company," he says. "These retreats are pretty draining."

I agree. "We don't have to talk about writing. In fact, we should avoid the subject. Believe me, I'm not looking for extra help or critiques or anything. I declare this retreat over. Now, on to other—"

He looks a bit bewildered. "I haven't seen much of your work, have I?"

"Writer-speak prohibited. You already broke the rule," I tease. I wait. I pick up my books, sigh, and cane my way to the door.

He softens his resolve. "Ah, sure. What the hell. One drink won't hurt. We can walk over from here."

I tap my cane. "Walking's not so good."

"Sorry. Right."

I love the fact that he doesn't ask about the cane. "It's okay. You can ride with me. Unless you want to meet me there."

"No, no. Let's go."

So we do. It's a short drive. The parking lot's empty. The pub looks out over absolutely nothing. I checked this out earlier. No distractions. Except when we walk in there are two other women retreaters. We pretty much have to sit with them. No way around it. I play it cool on the out-side. The inside, on the other hand, is really cooking.

Drinks keep coming. These other women, I can't even remember their names, are having a swell old time. They're giggling and revealing a little too much in the personal department, one with a penchant for in-tellectual men, the other with a sexually dysfunctional husband. They're fawning over Prof and he doesn't discourage it, but he's playing it close to his chest. That's right, breast your cards, baby.

Me, I'm in for the long haul. I know I can outlast them. And I do. They finally wobble out.

Prof's long ago forgotten his one-drink rule. We're warming up, but I'm not getting a very clear reading on him. Not clear at all. Figure I'll just quit messing around.

"So, attractive man, how about it?" I ask. "Just sex, right now."

"What?"

"I said, sex..."

"I got that part." He stares at the clock behind the bar.

Awkward. Impulse can be a bad thing.

He finally speaks. "I'll be right back. Hold that thought." As if I could do anything but. He heads to the washroom. Maybe he's consid-ering. But he does return.

"I should really go," he says, but sits down again, eyeing the fresh round of drinks I ordered. Aha, he's got a weakness.

"It's okay, not to worry. We all head back to our real lives tomor-row."

"Yah," he says, all thoughtful. There's a long silence. We sip away the minutes.

"My turn," I say, motioning to the washroom. "Be right back." I do my unsvelte cane-leaning drag-stagger walk to the door that says Gals. I'm thanking the universe—prematurely, it turns out. The zipper on my pants is stuck. Really, really stuck. That MS urgency, made worse by the booze, is getting beyond uncomfortable. In fact, I'm leaking. I weigh my options. None. I clutch and yank and finally just sit down on the toilet. The leak accelerates to a full-blown flood. My jeans darken like a big den-im wick. Even my socks dampen. And then I sit there because I cannot for the life of me think what to do. So I sit away the minutes now, alone.

Funny how desire goes out the window in the face of flooding. I'm making a vow to be sexless when somebody knocks on the outer door. I hold my breath till they leave.

Then the waitress comes in and talks to me through the cubicle door.

"Are you okay, sugar?" she asks. "Your friend is worried about you."

"I have a dilemma."

"Is there something I can do?"

"Indeed, there is," I say, as I dig in my purse, which now also has a soggy bottom. I explain the situation to her in detail, and then pass a hundred bucks of my gas money under the cubicle door to pay the bill with a huge tip for my new accomplice. She agrees to hide my car round back, explain to the Prof that I must have left (and seem to have already covered the bill—look at that!), then help me into my van after he's gone. Long gone.

m⁓◄

I sneak out of Climax nice and early with a bagel and a mega-cup of Timmy's by my side, eager to put distance between me and last night. The last whole bloody failure of a week. So much for writing. Now my only goal is to get home. I'm looking forward to the drive alone across that stretch of prairie, then the lift of highway through the foothills, up and over to the coastal side and back to my real life. I'm just out of town when I see some poor sod up ahead with a thumb out. She's leaning up against the Thanks for Coming sign. I don't pick up hitchhikers, and I can't wait to see the backside of that sign in my rearview mirror. I feign road concentration, grab a quick glance. Mistake, mistake!

It's bloody Yvonne, my dippy classmate, holding a sad illegible cardboard sign. I keep going. I'll never see her again.

It takes me a couple of minutes to break my rule, brake the van and reverse through the shoulder potholes until we're face to face through the passenger window. She's really glad to see me, she says as she climbs in, stowing a backpack and a case of pale ale at her feet. She missed the bus, the bus to Nelson. I offer to get her to a town where she can catch another bus. She looks wet-eyed like a thankful puppy. So I offer to get her all the way there. She bursts into grateful tears. So I stop thinking of things to offer her except a cooler to park the beer in, not that I'm interested in drinking today.

Yvonne is effusive. "This is so *so* great of you, Melanie. Like fate or destiny. You just showing up like that. Honestly, the bus trip is hell anyway. This is just so *so* much better."

"No kidding."

"You know I can drive if you get tired. And I've got a little gas money. Maybe I can get my ticket reimbursed."

"Yeah, sure. Let's just get moving. I'm ready to go home."

Then she talks. A lot.

I draw the line at writing. Nix anything Climax-related due to the fact that I never want to talk about writing again. Or think about it. Or fucking do it. And to tell her I'm physically and emotionally hungover would give her the upper hand. I'm more of a sick kitten than a cougar today, and it's going to be one helluva long drive, all the way to Nelson. But maybe, just maybe, this drive with Yvonne will take my mind off everything else.

Yvonne buckles up as we head for the Trans-Canada. Then due west. I drive, she chats, we stop for gas, then a refreshing rest-stop lunch—buns, cheese and one juicy tomato, sliced, out of the cooler. It's not totally unpleasant.

Yvonne volunteers to drive the next stint.

"You know, that would be great. I might just shut my eyes for an hour."

She takes over, adjusts the seat, puts on her massive shades, tunes the radio to a clear station playing the Eagles. It's "Life in the Fast Lane," and that's right where we are. She's comfortable with the van in moments. My eyelids are so heavy, my speech dull. I tilt the seat back as far as it will go—which isn't far.

We take the corners gently; smooth curves bend my mind to scenes, forgiving, familiar, then tender. Yvonne turns the radio off and practises a poem she wrote. I drift on the edge of sleep, listening, until I hear nothing.

I feel the van braking hard before I hear Yvonne cursing. My eyes pop open in alarm and there's this bright angel winging straight at us. It's a hang glider, with a wingspan looking to be almost as wide as the road. He's coming straight at us, flying, wobbling, floating earthward.

His long black hair blows back—darkly angelic.

Jesus! He tips to the right and his wing skitters across the wind-shield, a lime-green nylon whoosh and clatter, the snap of the radio antenna. Yvonne's slammed the brakes on all the way now. The green wing tumbles over and behind us, landing in a shallow ditch.

"Oh, fuck. Did we kill him?" she says. I mumble my uncertainty as we both try to look through the back window where a narrow strip of green nylon flutters.

"No, look," she says. "He's moving—I think."

She gets out and runs back. I manage to shuffle over to the driver's seat and reverse for the second time today to get a read on the situation without leaving the vehicle.

The guy untangles himself from the wing with some help from Yvonne. He's a lot less ethereal on the ground—a short, stocky, leather clad guy with long wavy locks, a heavy moustache and a nasty cut on his rugged brow. He opens his mouth and aims a foul stream of French and English curses in my direction. He assumes I was driving.

"His name is Yvon," Yvonne volunteers.

"Are you all right?" I ask.

The guy's livid. "You fucking hit me!"

I have to remain calm. "I'm pretty sure it was you who hit us. But hey, you don't look too good. Maybe we can help." I offer my first-aid kit to Girl-Yvonne. It's the least I can do.

"So *so* cool, eh?" says Girl-Yvonne, groovin' on destiny.

It takes a good hour, not just to bandage his minor gash but also to make a plan and put it into action. First, fold the wing so the hang glider can be tied to the roof. No easy feat. That massive green wing stretches from the front bumper to well past the rear like an oversized exotic insect. Second, rearrange stuff in the van and settle Boy-Yvon into the rear seat. I dispense Tylenol for his headache. Lots of Tylenol. Then I drive. Fast. Preferably somewhere with a washroom. And food.

It'll be me behind the wheel until we drop off Boy-Yvon, who says he's from Bigstick Lake, well behind us, but he's trying to get to Breast-work Hill, which sends Girl-Yvonne into hysterics. His bizarre method of travel—getting up to speed atop semis before catapulting his winged self into the sky—is his lifestyle, not his hobby. This doesn't even faze me. And the conversation's better than nothing since we can't pick up a clear signal on the radio on this stretch of highway.

It's only 6:00 and we don't have enough gas to make it to Breast-work Hill, so we pull in at a truck-stop motel with a congregation of big rigs, every colour and style. A lot of them are really flashy with bells and whistles up the ying yang. The gas pumps are down until the next morning due to a computer glitch. The motel, surrounded by oil-drenched pavement and chuffing engines and motors and reefers, is not inviting or particularly clean. There's no vacancy. Boy-Yvon slips away, and I'm kinda pissed about that.

Girl-Yvonne circles the winged van while I lean on it and smoke and contemplate sleeping in it as the only option—an undesirable one. My leg'll seize up, get all spastically uncooperative, refusing to bend or unbend. And my foot'll swell. I should elevate my leg right now, in fact, because extended sitting does the same thing. I'm just getting ready to tuck myself into my seat. There's no way I'm going to sit or socialize in the pizza joint nearby. Girl-Yvonne's trying to be sweet because she partly blames herself for the situation. I'm just cranky because I partly blame her too, and the real perpetrator has deserted us. I'm cussing him out under my breath when he strides across the lot with a wink and a dark cherubic smile.

Boy-Yvon, it turns out, has tracked down one of his trucker bud-dies, who's having a little sleepover with another trucker buddy, and he's managed to wrangle us a bunk. I couldn't care less how he got it or what he calls it. And it's no bunk. It's a full-on luxury sleeper, right behind the cab of a cherry Peterbilt. Boy-Yvon has saved us from a miserable night. Our own personal ark in a sea of semis.

I need a lot of help to get up the shiny chrome ladder into the thing, but it's worth it. All fancy-schmancy. Studded red leather. Clean sheets in a drawer. And a mini bathroom!

Over pizza and beer in our crimson abode we kick back. Girl-Yvonne's laughing at some joke I didn't get, when she starts to cough. It's that red-faced, teary-eyed coughing where you can't stop, and it goes on and on. And then it doesn't. And her face gets redder. And she's kind of beating at her chest. I don't get it at first, but Boy-Yvon jumps up and leaps behind her, grasping her around the belly. Now I get it. He's thrusting his fist up just below her rib cage like he knows what he's doing, and I guess he does because Girl-Yvonne coughs out a chunk of pepperoni. She's okay. The funny thing is Boy-Yvon's still fooling around and keeps thrusting but not with his fist, just his body. And Girl-Yvonne's gasping turns to giggling. Oh my! It's a good thing I'm no longer interested in sex.

I start to like Boy-Yvon. He saved the day. We're all really relieved and kind of euphoric about Boy-Yvon's safe landing and Girl-Yvonne's recovery after the semi-choking episode. Plus he found us a coolly unusual place to sleep, and we have decent pizza and cold beer. We have a little toke to celebrate—hot-boxing in compact luxury.

The Yvon(ne)s seem to have their own little something-something going on—drawn together by near-calamities—so I don't have to get involved. They take off for a walk, and I cuddle myself to sleep. And wake up chilly. And drift off, feeling slightly less worn out and a little more left out and wishing my name was fronted with a Y too, like a pair of tighty-whities.

I hear them come back. And I can see them all giggly and flirty and kissy. And then the light's out, and Yvonne pounces on me, all playful, and climbs over me, and they burrow in on either side of me. Brrr. Cuddle. Okay. Tickle. Not exactly okay. But I can't help but laugh. And I can feel them laughing too. Or more to the point, they're kinda feeling me feeling them laugh. I'm the "feeling" in the funny sandwich. Boy-Yvon's like thick coarse rye, Girl-Yvonne's like hippie sourdough. We start singing, "Sandwiches are beautiful! Sandwiches are fine!" by Fred Penner. I figure they'll quit tickle-touching soon. That doesn't happen.

I say in the dark, "Come on you guys, really," but I guess that could be interpreted in multiple ways by multiple minds attached to multiple lips and fingers. Before you know it, we're all rolled up in a kitten-ball, laughing and kissing and purring and kissing and murmuring and kissing. And being in the middle of spontaneous tickling and kissing is a pretty fun spot to be in. And then it doesn't matter anymore who's in the middle. Or who's doing what, but I can definitely tell the difference between hairy-everywhere Rye Guy and Hippie Girl, who has a carefully coiffed landing strip down south, which makes me wonder if that's what initially drew the hang glider to the van. Regardless, I have no complaints about either. Touchy-feely head to toe.

I'm feeling really generous. Downright selfless. It doesn't even bother me that both of them climax at least once and that I've had more than a hand in making that happen. And I don't mind staying on this drifting pleasure plateau for a good long time until sleep takes over. We're winding down one by one. Boy-Yvon fades first, but we're all still cuddled up. Oh. Did I say plateau? There seems to be a change in topographical altitude. Maybe Girl-Yvonne's the real angel. My oh my. Here it comes. And keeps coming. It's not one of those intense clenching orgasms but more an extended rippling circling wave of deliciousness.

Mmmmmmm...

mmmmmm...

mmmmm...

mmmm...

mmm...

mm...

m

Bye-bye, Number 4!

Maybe this whole trio scenario is so *so* good, as Girl-Yvonne would say, because it was unplanned, unexpected and sort of has a last-day-on-earth feel to it. A long, long day. One I won't forget. Until I try to, in the awkward morning, when cougars and kittens, angels and arks, shrink to tiny memories.

4

Darling Techno Love

I dropped the pretense that I was becoming a writer about the time Char and John and Jackie stopped pestering me about it. I'm more than happy to put not only Climax behind me but the whole sticky West Coast summer. It wasn't pretty, but I survived.

Heat intolerance makes an enemy of the sun. The higher its intensity, the lower my energy and the worse my MS. The war was on. I spent most of July and August monitoring my core temperature. Even a cooling shower became a daunting task. I got myself a shower seat after a couple of near falls, but even finding a safe way to clamber in and out of the tub without stressing, spazzing and further overheating was sometimes impossible. Defeat wasn't an option. I bought a startlingly unfashionable cooling vest, which quickly became my ultimate weapon of defence, but even that took organization: soak, wring out one-handed, put the dripping thing on, repeat—often. Other tactics involved closed blinds and windows, a massive fan, a bucket of cold water for my feet, a mister at the ready and a reminder to myself that night would eventually arrive.

My mood was another issue. It wasn't that I was melancholy. I was just fucking cranky all the time. My friends started calling me Bitchzilla. When the internet started targeting me with pharmaceutical ads, I was convinced I needed meds. My doctor was happy to help, but the anti-depressants left me feeling hazy, like I was missing a whole lot of something, though it wasn't sex. Sex had fallen so far off my radar that August 8—World Orgasm Day—passed by unnoticed. Selective, yes. Inhibitor, yes. But on those meds I'd been only half here, and it wasn't necessarily the good half. Peace and calm became synonymous with half-dead. Without desire, there was a gaping hole in my supposedly happy medicated self. Artificial serotonin, be damned. I needed a boost of the real thing so I stopped the meds and started talking to telemarketers. One in particular, Delhi Patrick, not only managed to lighten my mood with his cheery chatter, but he had no choice but to listen.

"Madam," he would always begin. "My name is Patrick. Are you interested on this fine day to purchase—"

"Of course, I'm interested," I'd tell him, not waiting for details about whichever cruise deal he was selling. Then I'd talk away until deciding that maybe another day might be a better time to make that purchase.

"But time is running out for this offer, madam."

"I lost my credit card, Patrick," I would lie, or, "Oops, I have a board meeting in ten minutes, Patrick. Got to run!" But I'd feel terribly guilty about misleading poor Delhi Patrick—until the next time.

Like lying to a captive audience of one who's trying to make a living at an Indian call centre, quitting the pills has an upside and a downside, too. The upside is the renewed feeling of Heightened Olfactory Raunchy Necessary Yearning (HORNY) and the downside is that I'm back to caring about those last few orgasms.

With the chillier weather here—in fact September's turning out to be one long series of storms—it's time to take action, commit to something, find a new purpose. Everyone has been on my case to take some kind of control of my life—all in different ways—and to, coincidentally, find something meaningful to do. Getting out from under the numbers game would definitely be a good first step.

Even if there actually is someone out there to assist with or share or do one of these last three dirty-sweet deeds, I'd have to find a way to attract that particular person or persons. And no, I am not open to mechanical or self-induced. But it's the attracting that's getting so much harder or—in the language of positivity—more challenging.

Fingers and hips and even the ass that wasn't half-bad—all seem to go off in odd directions. My body makes people nervous. Especially the younger ones. They can't trust it, and neither can I. They think they might have to *take responsibility* for me temporarily if I slip up or fall down. Attractions run the other way—and fast—at any sign of incapacity. I've experienced first hand the dampening effects of little things like leg cramps or wet pants.

And while the wheelchair can be a curious attraction in its own odd way, it's not, believe me, a sexual one. If that was all it took, I'd use it all the time. But the chair kind of demands its own set of rules. I become invisible if I'm with my pusher, and I'm not referring to drugs here. I mean friend, volunteer, chaperone. In the big socio-cultural scheme of things, the general consensus is wheelchair equates with non-sexual or infantile or stupid. Or all of the above, with the assumption of deafness thrown in. I abhor being yelled at, but if some good Samaritan screamed "yes!" in answer to my request for sexual assistance, I'd be over the moon and back.

Maybe I could just track down Marvin or the Yvon(ne)s or the cowboy from twenty-some years ago who was so fantastically acrobatic from hanging off the saddle. There was certainly something to be said for living in motels called the Flamingo or Saratoga or Western Star. Who knew that was as good as it would get? I bet John would even help me out of this pinch, but really—a childhood friend? That would be weird or incestuous or something.

I need a freakin' fearless lion tamer or an astronaut. No, too spacey. Maybe an all-star wrestler or a dominatrix or a ballerina or somebody who thinks outside the box. But you have to move in the right circles to meet these folks. And moving in circles usually takes a little money. Shrinking assets mean fewer options. I'm trying to think through this conundrum and also remembering just how long it's been since someone has touched my skin.

When the phone rings, I ignore it. I'm busy! I'm thinking!

When it rings again, I check the number and pick up. "Hello?"

"Madam, hello. My name is Patrick. Are you interested on this particularly fine day to purchase—"

"But of course! This is the perfect day. I should tell you, though, I've been thinking. Thinking about how I've done my share of paying people—a small fortune in fact—to touch me for years. Even small doses of touch...you know, *attention*...are therapeutic. Don't you agree?"

"Yes, madam, of course, but I'm calling with an exclusive offer and time is running out so..."

"You know, Patrick, the shampoos and root stimulation at the local hair salon were the cat's meow until they changed the name of the place to Curl Up 'n Dye.

"And massages...have you had a massage, Patrick?"

"Yes, madam."

"Well, the massages by Bob the Masseur were pretty sweet, until the fee went up and the government subsidies went down. And Tanya! Tanya the Pedicure Queen could have sent me off to pedi-heaven but my feet aren't, you know, *that* way.

"And let me tell you about Dr. Sounomono. He is my small but powerful pleasure/pain man. Forget those basic acupuncture needles, even with the electric current enhancers. Acupuncture, Patrick. Have you had it?" I love saying his name because it's *the* most popular tele-marketing name.

"No, madam, but I'd like to tell you about this incredible offer of—"

"Well, never mind. Dr. Sounomono adds moxibustion to his treatments. That's what makes the body sing, Patrick, and the legs bend and zing into taut bows. Small cones of herb burning on precise pressure points gave me so much more moxie, and such a damn huge hit of relief." I laugh and go on. "I did get a bit of a lift from the smoky smell on my skin and the small blisters."

"Madam?"

"Yes, Patrick?"

"Can I interest you in that cruise today?"

"Yes, but I have to tell you...it's the most amazing thing! The most amazing *thing* about all these professional sessions, especially with Bob the Masseur, was that my totally illegible handwriting improved enough for me to write exquisitely penned cheques immediately after the treatments. Like nothing was impossible. You know that feeling, Patrick? The improvements never lasted longer than the money, though. And if not healed or physically satisfied by any of the above, at least I felt damn good, at least for a short time afterwards. Oh no, there's a lion tamer at the door. I have to go, Patrick. But do call again."

The thing about touch, though, is that I want what I want when, how and where I want it, so I have to be careful about what I wish for. My future probably includes touch that's more about maintenance than desire. Hands that dress me and feed me, hands that rearrange me, turn me over.

And between now and then I do not want early-bird entry into the seniors' club, regardless of their welcoming me and anyone else with a cane or other mobility equipment. Even for discount Tuesdays. Ugh.

Too much thinking is detrimental to my progress. I should really get out of my head and talk to a real live...

The phone rings again. Enough is enough. I figure it's better to break it off with Delhi Patrick permanently before it gets out of hand and he either talks me into buying something or starts having feelings. I put on my mean voice. "Look! If you ever—"

"My, my," cuts in Charlene. "Aren't you in a mood!"

"Telemarketers."

"Ah, right. Nothing worse. How are you otherwise?"

"Otherwise, fine. You?"

"Oh, you know, busy busy. I just thought I'd take a minute and call. See how you are and..."

"And?"

"If you'd subscribed to my daily personalized horoscope blog, you'd know."

"Oh, um, I thought I did. What would I know? Can't you just tell me?"

"Just sign up now. See for yourself."

"Is it free? My budget's a little tight."

"Oh. Well, yes, Mel, for you. The first week anyway, if you give it a good review. I'll give you a promo code. Just go to my website. It's user-friendly. And follow the cues. I know you think it's a waste of time, but today's the beginning of something really important for you. I was doing up charts, saw yours and just *had* to share!"

"How important?"

"I'm sure it's about your book!"

"What book?" Geez, a spear to the dead heart of that bad idea.

"Sorry, I meant your...well...whatever big thing you want to apply it to!"

"At the top of my list?"

"Yes! That's crucial...if you're open to it, that is."

"Okay, okay. I'll check it out. I'll even be all open. What's the code?"

"Code?"

"Promo code."

"Right. Use PROMPTLY333." She spells it out for me so I have no excuse. "All caps," she adds. "And let me know how it goes, Mel. Don't forget the 333."

Well, I like those numbers. "Char? Charlene?" But the line's dead and I can already sense that she's waiting for my log-in, subscription and feedback. I'll have a look. What harm can it do?

I follow the steps on her sparkly website and after three email confirmations I get this:

> Now is your time for successful energetic activity! Your affairs will come to fruition through intelligent planning and foresight, which are available to you under this influence if you make a conscious effort to take advantage of them. Time to cross the finish line!

A few words stand out: *affairs, fruition* and *Time to cross the finish line!* I tag on PROMPTLY333.

Hello, orgasm number 3! But, how?

Jackie might have been right about my general concentration problem, not that I'll admit that to her, but in this one area of interest it is once again unswerving, relentless. Sex. Maybe sex through online dating, though it still creeps me out. But Jackie and a lot of other people use it. And maybe it's a better fit now for a misfit like me. I can sculpt my online profile, reveal the good and bad if and when I choose. It seems perfect. Char is an astro-genius!

I'm going to try it! No, I will succeed at it!

I reread the horoscope and notice something about *under this influence*, so I accessorize with a tall Bacardi Coke at my side and a cigarette behind my ear. It makes me feel nonchalant, like an after-shift construction worker in those faded, torn, too-tight jeans that I love to love. Before I even touch a key, ads and offers pop up. No! I do not want to see a Kardashian anything! But Click to Enter sounds kind of erotic. I consider my options.

There are two billion sites for sex, six hundred thousand for dating, half a million for lion tamer, and a hundred and fifty thousand if you google all three together. The possibilities are endless, unlike my current situation.

Research demands perseverance. I refuse to be overwhelmed or impulsive. I want to pick the online dating site that feels right. I dig, click and scroll. For hours. I swap out the rum for an energy drink. This is serious business. I miss lunch, dinner, four phone calls and the garbage pickup. Nothing exists beyond my computer screen.

It's easy to rule out a lot of these sites. I'm not into the Christian, Baha'i or Scientology find-a-spiritual-soulmate connections. I need something spicier and more forward than Friends-Reunited dating. I'm over the idea of success at Cougar dating. Nothing about Sports dating interests me, but I bookmark it because you can classify yourself as "spectator only" or even "team mascot," and you have the option to communicate with an armchair tennis aficionado or a retired pro footballer or an active hockey-pucker or someone who's into fishing, but the hooks could get messy. Maybe they fit more into the Fetish-Mate love sites. Harley dating is out, too.

Liberal Hearts, which claims to bring together like-minded politicos, Greens and environmentalists, doesn't do it for me. Neither does exclusive racial or ethnic dating. I mean, really, I'm a mongrel and an open-armed Canadian. I've never been a nurse or a firefighter or a soldier, so Uniform dating is out, but I notice that there seem to be a lot of the same lookie-loos poking around in there as on Fetish Love. Vegetarian, vegan and raw-foodist dating sucks and so does dating for "thinking people"—I'd really prefer less affected conversation, no matter how brilliant, and a little more fruitful action.

Finally, an interesting one—radiocarbon dating! But surprisingly, my MS disease shares two-thirds of the AMS acronym for Accelerator Mass Spectrometry dating. And this facility guarantees the same kind of thing as all the other dating sites: excellent service, rapid turnaround time, liaison with submitters and confidentiality. But I can't even fit in there. I'm not a traditional Kwakiutl totem pole or an ancient Akrotiri fresco.

The Darwin Dating brings on an overwhelming wave of despair. I feel wretched enough to wash a few dishes, straighten the sheets on my empty bed and notice the rising sweep of wind-tossed branches against a fierce sky. I've lived through my share of selfish, shallow vanity and arrogant youthful immortality. And survived it. So I turn up the heat, pluck my eyebrows, dab hemorrhoid cream under my eyes, attempt to stand on the bathroom scale, then apply anti-wrinkle lotion—everywhere.

It's not just that I'm way over the thirty-five-year age limit of the Fittest site. I would never have been allowed in even before my disability took hold. Although the Darwin Dating site doesn't specify physical abnormalities in its list of entry denial criteria, applications get a big red X if you admit to having red hair, too many freckles, too many pounds, too much body hair, pale skin, etc. The list goes on.

The regular route looks more appealing. Match-dot or Date-dot or Plenty-of-fish-dot or Charmony, which claims to use scientific techno-chemistry. This means I have to look at myself—answering reams of questions—with some kind of honesty while marketing a desirable image. I have to concentrate, stay on task, which is too much like a job. I can't help searching by city to see what other kinds of people are listed and if I recognize anybody. Sure enough, here's my first husband—so that's what he looks like now—and my old neighbour, Carol.

I fill out the form to the best of my ability, lying only a little about my age. Failing to mention the fact that I have a dysfunctional body that relies on a cane or a wheelchair isn't even a little white lie because there is no question about that. Later for confidential revelations.

I submit my profile—goodbye, privacy!—and within hours I become a non-fetish submissive, a prisoner to the habit of checking for responses obsessively. And lo and behold if they don't come and keep coming. But after a couple of weeks and a few dozen people requesting emails, before I even seriously contemplate opening communication lines, I notice a trend. A few prospects—both male and female—want to spend time in their boats or on their bikes but the majority suggest a walk on the beach or a hike in the hills or a bloody weekend of camping, which makes me rethink disability dishonesty. I'm just not prepared to come out of the disability closet before I even meet somebody. It's obvious that normal dating channels are not open to me.

But what's this? A disability dating site? This could be for me! The only obstacle is that there are 325 conditions to choose from. So here's a new dilemma. Do I make a selection by my disease? I suppose it would make sense to share common problems as a way to break down that first big barrier, but maybe a mixed-disease "relationship" would be more interesting. You'd have differences rather than commonalities to talk about.

I notice the wind in the treetops has picked up to gale-force magnitude.

If I were braver and more marketable, I could just build my own website advertising the fact that I have three orgasms left and I require a trio of hearty, sensual souls to rise to the occasion. I could have a TV reality show with games and competitions and a cash prize generated from membership and application fees, just like a literary contest. I could market mugs and hats. But I'd need an assistant for the business end of things and a decade to accomplish it all.

This is defeating, weird, frustrating and, do I dare say the D-word, depressing. Now all I need is a twelve-step program to battle this addictive online dating business. And I haven't even answered an email or talked to anyone in a chat room.

I need a break. No, I have to stop. I pull up Confessions Online and type in: I am a hedonist, a deviant, and I am an internet-dating site addict.

That's when it hits. A great crash, total darkness, a blank screen. It must have been a tree coming down. I hear the howl of wind and slashing rain. No white noise, no refrigerator running or radio hum or electric heater. But there is no gaping hole in the roof, and I feel relatively safe. I do what any survivor of addiction does. I find my wheelchair, a flashlight, two extra blankets, my cellphone (which has slipped out of the service area all by itself) and go to bed.

I did it. I turned my still-solitary back to the blank screen without another hopeful glance. Without tomorrow's horoscope, or tea leaf reading, or even a finished submitted online confession. I slide my cellphone under my pillow and for the first time in days, I dream of absolutely nothing.

5
These Three Things

I survived September—even that last week when I steered clear of the internet. Then I killed that month off with a bang.

I fell.

In public...

...while window shopping.

My cane failed me and down I went. I wasn't even trying to make eye contact with that guy. I didn't split my chin open, but I did suffer. Indignity was involved. Said guy helped me up, sat me down on a bench and before he left, he patted my shoulder like I was his grandma.

It took a bit of time—three inquiries by mall security—to quell my snivelling and gather my thoughts. I had a few realizations. One, that there's also a limit to how many headers I can take before reaching the breaking point. Two, that it's time to lay bare to the world the extent of my disability regardless of the effect on my level of desirability. Three, that disability and desirability are both "d" words with a difference of "e" and "r" and if you put those three letters together you get "red," which is more exciting and less disconcerting than the black and blue on my knees and elbow.

Shopping was the obvious remedy. It was time to rack up some credit card debt to buy some equipment, starting with an uplifting, very crimson underwire bra. Next, I purchased a motorized scooter. It's awesome! It's also red! And it's petite and zippy and versatile. Right there in the shop, I named my new wheels Adele so I can sing "Rolling in the Deep" and "Hello" when I take her out. They even delivered Adele!

I'm all excited about this new freedom—outings without the stress and anxiety of falling. But with steady days of rain on their way, I realize Adele's a fair-weather scooter, and one with a distance limitation. Rather than learning to love her despite these disappointments, I decide to enhance our relationship, spending another few grand to have a motorized lift for Adele installed in the back of my van. Push-button in, push-button out sounded easy. All I have to do is roll her on, get her into position, buckle her up and manage the door—without falling. More options for my disabled future.

It's only the first of October and a Friday to boot, with a weekend of isolation and empty arms hovering on the horizon. This whole orgasm thing has me by the non-existent balls. I can't concentrate on anything else. At all. *Three.* If I could resolve this satisfactorily, I'm convinced I could actually get on with the rest of my limited life.

I need a refined plan. Something I can take step by step. So I get busy. And procrastinate. I worry that if I wait too long I'll risk losing the option of any more orgasms at all, but I rationalize that they're always bigger and better after a sexual dry spell. And I'm bloody well parched. I plan to space them out, and although each one may work up to fruition over a series of episodes, I'm ultimately looking for three unique experiences.

I attach myself to the number three until I can adopt another field of interest that's non-sexual. Fortitude and tenacity—even I can manage short term if I'm not interrupted or sidetracked. Of course, that's when a message pops up on the screen. It's from my friend John, who promises to stop by for a beer if I'm up for it. He'll be in the neighbourhood Thursday, he says. October 7, I realize, which is six days from now—two times three. I message back an enthusiastic affirmative. More than anyone else, he's the friend who seems to practise disease—mine—avoidance. I wish he'd get over it, quit being uncomfortable around my physical changes, treat me like he used to—like a buddy—regale me with tales of his latest nymphomaniac girlfriend. At least he'll be company for a couple of hours.

In the meantime, I figure I'll make myself presentable and available every three days for the month of October, which gives me eleven hot opportunities—including today, and ending on Halloween for a no-holds-barred wild possibility—to bring about a successful outcome. Three orgasms out of eleven attempts make for decently optimistic odds.

While I'm not exactly lazy, I get overwhelmed with the preparation for and execution of social contact. Still, I'm ready, really ready, to put myself out there. In order to avoid utter exhaustion, I am allowing myself two days between each foray to chill out, make crisp notes, make myself cool all over again. If things work out ahead of time, all the better.

I ask the universe—Char's kind of universe—to assist me, maybe even give me a sign. Sure as guns, in a matter of minutes, three ravens swoop through the scant trees across the way. Okay, that's not true. But I do find three hangnails on my left hand while I'm waiting for the miraculous sign. Then it happens. I get three text messages. They're from a number I don't recognize but it contains three threes and is local.

Hey, reads the first.

The next is a little more interesting.

Im softly kissing your neck

And, oh my.

Now slowly moving down your body. Nibbbling

I can't help but notice three *b*'s.

I figure this is a way better sign than the hangnails, regardless of the fact that the words aren't meant for me. After all, technology is a big part of our universe. I do a reverse search, but it's a cell number so there's no listing. I think this stranger must have realized my number isn't the right number. I wait, half-thankful, half-disappointed. I give up, light a cigarette, thinking about places to meet people. Three more texts stutter in. Anticipation rocks!

working side to side down your body with my

I realize that the texts must be character-limited, or the sender likes to build excitement.

tongue to your inner thigh kissing softly every now and then

I'm kind of speechless, a little flushed even.

One side then the other working to the middle where I blow softly

Then nothing.

It's okay. While I cool off, I save the number in my contacts just in case I have the guts to text them back.

Anything is possible and nothing is off limits, so in preparation I charge up the 12-volt scooter battery in Adele—12 is a multiple of 3! Bingo! Maybe bingo's a good place to start—all those daubers and balls and numbers. I notice, too, the number 3 key on my phone also stands for D, E and F. Is this a sign that I should look for somebody hearing-impaired at the local bingo hall?

It's time to get excited. While I'm waiting for bingo o'clock, I make a list of possible ways to meet people—aside from Craigslist and internet options. And counting to three often signals some synchronous act, like one, two, three—pull! Or one, two, three—open your eyes! Or one, two, three—jump! Rock-paper-scissors may dictate the order.

1.   Three wishes (someone wearing a turban?)
2.   Three witches (Boil, Bubble & Trouble?)
3.   Three strikes, you're out! (What I'm aiming for...)
4.   Three strikes in bowling, called a turkey (Thanksgiving holds promise)
5.   Three bears (hairy guys?)
6.   Three little pigs (straw, wood, brick—maybe carpenters?)
7.   Three blind mice (if the deaf option doesn't work out)
8.   Three stooges (Comedy Club?)
9.   Roman numeral III (all upright, phallic)

The community hall is about half a kilometre away, well within Adele's battery capacity. This is the same hall that holds Fetish Night once a month, so I wonder if I'll find any souvenirs.

The atmosphere leaves something to be desired—long folding tables, only twenty people so far, but others follow me in. I look for attractions and hearing aids while I purchase a paltry four bingo sheets but end up sitting alone with Adele at the end of a table, leaving fate in charge.

It isn't long before several serious aficionados pull up their chairs. The woman beside me in long black leather seems overdressed, out of place, but she's all business. She arranges thirty or so sheets and a rainbow of ink daubers. I take note of her large frame and bleached blond hair. She doesn't have hearing aids but every time I ask her about numbers that have been called I have to repeat my question, so maybe she needs them. I can't guess black-leather Blondie's age. Somewhere be-tween young and old. Like me.

As the games proceed and the jackpot continues to grow, I find myself falling behind and Blondie's leaning in to help. She's quick and practised and I don't mind a bit. She seems to be touching my arm a lot, gently nudging me when I miss the numbers, which are sadly lacking in the number three. She wears three serious silver rings, those extended knuckle ones with hinges. By the time the last game's done, Blondie has won several times and I've won nothing. We haven't even exchanged names, but she suggests coffee and she'll buy.

It turns out coffee doesn't mean a cozy café but the back corner of the local Starbucks patio, which is really empty and chilly but, at least, we can smoke. She sits close, drapes her arm around me—for warmth, she says. We clutch our uber-hot coffee cups. It isn't until I find her mouth on mine that I think the night may not be a total bust after all.

"Let's walk," she says. "Around the corner."

"Not really an option," I reply, finding it so odd that people forget to pay attention. I tap on Adele. "But I can scoot."

"Well, we can't do much here."

"What do you have in mind?"

She doesn't reply but pulls out her multicoloured bingo daubers and draws a red arrow on the palm of my hand. It feels weird—cool and moist.

"It's washable," she says, loosening the cotton scarf around my neck, and draws in blue what I figure to be an arrow from my ear down my throat, ending in my red satin-clad excuse for a cleavage. I'm not sure what to do, so I do nothing.

Her eyes scan the empty patio and the lit interior. There's another kiss. No, more than a kiss. A nibble. No, more than a nibble. Her lips are on my throat. And her teeth. A nip. No, not a nip. A small bite.

"Bite me or I'll bite you harder," she hisses, pulling my head to her. I can't get away. I consider reasoning. I consider pleading but don't because it turns me on a little...until it scares me more. Ouch!

I try to pull away, thinking scream, thinking run, but Blondie's strong and she's holding me tight. I'm stuck with fight over flight, but I'm not good at that either. I think semi-friendly biting must beat out fighting so I nibble just a little. She nips at my lips and throat and ear lobe. I don't know if it's the biting or the chilly October evening, but I'm all shivery. This is a new thing...terror.

Must go. Now.

My coffee cup flips its lid, thanks to the nimble fingers on my good hand, and splashes enough steaming brew to make her jerk away. I race Adele inside, where a barista with dangerously long nails calls me a cab—a wheelchair cab that'll take an hour. I say that's fine. I'll wait. I keep my back to the wall, hold my breath, not wanting to look in the direction of the patio. Then I look. There's no one there. No coffee cup. No spills. I convince myself I'm delusional, that it never happened, that binge-watching vampire movies has had a detrimental effect on me.

As the cabbie buckles me and Adele into the van, I find my voice, the semi-sultry one, and say, "I love it when you do that." Proving to myself I'm not really rattled and am still on task. Neither of us speaks on the short drive. He's got another fare waiting. Too bad. He ramps me out and I pay and tip and smile and he smiles back.

"Another time," he says with a mock salute. I notice a toothy glint.

I deadbolt the door and go straight to the bathroom. If I couldn't see proof in the mirror—the fine necklace of angry little bite marks at my throat, I'd still believe it was my imagination playing tricks on me. The coloured arrows are still there. Waterproof, it seems. I scrub and cringe and scrub until my skin's as red as my bra. I apply calendula oil to ease the inflammation. Calendula has nine—three-squared—lucky letters. I check the locks three times before I curl up in bed to chow down on Lay's chips 'n dip.

After two days of recuperation I peruse my evolving list. I cross out mice and witches—considering the semi-deaf bingo succubus, the semi-boiling liquid that was involved and the amount of toil and trouble it took to make my getaway.

Number 3 on the list—*Three strikes, you're out!*—holds promise. The city's ball diamonds may just be *this* girl's best friend. I cover up the lingering string of tooth marks on my throat with makeup and a turtleneck sweater. I decide to play it a little safer this time, leaving Adele at home so I can cruise in my warm, safe, comfy van. But the baseball diamonds are empty because it's October.

Pulling over next to a deserted ballpark, I consider the ways I could have misconstrued the third directive. Maybe baseball was too obvious. Maybe the word "strikes" is a puzzle that requires an unconventional approach. I try scrambling the word but come up with nothing. I consider other definitions, but I haven't seen a picket line lately and air strikes only show up on the news. Direct hits of a personal nature aren't even a consideration. While I'd love to be desired and satisfied ferociously, I don't want to be punched in the head or anywhere else. I've overlooked ignition...spark...fire. Yes! So it could happen anywhere with cigarettes or wood stoves or candles.

I cruise out toward Yellowpoint, looking for a sign, until there's a cranky bunch of motorists behind me. Retracing my route, I finally spot a distinct drift of smoke. It's a backyard bonfire, but it looks to be far too family-oriented for my mission. I consider a bar closer to home with a smoking stone chimney, but I need to find somebody who's sober enough to ensure success.

I go home slightly deflated but still determined. I haven't ruled out the bar but have ruled out the probability of sobriety. I order Viagra online, with an auspicious three-day delivery guarantee. Little blue pills might be handy—even necessary—to have around.

m~◦

Three days later, my phone rings. Right while I'm unwrapping my delivery package. It's John. I'd almost forgotten.

"Hey, Mel. How's tricks?"

"Non-existent," I say, half thinking that turning a few might be an option. "John, don't tell me you're not coming. A-fucking-gain."

"Uh, I'm not coming."

I don't say anything because I can't be sure which of my voices— furious, disappointed or hurt—will have the desired effect.

"I'm kidding. Just kidding," he says. "Beer and hockey sound okay? I'll even bring a pizza."

"Hey, that actually sounds good. Great. Like old times. Triple cheese?"

"Sure. Puck drops at six. Hopin' for a hat trick tonight."

"A hat trick! Of course! I hadn't thought of...sorry, never mind. Just..."

"Just what?"

"Just thinking about...hat tricks and game nights. Whatever. See you at six."

"Right. See you then," he says.

I make adjustments to my list, replacing *triathlon* with *hat trick*, and crossing out a few more while I'm at it. What the hell. Maybe I will just put it to John—my dilemma.

"You seem preoccupied," says John, three beers and half a pizza into the game. Second period's ended and the Canuckleheads are down 3–2.

"Really? Sorry."

"Wanna talk?" John asks, settling back like I'm going to hit him with something mentally heavy.

"Talking is the last thing on my mind."

"Meaning?"

"Meaning I don't want to talk." I pout.

"Okay. Well, what do you wanna do? We've got eighteen minutes."

"What I want to do is have a hat trick." Preoccupied is an understatement. I am cranky and starting to feel a little desperate.

"You might be in luck. Sedin's on his way."

"No, John. Not Sedin. Me. Before I'm sent down to the farm team." And with that, I dissolve into tears. Pathetic blubbery tears that demand a hug. At the very least, a hug. And I get it, because John has no idea what else to do. He pulls me close, attempting to calm me, defuse the baffling emotional situation. I comply, wiping my nose on his shirt. It's all comfy there and so soothing—the aftershave, the warmth, his hands resting against my back. But that's it. I'm in a fix and comfy just isn't going to cut it.

"Kleenex," I demand.

John passes me the box, looking simultaneously concerned and relieved, just waiting—for me to compose myself. For the third period to start. For a return to normalcy.

"Phew," I finally say. "Enough of that."

John pats my knee. "Any time you wanna talk."

"Thanks," I say, knowing my desperate sexual situation is not appropriate or comfortable or smart to discuss. I also know the differences between men's and women's listening skills and which part of the conversation is taken seriously, especially when hockey's involved. I know what he's thinking, that it's the MS thing, which is a perfectly acceptable excuse for misery in John's books. He probably expects tears on a regular basis from me because he's not around to see that it's not—not regular, at least.

Sedin fails at the hat trick. So do I. For now. I feel better after my teary little episode though—all that self-pity flushed out. A fresh slate. I even manage a mysterious smile when I hint that I've got plans for Thanksgiving that don't include him or Charlene or even Jackie. I keep my plans secret. Even from myself.

We hug good night, mutually reassuring. There is not one iota of spark. I'll save that for some unsuspecting turkey on the tenth. The tenth day of the tenth month. If I add 10:00 p.m. that makes three tens! This cannot be anything but lucky, considering ten is a symbol of perfection, and in temporal binary it equals forty-two, which is, of course, divisible by three—a rational number.

Again, I ready myself—get a little dolled up. Between hair and makeup, I text the mystery texter with three quick before-I-change-my-mind messages, allowing for slightly more honesty than I can muster with friends, acquaintances or medical professionals.

> recruiting volunteers to have sex
> with hot disabled chick
> position open immediately
> sliding pay scale

Flirtation and assertiveness have their place. So does anonymity. I'll never meet him face to face. I don't even expect a response but have fun sending the texts. It's not even a novel idea—the volunteers. They've been doing it in Switzerland for years.

In the meantime, the bar may have to suffice for doable options. The only problem with this is that a female sitting alone in a bar on a sentimental statutory holiday looks pathetic—a disabled one, even more so. So I go early—mid-afternoon—as though I have somewhere else familial to be later. I'm feeling so good that I decide to leave Adele at home, relying on my cane between my van and the bar stool.

It's dead but for a few late-lunchers and a couple of sad-sack permanent bachelors, until the boys roll in from the Rod 'n Gun Club turkey shoot—all plaid and flannel joviality. A couple of them that I know a little pull up bragging chairs, happy to talk buckshot. I'm willing enough to listen, question even, waiting for a sign from somebody, almost anybody. Attentiveness takes work.

There's one particularly dark furry guy who's got curly chest hairs spilling out over his Stanfield's, which could be a good sign for the three bears on my list. But he also has hair on the back of his hands, which filters down to a bare white patch on his ring finger where a ring should be nestled, pointing to a turkey dinner with all the kids and grandparents. The other guy is barely drinking age. I probably know his mother.

When the lot of them leaves, I'm not overly disappointed. Resigned is more like it. The work of seduction is exhausting. Today is not the day, and sex is off the menu. People suck. I hate my life.

I'm buttoning up my coat when I see someone else on the approach. *Too late. Not only has my mission been aborted, my aversion to people has returned.* More plaid. Tall. Hefty. *I wish I was home already.* A thick plait of carrot-red hair over one shoulder. Oops, no, I was wrong about hefty. Buxom, maybe? Chubby? Heavy? I don't know what word I'd use without it being wrong. Okay, she's a big woman with the plainest of faces. Raised eyebrows above small but sparkly eyes. A shoulder bag the size of a kayak.

"Would you mind some company?" she asks. "Just until my friend shows up?"

I cringe. "Sorry, no, I was..."

"I hate sitting alone in here is all. And I've been waiting for an hour. And..."

I gesture to the exit. "I was actually just..."

She offers an unpretentious smile and a firm hand. "Fiona. No Shrek jokes, please. And, don't worry," she adds. "I wasn't at the turkey shoot, so we'll have to find something else to talk about."

I can't help but laugh. A little girl talk might be the best antidote for my failures. Nothing like diversion, especially with an exit point. I quit sucking in my belly and relax. "Melanie. I was just about to...order an early dinner."

Fiona settles herself into a seat, doesn't judge my solo dinner or solo drinking on Thanksgiving, so I silently give thanks for that. She's casual, single, more interesting than I thought, and more complicated.

She's been a potter, a barber, a baker and worked construction. "It's all about the hands," she says. She slips on a pair of sequined glasses to examine the menu. We have a couple of drinks while she checks her phone, order hot turkey sandwiches after. Fiona talks clay and dough and carpentry.

"Straw, wood or brick?" I ask, enjoying my private list-joke.

"Wood," she says. "I was more into fine finishing."

"Was?"

"I'm back at school. Just started in health care...home support, eldercare, that kind of thing."

"Wow. Good for you."

She squints her eyes but doesn't comment.

I've fed Fiona the same atta girl type of response that I resent. "I mean good for everybody. You know, good for the whole world." How lame.

When Fiona checks her phone for the thirty-ninth time, it gives me a chance to change the subject. "No word from your friend?"

She sighs. "Ghosted again."

"Friends can be..."

"To be honest, it's a date. Was supposed to be a date."

"Bummer."

She gives a wry smile, patting her substantial derrière. "That's usually the problem."

"No!" I protest, blushing. "I didn't mean..."

"Don't sweat it. It happens...all the time."

"Well, he doesn't know what he's missing."

"Right. Ugh. People's expectations...versus image...body issues...you wouldn't know."

"But I *would* know. I *do* know!" I show her my cane.

That's how we end up talking about less-than-ideal bodies and their complications. We talk about fat—Fiona's—and disease—mine—which leads to conversation about desire—everybody's. I mention the Swiss volunteer experiment and she gets a funny look on her face before bursting out in jolly infectious laughter. "I can't believe this!" she keeps saying.

Fiona presses a couple of buttons on her phone and lays it on the table between us. I swear the thing is smoking. There's my text starting with *recruiting volunteers*.

"Oh, that..." I say, blushing wildly.

"What are the chances?" she laughs. "Your texts...I thought you were some guy just—"

"I thought you were too."

She gives her head a shake, replacing laughter with a laser beam of focused empathy. "How long has it been since you..." She must be reading my confused face as a very long time. "Lady," she says, standing and pulling me to my feet, "forget the turkey sandwiches. Come with me!"

In my van she says, "Think of me as your good Samaritan."

When we get home Fiona extracts a clipboard from her monster bag and displays a take-charge persona I couldn't have imagined. "First your stats, then we'll get you looked after."

I feel awkward. "We haven't talked about...money."

"Oh, no money. Fair exchange," she says, taking off my coat. "I have a paper to write and need a subject, a more interesting one than I've been assigned."

"Your bedside manner?"

She smiles. "Exactly. Let's keep this professional."

"Professional?"

"Home support. Health care. Now..." Fiona takes notes while she slips off my shoes and socks, every bit of clothing. She's adept and natural, arranging my klutzy incompetent body face down on the bed, covering me and telling me to relax while she gets ready. I lie there like a stiff, listening, wondering—until she returns in her maroon scrubs, sequined glasses and sky-blue latex gloves. This makes it clinically erotic. She's carrying her adorable clipboard, an armful of extra pillows and a bottle of my own lotion. "It's all in the hands," she reminds me with a big smile, and my awkwardness disappears.

Human touch—such a luxury. "Here?" she asks. "Too hard?" she asks. My body and I tell her the answers.

I become Fiona's clay as she stands over me manipulating my neglected leg muscles, Fiona's bread as she kneads my back, neck and shoulders, my good arm and hand, then my bad. Even my hips and bum muscles. I tell her how it feels and where it doesn't. She takes notes, then turns me easily onto my back, leaving room for her own generous hips and impressive thighs to sit next to me. She works on my feet, my toes, my lopsided legs, my belly, my Ohhhhh! Sky-blue palm and fingers say hello to my clitoris. I shut my eyes, hold my breath. Little twinges... slightly bigger twinges...

But I don't seem to be progressing. I open my eyes and look at Fiona, who seems to be in a trance. She's rubbing me the wrong way and then not rubbing me at all. Her smile has disappeared. "Fiona?"

She snaps out of it. "Sorry. Where was I?"

I pat the bed beside me, take her sky-blue hand in mine. "Why don't you just—"

"So much for professionalism!"

"You have a whole career for that. Now, lady," I say, turning the tables, "let's get you out of that uniform and into some R-and-R nakedness."

"Don't look," she says, blushing like only another redhead can.

After the last hour of baring all, I want to laugh. Instead, I suggest she turn out the light. Then we laugh. And laugh. And giggle her out of her scrubs and under the covers. What a beautiful mouth! Between her voluptuous roundness and my post-massage-but-still-uncooperative body we invent a hot new game of tit for twat. It's a win (*mmm-mmm-mmm*) win! So we play another round. And, voila, we pull off another pair of coups without too much effort. Gawd, we're good! And we're beautiful! And exhausted in the best way. After cuddles and kisses and wishing her luck with her paper and paying for her cab— we say good-bye.

It isn't till lunchtime the next day, when all the warm fuzzies have worn off, that I realize I've used up my Number 2! It was even better than Number 3, but I admit I would have gotten a kick out of another list of possibilities. Good and evil. Hot and cold. Pairs and pears, cuz now that my second-to-last orgasm has been used up, I'm incredibly hungry for sweet curvy October fruit.

6
Liberation

I'm down to *one*—an orgasm number I refuse to spend alone. And I demand champagne, canapés and a cigar from Havana. When I call Char to ask about the symbolism of the number, she gives me such an overblown assortment of interpretations that it might as well be a bag of jellybeans.

"Can you pare it down?" I ask.

"Well, basically, it's a reminder that we create our own reality. You know, thoughts, beliefs, actions, that kind of thing."

"More basic?"

"You need a full reading."

"Please?"

"Step out of your comfort zone."

I tell her, "Thanks. Perfect."

Then she adds, "It also means goodbye. Are you planning a trip?"

I laugh. "Not any time soon."

So, I think, after hanging up, I just have to get out of my comfort zone to get my last bell rung. And goodbye is what I'll happily say to sex once that's been accomplished. It still feels overwhelming. My list isn't particularly helpful. It's almost extinct.

9. Roman numeral I (all upright, phallic)

One's not a bad number, in Roman numerals or otherwise. I like the shape. Pure simplicity—like a bullet, which I'm more than a little prepared to bite for the sake of freedom or liberation or even deliverance from this numerical blessing-curse. And it symbolizes so many apropos characteristics for my final climactic act—urgency for new beginnings, action—both mental and physical, positivity and strong will. And I read somewhere that if one urges us to some pure urgent natural action, we'll be rewarded in kind.

All my senses are heightened as I prepare for the biggest, best finale. I look in my closet, thinking a dress is called for, nothing bridal but the opposite of that, black. No, not black. Too funereal, and it makes me look sallow. Red, then. Again. But with black boots and the biggest earrings ever. I make sure I have cash in my wallet in case I have to pay for the privilege of achieving Numero Uno.

I can't decide where to go, to look, to hook up. It's a real issue. I could call a cab and ask the driver, but the cabbie the other night was a little too creepy. On the other hand, they do know where to find any and every thing. They tell me the wait'll be over an hour. Now I have time to waste.

I twiddle my thumbs, check my nails, reapply my lipstick. I could use a sign right about now. Nothing happens. It's too quiet, so I turn on the TV and watch the news. More about lost hikers, more about floods and fires, more about hockey. After the commercial, a report on a medical breakthrough. I wait for it and hey, it's about multiple sclerosis. They describe a new theory about a condition that could play a role in the development of MS, and it's quite a mouthful: chronic cerebrospinal venuous insufficiency (CCSVI). And they mention the doctor who developed a medical procedure to tackle it: Dr. Zamboni. Zamboni! How could this Canadian not embrace the quasi-hockey relevance? Now they're talking about a small Italian study with remarkable results. They show before and after clips of MSers. Some remain static with no progression, while others are doing better, much better! The story's not that exciting until it suddenly is.

They're calling it "Liberation"—this angioplasty. A minor incision, a catheter, and poof, they open narrowed areas in the veins. The theory is that the blocked or narrowed veins have been preventing excess iron in the brain from draining away. I like the idea. No toxic drugs. No injections. No hopelessness.

I'll believe it when I see it, but I really want to see it or see more about it at least. I boot up the computer. Holy crap. Liberation is everywhere. It's going viral. They're already doing it in Poland and India and Egypt and other medical tourism hot spots in Central America, like Costa Rica and Panama. Not in Canada though. Far too experimental, they say. But life is one long experiment. I dig and research and read and research until I'm nearly cross-eyed. Screw the orgasm dilemma. This might be even bigger. Like health, or something closer to that. Imagine.

There's a knock at the door.

"What?" I call, totally put out at the interruption. "Who is it?"

I hear a muffled voice, a man's voice.

"Oh, shit. Just a minute."

I wheel to the door, open it a little and see a darn nice-looking fella. I open the door a little wider, taking a good look.

"You called a cab?" he asks.

Well, well, I think. But what I say is, "A cab? No I did not call a cab. Must be some mistake." I shut the door on the puzzled good-looker. He knocks again. I don't answer, hear his receding footsteps and spinning gravel as the taxi peels away.

I get right back to the computer where I slip off my earrings, stockings and special-occasion garter belt. Down to business. I crumple the old list and toss it. I fill out applications for six countries. The wait times are atrocious—up to eighteen months. It's incredibly expensive—in the thousands, which is way out of my reach, but I'll worry about that later. The possibilities are endless. I'll make a list! But first I think about my life, and what I can quit—like drinking, smoking, being a couch (wheelchair) potato—while I'm waiting to improve my outcome.

I get the call on the thirteenth, a seriously lucky number. I have a date three months down the road with Costa. Costa Rica, that is. I can't wait!

6 1/2
Hurry Up and Wait

Three months is a long time to wait for a life-changing medical procedure when your disease is progressive. On the other hand, it's a mighty short time to jam all the square monetary and medical pegs into the round holes required to see it to fruition. The list I started three months ago is almost complete.

1. Passport √
2. $20,000 or equivalent credit (yay, Charlene! Credit, it is!) √
3. Wire $10,000 asap to Travel-Med Company √
4. Referral for private clinic pre-op MRI/sonogram from doctor/GP X
5. Fire GP √√√√√√√√√√√√√√√√√√√√√√√√√√√√√√ √√√√√√√√√√√√√√
6. Find new GP √
7. Private clinic pre-op MRI $$$$ √
8. Private clinic sonogram $$ √
9. Find travel companion/caregiver (yay, Jackie!) √
10. Book flights (x 2) Vancouver/Houston/San José, Costa Rica √√
11. Pack √
12. Go!

7

Lost in Translation and I Can't Find My Hand

We're on our way!

Jackie and I breezed through the pre-dawn economy flight—pretzels only—from Vancouver. We logged five hours in the air and then another six in the Houston airport. The terminal is massive, but we were limited to Concourse B, which was just as well since the airline held my scooter in transit. Jackie had to push me around in a wheelchair, dragging our carry-ons, and I didn't want to wear her out too early on. We have ten days to go.

Concourse B was enough to see anyway. We were surrounded by red, white and blue banners, bunting and flags. Hoping for some relief from the Stars and Stripes and Texas Lone Star, we searched the crowds for Canadians—a Moosehead Brewery T-shirt or a backpack with a discreet maple leaf or some mention in overheard conversation of Montreal or Chilliwack. We found a near-empty salad bar and nibbled on limp greens, resisting the aroma of barbecue and Tex-Mex. We whispered to each other about the NRA. We counted stetsons. We discussed the word *potent*. We did crossword puzzles together and then separately until our departure flight was called. Cordiality is exhausting, y'all! It also ends at the security gate.

We got my shoes off okay but the pliers I use to get them on and off were confiscated. My incapacity to walk through the metal detector without touching its walls didn't go over well. When Jackie got all indignant about the situation, things got worse. They hustled me into a clear cubicle for the inevitable pat-down and spent an inordinate amount of time trying to find something nefarious inside my suspiciously hollow cane. They dusted the underside of my wheelchair for explosives. The hefty blonde Homeland gal was finally convinced that I wasn't the underwear bomber, and I was glad for her sake and mine that I hadn't succumbed to the draw of the Tex-Mex chilied frijoles.

The bonus of disability-related early boarding and semi-private lurching down the aisle will be negated when Jackie and I are stuck on the plane after landing till every other soul has departed. But then again, I'll get to take the arm or hand of a variety of hottish pilots and stewards and even baggage handlers when they deliver my scooter—hopefully—to the door of the plane.

m⁓

We're in the air again and, with Jackie asleep beside me, I have time to think on the final southern leg. I'm imagining my hot date with Costa Rica. It's on Valentine's Day. And I can hardly wait! I try not to think about the procedure itself. Anxiety, fear, hope and excitement—in one overwhelming combo—make it hard to know what my erratic emotions will tolerate best: thinking hopefully ahead or thinking analytically back. I keep trying to do none of the above by examining a paperback, my grotesque passport picture, even the vomit sack, but "trying," as Homer Simpson would say, "is the first step to failure."

I look around at the other passengers. The thing is, I'm different. I'm not like the vacationers and business-trippers crammed in around me. I'm a medical tourist, and my date is with a doctor at a hospital in San José. My date, this procedure, could theoretically be life-changing. And there'll be balloons, but no party, because they'll be tiny balloons, expanded inside the blocked veins of my neck to release the overload of iron in my brain. That's the concept anyway.

My homework's been done, including research into the vascular procedure, the handful of countries like Poland and Egypt—not Canada—making it available, before-and-after care, the San José hospital—and I'm cautiously and terrifyingly optimistic! I've paid my thousands up front and signed the liability waiver. And seriously, at the moment, I don't give a flying fig about risk.

I just want the basics back. I want to walk. I want to have two good hands to accomplish tasks. I want to move and do and make and feel and be what I was like before. Simple things.

My watch confirms my suspicions. Still an hour to touchdown.

Hope can be a wonderful but dangerous thing. So I look to the past. Like to past trips, discreet airplane sex under a blanket, becoming an official member of the mile-high club. Wrong thought direction but entertaining nonetheless.

Looking back at my last mother-of-a-roller-coaster year is pretty surreal. I'll admit it. Finding out that my MS is past the halfway mark and that my body was only capable of having six more orgasms threw me for the kind of loop that cinches you up tighter and tighter every time you try to wriggle out of it.

But I did have a five-out-of-six success rate. And I did have that timely shift in libido—less hopeful sex for more sexless hope. And I did come across this treatment and continue to pursue it. I'm fairly sure I'm justified in thinking that replacing one obsession (orgasms) with another (remission) can't be all bad. But balance has never been my forte.

I check my watch six more times.

$\sim$

We circle San José—all those red roofs getting closer! Red for the heart! Red for healthy blood and veins, for flowers, fruit and fire.

I nudge Jackie awake, which pitches her into her practical mode, with anxiety on the side. "Okay," she says, smoothing her newly blond-highlighted hair. "Passports?"

"Check."

"Declarations?"

"Check."

"And there'll be someone waiting for us, right?"

"Alejandro, like the Gaga song, yes," I assure her, scanning over our extensive itinerary. I pat her hand to reassure her—and me—because her unease might be contagious enough to exacerbate my symptoms. Botheration can throw me into spasms—and not of laughter—which could make our exit from the plane a snail-paced nightmare. "He'll be right by the baggage carousel with a sign."

"Cash?"

"American and colones."

"Hotel phone number, just in case?"

"Right here. Jackie, we've been over this a million times. It'll be fine. This medi-tourism company looks after everything."

When the plane makes a bumpy landing and taxis to a stop on the San José tarmac, she squeezes my hand back, gives me a dazzling and uplifting smile like a warranty of support. "Are you ready?"

"So ready."

We gather ourselves while we wait for the other passengers to vacate, breaking simultaneously into our Vince Vaccaro theme song, "Let's go-o-o to Costa Ri-i-ca!" Despite my uncooperative stiffness, I manage to lurch to the exit door assisted by chair-backs and Jackie. My scooter's not there waiting for me. Neither is my wheelchair. In fact, there's nothing there but hot air, stairs, tarmac and a distant building.

"A moment, please," says one of the stewards hovering near me.

I see this big contraption rolling toward us. It's got a little human-sized compartment at the bottom that looks like an elongated fiberglass egg attached to a metal tower. It's rolled up to the platform atop the stairs, and the egg rises to my level. There's a decrepit standard wheelchair inside.

A second steward offers his hand. "Your elevator, Señora. Costa Rica awaits you."

Holy hell.

They help me into the egg and buckle me in and shut the half-door and I'm alone but I can at least see out. I wave goodbye to Jackie. For all I know there's rocket fuel under my little egg that someone's going to light and I'm about to experience a Cape Canaveral blast-off. Sometimes you just have to trust people. A lot of people. So I do. My egg descends noisily and slowly till I hit bottom and am released into the welcoming arms of my scooter. I love you, Adele!

Next adventure, please.

We make our way into the terminal, use the washroom, follow the arrows, look for Alejandro, gather our bags, search for Alejandro, question a couple of sign-holding guys about Alejandro in really minimal Spanglish, and realize we're missing my personal wheelchair. We finally find the *especialidades* baggage pickup area for surfboards and caged Chihuahuas and mobility equipment.

"Airline?" asks the guy behind the counter.

"Incontinental," says Jackie, and we both burst out laughing. "Another trip to the washroom?" she asks me.

I have to agree. We take turns guarding our belongings.

It's beginning to look like Alejandro is a no-show. Neither of us mentions how worried we're both starting to feel. Two women. And half of us are kind of vulnerable. In a foreign airport. With a wheelchair now loaded up with our luggage.

"I need to smoke, Jackie."

"Can't you wait? You'll have to go *outside*. Of the terminal, I mean. And *supposedly* this Alejandro will be *inside*."

"Right. I can wait."

We give it another thirty minutes. There's a wee bit of testiness in the air. I remind myself Jackie hasn't travelled much.

All of a sudden, through all the unfamiliar faces, another unfamiliar face (under a frantically waving sign) stands out because it's a super-friendly face and it's calling my name. "Farrell? Melanie Farrell?"

"Alejandro!" we both call out as he approaches, sweeping us into his genial thirtyish—give or take five years—assurance. "Ladies, José at your service."

"José?" we chime. "Where's Alejandro?"

José explains, leading us out to the parkade through a sudden heavy rain, that Alejandro took sick and that he, José, will be ours for the ten-day duration. Our transportation. Our tour guide. Our translator. And our concierge, if we have any special or unusual requests. He winks, then sighs as we arrive at our well-travelled van, the kind you can roll a chair or scooter into through the rear door.

"We have a little *problemo*." He loads our bags and my wheelchair. "With the starter."

I stay put in the scooter, fumble for a badly needed smoke.

Jackie raises her eyebrows.

We look on as José's failed ignition attempts almost murder the battery. He has a back up plan, to jump-start the engine. I move well out of the way and Jackie and a parking attendant push. Success! I refuse to roll into the back where the view is restricted so we climb in, me with a lot of assistance. José stows the scooter, and we're off. Jackie, grubbier and sweatier than I've ever seen her, asks how far the hotel is. José passes us bottled water from a cooler.

"*Pura vida!*" he toasts. "Pure life! It's our...how do you say...motto? Yes, here in Costa Rica, we use it for everything."

We raise our plastic bottles together. "*Pura vida!*" we say in unison, though Jackie seems to be somewhat lacking in the exuberance department.

José smiles at me in the rearview mirror. "Oh, and we go to the hotel later. First, the hospital. You have an appointment in forty minutes."

I smile back, feeling special. And confused. "I do?"

"Just for the tests," he says. "And signing papers. See the doctor."

I'm game, trusting, but I need answers. "So a couple of hours?"

"Sure, yes. It's good. They moved you forward a day. Don't worry. We coordinate everything for you."

"Okay then," I say, glancing at Jackie, whose eyebrows are still hidden somewhere up near her hairline. "I guess we clean up later."

"I guess so," says Jackie, brushing soot or something from the sleeve of her shirt. "The hospital *is* why we're here."

"Right. And we'll *never*..." I whisper, pulling out a sanitizing wipe for her hands.

"Have to do this..." Jackie whispers, pulling a comb through her hair.

"Again," we both say, oh so quietly.

When José's not talking on his cellphone—in thousand-mile-an-hour Spanish—he talks an impressive and informative streak of really good English, patting his chest every time he says the José in San José. Mostly we just double-take and half listen—the random careening and blaring interspersed with random pedestrian pedlars, the vivid colours, concrete houses, barred windows on everything. Poverty. I almost forget myself.

"Here we are," says José, pulling into the entrance of a six-storey ultra-modern structure. "And there's Gloria, your team coordinator."

Wow! I have a team! A team that includes Jackie and José and Gloria—middle-aged and bespectacled—and I expect my team to swell shortly to include nurses and neurologists and vascular surgeons and anesthesiologists and pharmacists. And accountants. You don't get all this for nothing. You get it for thousands of dollars, and in my case, it's dollars that aren't exactly mine. Despite feeling uber-positive I'm also feeling the overlapping responsibilities of borrowed money and expectations here and back at home. My team is only as strong as its weakest member, and I'm it.

Gloria leads us into a room, biggish for the single bed and minimal equipment. Jackie opts to exit following Gloria's cafeteria suggestion and a promise of sandwiches. I flip through a magazine—*Neurology Now*—until I come across an article about a condition that's far stranger than mine, therefore freakishly fascinating. Enough to take my mind elsewhere. Apotemnophilia. It's sort of the opposite of having a phantom limb. It's not even that rare. It's a strong aversion by an otherwise perfectly sane, functioning person to their own perfectly good limb. Voluntary amputation is their answer, their resolution. Wow. And they want it done in a very specific way.

This one guy, I read, would frequently take a pen and draw the same very precise irregular line around his arm and say that he wanted it gone, amputated exactly along the line—no less, no more, or it would feel wrong. And when he was tested a year later he'd draw the same wiggly line—a line he couldn't possibly have memorized—which seems to indicate that it's something physiological, not simply psychological.

Neurologists have developed a complicated mapping explanation for how they think it works, and I read it about six times because I like maps and I'm trying to get it. The article goes on to explain how this brain imaging technique is used to map out the body and how normal people have a complete point-by-point map on the surface of a particular strip of cortex. But there's another region behind that—the superior parietal lobule—which actually creates your body image.

When a person closes their eyes they have a vivid sense of their different body parts, mostly from joint and muscle sense, partly from the vestibular sense—whether you're standing erect or tilting your head—and partly when confirmed by vision. This convergence of signals to your brain from touch, proprioception, vestibular sense and vision enables you to construct a vivid internal picture—your body image.

For the apotemnophiliac, that map does not include the arm that the patient wants to get rid of.

I do not want to amputate anything! But the mapping is interesting, because of my MS symptoms—like my failing vestibular system, that lack of balance, which is why I fall over in the dark or when I shut my eyes if I'm not touching something stable. I put down the magazine and try to visualize my limbs. And muscles. And even my veins. And my brain. I visualize them healthy. I don't think I really understand it all, but I still like the idea of a body map between my ears.

I contemplate the strangeness of the brain just as the first of several male medicos begins what will be an afternoon of repetitive interrogation about my medical history, interspersed with a few minor tests—blood, blood pressure, kidney function, spasticity, mobility, ultrasound—mostly in English but with that melodious Spanish flourish. The young neurologist is tall, his intern sidekick looks about twelve, the nurse is swarthy, the accountant is, um, forgettable and, finally, the vascular surgeon is none of the above, meaning he's very attractive. Even his longish oiled hair. And his reassuring smile. And his agile fingers at my wrist. His name is Falik. Dr. Falik.

I think of the phallic Roman numeral I on my list at home. I start talking because somebody has to. "Phallic?" I ask, admiring his aquiline nose.

"That's right."

I get back on track. "My appointment's been moved up to tomorrow, I hear. Is that right?"

He looks at his watch. "Tomorrow, yes. The thirteenth. In the afternoon."

"I was all geared up for Valentine's Day."

"Oh, you're romantic. Like my wife." He smiles.

"Not really. I was just making the heart connection. Vascular. Venous. Valentine."

"We don't touch the heart, but I see." Dr. Falik explains the procedure. It's not surgery but I'll be in an operating theatre. I'll have an IV for saline and the contrast dye.

"Okay," I say.

He tells me that I won't be anesthetized, but I won't remember anything either because I'll be under twilight sedation.

"Sounds nice-ish."

"No pain," he assures me.

"Excellent."

"There will be a small incision in your groin. Local anesthesia. Okay?"

"Right. Yes."

"A thin catheter—imagine a spaghetti noodle—will be threaded up through a vein in the neck. Near the spine. The fluoroscope—like an x-ray—shows the dye, the vessels. It's a living map."

"Can I watch?"

"Of course," he says, "but you won't remember. What we will do though," he adds, "is take photos for you. You'll have a souvenir CD to take home with you."

"Cool." Just like a skydiving video, I think.

He continues. "A balloon on the tip of the catheter will be expanded."

"Yes."

"After a short time, it will be deflated."

"Okay."

"And removed. Along with the catheter."

"Awesome."

"Then the procedure will be repeated."

"Repeated?"

"As needed. Left side, right side."

"Right. Of course."

"Then rest. Stillness. Wake up in a nice patient room, a nurse, a cot for the sister."

"Sister? Oh, Jackie. No, she's my friend."

"Ah, good," he says. "Questions?"

I shake my head. Not a one. Sounds like a breeze. I smile. So does Dr. Falik.

And then he's done. And seeing as I've been on the move for the last eighteen hours, so am I. Beat. Stressed. Nervous. Excited. Hopeful. Optimistic. Exhausted and dog-tired.

8
What's Not to Love?

Gloria gathers Jackie and me up and leads us back to the hospital entrance, where José waits with our little van and two other very pink women. Moira's maybe forty and waiting for the same MS-related procedure as me. Pyjamaed in her wheelchair, she takes her MS and medical status seriously. Jinx, her companion, is somewhat younger but not as young as her attire suggests. Apparently we have to share José with these two for our whole ten days. I don't usually mind sharing. It's just this sense of slight diminishment, a little tarnish on our postcard experience—especially when Jinx lets go of Moira's rolling wheelchair and hollers, "Shotgun!" lunging past Jackie into the front seat. Moira, thankfully, is rescued by José before she rolls out into traffic. The rest of us cram into the back.

Just then the skies open. The rain is frenzied, as is the rush-hour traffic. José bamboozles the van into the streaming vehicles and we attempt to relax in our own steam. There's lightning. And honking. And thunder. With undertones of diesel. I like it. Everything about it.

"Every afternoon," José says, gesturing to the sky, "a show for you."

"Rain every day?" asks Jackie.

"Every bloody day," says Jinx.

"Oh," Jackie says. "How long have you guys been here?"

"Day before yesterday. See my burn?" She lifts her T-shirt and shows us her lobstered belly. "That's one morning. Watch out."

"Right." Jackie dismisses Jinx. Redirects.

"José, really? Every day?"

"Hot hot sun in the morning, rain in the afternoon. All days like that."

I see Jackie behind José thinking. She likes to have control. I'm wondering how flexible her comfort zone is and hoping it's like a pair of Vancouver-friendly yoga pants. Have Zen: Will Travel. She strains forward, grasping our driver's shoulder to override the racket outside.

"How far to the Holiday Inn, José?"

"Oh, no Holiday Inn. A better place."

Jackie twists around to catch my eye like I'm automatically responsible for any screw-ups or disappointments. "Ohhh? A better *closer* place?"

"Not so far. Maybe, mmm, an hour. Because of the traffic."

"It's here in San José though, right?"

"Not exactly." José smiles. "Alajuela."

"Hallelujah! Fucking perfect." Jackie's eyebrows are up again and her mouth is turning down, getting all pinchy.

I am mute. So is Moira but for her whimpers as we corner.

José laughs. "Not hallelujah. Ala-who-aila. Not too far. Better than San José. Beautiful hotel. Big gardens."

"I bet," says Jackie, staring into the distance and crossing her arms, then quickly changing her mind to clutch at the armrest and José as we hurtle through a red light, a newly formed curbside lake, and round another corner.

"*Pura vida!*" José exclaims, waving both hands through the steamy interior air. "Full of life. Plenty of life, yes?" He steers with his knees.

Jackie responds. "Just enough life to get to the bloody hotel would be good."

I blot out everything but the present. Me. Breathing. Possibilities. Dying inside this van. Dying outside of this van before the good possibilities have a chance.

I snap to when we veer up into a cobbled driveway. I didn't see it coming—the hotel. Villa Flora. We're stopped at a little guardhouse. José's checking in. Security makes me feel funny, especially as darkness falls—simultaneously more safe and more at risk. The rail-crossing-type barricade is raised. We follow the driveway up. I smile at Jackie. She smiles back. And so do José and Moira and Jinx. We are in paradise.

Hallelujah! Alajuela!

The air is heavy with perfume. Redolent. Ambrosial. Spicy and musky and sweet all at once. José points out the surrounding trees, their massive pendulous blooms softly white in the dusk, as though moonlit from within. Angel's trumpets. Each one large enough to cloak a whole hand. Foliage everywhere. Settled solidly in the midst of all this abundance is Villa Flora, our delightful home-away-from-home hotel, just the kind I might choose myself if I could afford it—clean simple lines, low-slung, white stucco, Spanish tiles, stained glass, boutiquey, only a few dozen rooms.

The luggage is unloaded and so are we—me back in my scooter, which gives me some independence. I don't need to wait for a push or a pull. Despite the incredible fatigue, I don't want to go inside but we do. Wood and white walls and welcoming smiles. The check-in's a breeze. We say good night to José and give a quick wave to the other MSers in the lobby—all ages with wheelchairs and scooters and canes. I wonder who's already had the procedure done. And if they're better for it. But time enough for that.

"Jackie," I say, and point past the gift shop to the elevator. No need to explain.

She nods. We go.

What a sweet room! Clean and fresh, big and bright, the night breeze. We're too tired to unpack. Jackie doesn't even check her cellphone. Wow. We collapse into bed and drift off with the scent of angel's trumpets wafting through the open windows, hardly a care in the world.

A persistent knock at the door drags us out of travel-weary sleep. Holy shit! Today's the day! My mind's wide awake but my body—as usual—is sloth-like before coffee. I peek over the covers to make sure Jackie's on top of things. She fumbles around for a robe and opens the door a crack. I hear a man in the hallway. The only word I can make out clearly is "*problemo.*"

"What?" I ask when Jackie closes the door.

"A change in schedule," she says matter-of-factly, pulling back the blinds to flood the room with sunlight. "Don't panic."

"Another change?" I'm not that good at change, especially last minute, and we survived a lot of that yesterday.

"It's been postponed."

"Postponed?!"

"Stop repeating everything I say. Yes, postponed. Not cancelled."

"Tell me!"

"I'm trying, Mel. Calm down. It's just for one day."

"Calm down? *Just* one day? And what if it's *just* another day? And then another..."

"It's tomorrow, for sure. Back to your original appointment. I'll tell you everything but remember our little rule?"

I get myself upright. "No talking before coffee."

"That's the one." Jackie pulls some summery item from her suitcase and heads for the bathroom.

"But, why? The doctor died? Somebody jumped the queue?"

"No talking!" she calls back. "They're out of balloons, okay? Let's go. Coffee. Brekkie. Talk. In that order." She shuts the door between us.

"You forgot smoking. In the no-talking-before rule." Just as well she couldn't hear me. As far as smoking goes, she's one of the obnoxiously reformed.

Humph. Back to waiting, just when I was all geared up to go.

I give my head a shake. I can't afford stress or upset or dwelling. Maybe, just maybe, today's a bonus. A free day. A day to get familiar with our posh digs, the acres of gardens, the pool, the food, the language, the people, the sun. I am here and I am Lucky—with a capital *L*. And, hey, I'll get my date on Valentine's Day after all. Oh, yes I will.

Jackie and I swap spots. She comes out and I go in—without a word. I wake up enough to brush, wash and flush. I use Jackie's lipstick to draw a heart on the mirror with an arrow and a little balloon before I vacate. I put on my swimsuit, that despicable necessity for getting publicly wet and refreshed, cover it with a sundress, decide against footwear—too time-consuming without my confiscated pliers—and arrange myself in Adele.

"Ready!" I announce.

Jackie's gone. Oh, she's out on the sundeck in her bathing suit. She looks way younger, more fit, way better all-round—damn it!—than me, which makes me feel old and unfit and rounder than the generally able-bodied population. Jackie's talking on her phone. I can tell who's on the other end—Cameron, her boyfriend back home—by the way she's smile-talking and running her hand ever so slowly along the railing. It'll be a long schmoozy call.

I signal to her that I'll meet her downstairs.

The fragrant lobby is quiet, a pretty young woman busy at the front desk. I motor into the near-empty high-ceilinged dining room. Windows flung open. Casual elegance. Flowing white tablecloths. Essence of coffee.

Several white-shirted toothsome young Hispanics, one standing on a chair, wave white linen napkins in the direction of a small brightly coloured but unwelcome bird. They laugh and banter and fail happily at their task, come over to greet me, a little embarrassed at being caught out. The boys are lovely, sweet, eager and ready to serve.

A sumptuous buffet is laid out on a long table with everything internationally breakfasty and typically Costa Rican: beans and rice and fresh warm tortillas the size of my palm. There are massive platters of fruit: mango slivers and nuggets of pineapple, slabs of papaya and heart-shaped—symbolic, no?—strawberry halves, quartered bananas and a rainbow of sliced melon.

The boys are disappointed when I ask only for the biggest possible coffee to go, but I promise to return. I think I am in love with each and every one of them. And the little bird. And the coffee. And the flowers everywhere inside and out.

But I'm on a mission. As much as I enjoy and need and appreciate Jackie's company, I also badly and frequently crave solitude. It's what I'm used to. So I tootle out to the farthest corner of the parking area. Angel's trumpets, here I come. I bypass orchids galore and bromeliads and a dozen or so cars. I park myself under the biggest trumpet tree where I can oversee the unfamiliar street, the sidewalk, a small public school next door. There is a high wrought-iron fence between me and all of Alajuela, but I can see it and taste it and smell it. Travel is a wonderful thing despite the medical reasons for doing it.

I light a smoke, sip the rich coffee, soak up the luxurious-in-February sun. By...my...self. Ahh. I see a woman near the hotel entrance searching around for someone, her hand shading her eyes. She's wearing pastel-blue pyjamas. Oh, not pyjamas, scrubs. And she's coming my way, waving and smiling.

"*Buenos*," she says. "*Buenos días, Señora.*" She's carrying a clipboard and a blood pressure cuff. There's a stethoscope around her neck.

"*Buenos días*, indeed."

"I'm Isabel, your hotel nurse," she says, taking the coffee and cigarette out of my hands and popping a thermometer into my mouth. She takes my wrist, checks my pulse, counting.

As badly as I want to, I can't interrupt.

"I'll see you each morning. I tried calling your room but..." She removes the thermometer, nods, jots on her clipboard.

"How did you...?"

"Oh, you're easy to find. I just ask around."

"So my procedure's been postponed until tomorrow?"

"I heard that, yes."

"Do you know..."

"*No sé, Señora.* I just see you here at the hotel. Every day at the hotel." She takes my blood pressure.

"Every day, okay. So how am I this morning?"

Isabel smiles. "You're very good."

I smile, too. "So is the coffee."

She places the coffee cup back in my hand, then the cigarette. I feel guiltier about that because she doesn't say a word about it. I joke about the novelty of a drive-by checkup. She laughs. "Whatever works."

"Indeed."

"Okay, bye-bye, Señora," she says. "See you tomorrow." And off she goes.

Efficient. I like that. Now where was I?

Uh-oh. A man and woman, also in scrubs, are waving at me. I wave back. Here they come. I gulp my coffee, put out my smoke.

It's the physio folks, and I know exactly how they found me. Word travels faster than I do at Villa Flora. Carlos is built like a tank. He tells me he plays rugby, which should make him a good candidate for manipulating my uncooperative body. Abby, who I take for his protegé, is petite and feminine and proficient at therapies involving balance balls, fitness equipment and the swimming pool. When I query them about tomorrow's procedure, they nod yes, say they know and tell me not

100   A One-Handed Novel

to worry. I'm heartened by this and even more so when they give me
the lowdown for post-procedure days: check appointment times each
morning at the front desk, potassium-loaded bananas before and after
each one-hour morning session, which will involve a personal regimen
just for me. They're super pleasant, all talk no touch this morning, but
I know that will change. They're keen to get at me, bend me, make me
improve. Abby shakes her finger at me when she sees the cigarette butt.
Carlos says coffee's okay though. Good physio-cop, bad physio-cop. I say
bye-bye when they leave. I like them a lot but wonder if some mole on
the inside will count my banana peels after every meal.

Now where the heck was I?

I light another smoke because I barely had time to enjoy the first
one so it didn't even really count. The kids are out for recess next door.
They're rambunctious and fun to watch. A couple watch me back.

"Mel!"

I hear Jackie across the parking lot before I see her. "I'm starving!"
she calls. "What are you *doing* out here?" She keeps her distance.

"Nothing. Nothing at all."

I scrunch out my smoke and scoot right past her to breakfast.

We have the late-morning dining room pretty much to ourselves.
Jackie fills me in on what she learned from our door-knocker while we
luxuriate our way through the delectable array of fresh bright fruits. I
ask all five of the standard W questions, but she's already basically told
me the Why and the What. I'm mostly concerned with the When.

"Tomorrow for sure, right?" I keep asking.

"That's what he said. For sure. Front desk will call with the time.
Probably afternoon."

"And the Who?" I ask, just to get my information all lined up and
attempt to keep it that way.

"You. And your twin, Moira."

I cringe a bit. "Moira?"

"Your patient-twin. Remember? We have to share."

"Everything? Even appointments?"

"Seems so. Okay?"

"Okay."

"Good?"

"Good." I finish up breakfast with a strawberry heart. "So we have all day."

Jackie checks her phone, her email, her Facebook, her linkage to home.

Somebody needs to be polite. "How is Cam?" I ask. "Managing without you?"

"Fine," she says, distracted by something on her phone that's far more fascinating than me, the restaurant, the country or the reason we're here. Thankfully, she snaps out of her techno-world fairly quickly.

We head for the pool, intent on making the most of our bonus day, but in the lobby we run into some regular tourists and a small herd of MSers. Some of the same ones I noticed last night and some new younger faces and, of course, there in the middle are Moira and Jinx. Everyone's in pairs: a farmer from North Dakota pushed by his daughter, a well-heeled Albertan foot-dragger with his overly solicitous wife, a wobbly but upright jaw-dropping young dancer from Montreal escorted by her diminutive mother, and a couple from Saskatchewan, who look like they're on their middle-aged honeymoon except that—or in spite of the fact that—she's been dependent on her hubby and her wheelchair for quite some time. There are more, too, around and about who span the age range of twenty to eighty. I guess, here in the hotel, there must be about fifteen patients and their significant others. I'm not just talking "significant" as sexual or substantial or statistical. I'm talking "significant" as invaluable, like these vitally important helpmate attendants. The ones who often have even less of an idea of what to expect out of this medical adventure. Like Jackie. I mean she knows quite a bit about me and my MS but she's never *lived* with me. Or the MS. Or the combination 24-7.

At the moment I love her more than anything.

We both learn a lot of stuff in a very short time. Like who's where—pre or post—on the procedural timeline. And who's doing well. And who isn't—yet. There's talk about the delayed balloons, so I know I'm not waiting alone. There's talk of shopping—high on the group agenda today—and zip-lining for the more fit and bus tours for the less fit and

what you shouldn't risk doing post-procedure while your body recuper-
ates and adjusts and you concentrate on wellness and physio.

There's also frequent mention of an all-star—a young BC woman who had miraculous results and is ready to go home, and she's now
walking, not even lopsided or anything. We all want to be as good, lucky,
blessed, determined as she is. Each of us wants so badly to succeed at
this. Just accumulating the funds and hope and scientific—or whatever—faith to actually get us here is like making it through the first cut of
Canada's Got Talent. We pump each other up. We're all kind of high on
the prevailing optimism. And as humans do, we gravitate to each other.
We are a group. And in this exotic secure setting, right here right now,
we're a majority. A gnarly bunch of cross-section misfits. And there's
such comfort in that. Until there isn't.

"Jackie," I say, "I'm getting too hot."

Several discerning folks nod. They get it. I've pulled the symptoms-
exacerbated-by-heat clause. Most MSers experience this, so it works like
a charm.

Jackie pats my arm. "Lead the way, Mel," she says, showing off her
helpmate skills to the group.

I give a little wave. Destination—pool. Directly, *por favor*. Do not
pass Go. Do not collect anything from the gift shop or the front desk
or the guy with his arms full of mangoes. We go out the back doors
this time. It's like falling down the rabbit hole, thankfully without the
falling. A mile of curving, dipping, wheel-friendly pathways in acres of
garden. The colour, the fragrance. The birds, the butterflies. Enough to
kind of daze a person from Canada in February. Hardly a soul around.
Now we can really relax.

There's a young Hispanic family with little girls in one end of the
huge pool. Jackie finds sunny loungers for us because those daily afternoon clouds we were warned about are already lurking off to the west.

I loiter around the steps in my scooter, decline Jackie's offer to
help, take my sweet time figuring out the spatial logistics of getting into
the water via steps and much-appreciated railings. And then even longer
actually performing the movements. It's like a slow-motion dance with a
new static partner and none of the grace. Stand, lean, grasp, lean, shift,

rotate, lean, step, repeat, until my feet touch bottom and I can sit on the step. Immersion is the best way to cool off so I get all the way in. And I look and look and look because it's easier than thinking or worrying or hoping, especially when everything in sight is so damn pretty: a bamboo grove, richly tiled mosaics, ferns and fronds and vines, a thousand speckled flowers, leaves of black and red and every green imaginable.

One of the little girls slides shyly into the water beside me. She's curious about me and particularly my operable scooter and my inoperable leg. We have a language barrier and blunder through a brief conversation helped along by nods and gestures. Her empathy is sweet and apparent. Sentimentality usually makes me gag, but kids have such an honest way of expressing it, I'm touched. She hops out, smiling, and fetches one of the fluffy pool towels and leaves it on my scooter while I dip back in.

I swim a little, which sounds like an easy thing, but even when afloat balance is required. I list to the left like I have a bilge problem. It's a bit freaky, that lack of control, even in shallow water. I do my ponderous exit dance and dry off. The girl and her family are gone and so is the blue sky.

"You look a little pink," Jackie says, gathering up her stuff.

"You, too. The sunscreen..."

"We should have..."

"How long have we been out here?"

"An hour?"

"Two?"

"Shit."

We make it back through the garden to our room just as the spectacular storm breaks and spend the rest of the sweet day and evening in hotel comfort. It's easy to forget—off and on—what I'm really doing down here. We have an unsociably early one-bottle-of-red dinner and then retire to our room, where we compare strap marks, apply aloe where necessary, crank the ceiling fan and lie on the fresh white linens giggling over nothing like we used to. By the time our anxiety-induced hysteria subsides, it's well past midnight. I go to sleep smiling. For all the most unromantic reasons, I already heart the promise of this Valentine's Day.

9

Dread or Alive

The bedside phone rings early, just after 7:00. Appointment time 3:00. Pick-up at noon. No solid food after 8:00, leaving us an hour to grab breakfast. I'm so excited and nervous I can't even decide what to wear.

"Go with comfy," instructs Jackie, happy to slip into her role as caregiver, while checking her phone.

I notice a little net bag of heart-shaped chocolates dangling from our doorknob when we leave the room. There are red roses on the dining tables. And heart-shaped pancakes smothered in sliced strawberries, the same pink as our skin. No sun for us today, but Jackie and I agree to meet at the pool anyway after she does her Cam call and I get my quiet coffee time under the semi-shady trumpet tree at the end of the parking lot. I commandeer this little territory, call it "the office," which surpasses any past bar stools I've called by the same name. Isabel arrives as if on cue. The routine is quick and painless. The sun is not. I dart my scooter from shady spot to shady spot.

When I get to the pool area, Jackie's already there, reading in the shade near the deep end. She looks up long enough to shake her magazine at me and say, "No woman will ever be truly satisfied on Valentine's Day because no man will ever have a chocolate penis that ejaculates money."

We both pause to imagine that.

The half-MS honeymoon couple is also there in their swimsuits but far enough away that we just wave. I settle into a lounge chair and try to read. Hopeless. I'm in countdown watch-checking mode. I can't help but watch the couple, how they are together, the way he kisses her, reaches for her hand. I know the woman follows me on the hospital list, probably booked for tomorrow. They must have come down to Costa Rica early because they're both really tanned—as in not pink, like silly us.

They head for the pool steps. I wonder how this is going to go, considering my own difficulties yesterday. Wow! He's going to lift her up and carry her in—like an oversized toddler. He's a squat hairy guy, hefty in comparison to his diminutive wife, so I figure he'll manage fine. He turns away to position himself, and I can't believe what I'm seeing. I can't stop giggling.

Jackie looks up. "I bet *that* hurt," Jackie sputters, cocking her camera to snag a discreet shot.

"Ya think!?"

"True love."

A huge white heart has been waxed from the centre of his back. We are hysterical, beyond hope. Ouch! It's obscenely romantic. Or romantically obscene. They're in the pool now, seemingly oblivious, maybe even proud. I guess this is something folks strive for.

Uncontrollable laughter is dangerous. "I can't just sit here, Jackie. I have to go."

Jackie bursts out laughing again, points directly under my chair. "Looks like you already did."

I'm embarrassed all over again but for a different reason. I can't even stand up when I'm laughing, never mind move around, so I get sober pronto. Jackie drops a towel over the spreading puddle. We avoid eye contact with the honeymooners, zoom in and out of the poolside washroom and resume our giggling through the gardens. We serenade the birds with the classic "Love Hurts."

For well over an hour, we sit outside the hotel entrance with Moira and Jinx waiting for José. At least there's a bit of shade. It would be a bitch of a thing to pressure-cook my grey matter and stroke out just before the hospital trip. I'm trying to keep my heart rate steady when a concierge comes out to tell us my appointment time and Moira's are postponed again. A few more hours. Pickup is now at 4:00 p.m. Ugh, more waiting. And no solids since this morning...which was already a while ago.

Despite hunger, nerves and growing animosity, our second departure goes like clockwork.

~�—

Finally, I'm in a hospital bed, after another careening van ride with José in a sudden and predictable drenching rain. Never mind the downhill detour we had to take because Jackie and Jinx refused to push the van even an inch in the mud. We are here, and I'm ready.

It's a little different than the last visit—less English, more Spanish—and Jackie's here reading on the cot next to me. At least Jinx and Moira are in a separate room.

There are a lot of bustling nurses, mostly male. One inserts an IV in my left hand. Another asks me if I've shaved the area.

"The area?" I ask.

"Your groin. For the catheter."

"Oh, um, no. I'm not very hairy."

"Okay. I can see by your arms."

I try to clarify things with the wannabe shaver. "It's my leg, though, right? Not my, um, groin."

"*Sí*. No worry."

"Okay." I worry. And we wait, and Dr. Falik stops by to reassure and remind me that I won't feel pain or remember anything, though I'll be awake. And we wait. It's about 10:00 p.m. when I say goodbye to Jackie and they roll me down to the prep room outside the O.R. where it's really cold, shaky cold. And I wait. And there are different male nurses, even busier, in poufy hats.

They strap down my arms so I won't jerk the catheter around while it's in there. This visual really creeps me out. They roll Moira past me—she's already done! I wait. And then they take me in.

Surreal.

~⌐—

I wake up back in my room at the hospital, and Jackie's there. Well, maybe wake up is an exaggeration. I'm zonked. Immobile. If this is light sedation, I can't imagine the heavy stuff. I try to fight my way out of the stupor, keep commenting on how drunk I feel. I keep trying to sit up, which the nurses don't like.

"Rest. Rest. No worry," they say as they press me back onto the pillow. "A couple more hours—this position. Only on your back."

We suffer through the bedpan routine. I'm no help at all. I notice my voice is getting whiny, and I'm reminded of Moira in my jumbled brain and stop talking for a while. I don't even want to sit up anymore. But there's a problem. A weird, freaky, inscrutable problem. I wrestle with myself silently, then I blurt it out.

"Where's my hand? I can't find my hand."

Not a nurse in sight, but Jackie's here. "You're just all tucked in under the covers, Mel. Here..."

She extracts my arm, which looks the same as always. But it's not moving when I tell it to. My left hand can feel my right hand touching it. But it won't move, no matter what I try. Jackie, hiding her panic, finds a nurse. I get kind of frantic—there may be crying involved—and I keep using my right hand to lift up my left hand and my whole arm to show the nurse how it falls unnaturally to the bed like a stone, something heavy and dead. The nurse finds another nurse, who in turn finds a doctor, who in turn finds a neurologist. Somewhere along the line I'm convinced it's only temporary. And relieved it's only temporary. And so is Jackie, relieved I mean. Everyone tells me to give it time, so I do. I'll give it time and I'll give it sleep and I'll even tuck it back under the covers to give it darkness if that's what it needs. But first, I'll tell it a little bedtime story—a grim fairy tale. That directive, *talk to the hand*, takes on new meaning.

I tell it my version of the apotemnophilia story I read in that neurology magazine—about brains and maps and undesirable limbs, both phantoms and their opposites. It's my subtle way of telling it to smarten up, to get its fucking shit together or else.

Once upon a time...

Someone's stroking my arm. I struggle to open my eyes. It's Dr. Falik. He's leaning over me, looking quite delicious. His dark eyes are sparkly, his white coat is half undone and his slick dark hair is, well, slick and dark. His aftershave is intense and rather pleasant.

I mumble, "Where did *you* come from?" Geez, I still feel slurry. Better to shut my eyes. I feel that weird out-of-control stiffening of my legs and back that I get when my libido's activated. Whole-body hard-ons have been known to stiffen me right out of my chair. Thank gawd I'm lying down. It's my favourite place for planking.

"I came to help you," he says, still running his hand up and down my arm. "You have a problem, no?"

"A problem?"

"Your situation."

"Oh yes. My arm."

"Sure. Yes, your arm. But the other one, too."

"My other arm?"

"No, that's just fine."

"There's something else?"

"No, no. Nothing new," he reassures me. "Rather, it's your sexual pickle. Your orgasm troubles?"

"Oh...that." I'm sort of embarrassed, but his presence is so heartening. "How did you know? Is it that obvious? Like medically?"

"No, Miss Melanie. You told me with your eyes. And I have something for you."

He slides in, white coat and all, under the covers.

"A present?" I say into his sensuous mouth.

"Mm-hmm. A Valentine."

He leans above me, slowly lets his chest meet mine, his knee inches its way across. His sizable, um, package is suddenly pressing against me in the vague vicinity of my cha-cha muffin. It feels nice. And then nicer. I groan a little as he bears down.

"Take off your clothes," I say. "Hurry."

"Mel...Melanie!"

"Yes. Hurry up," I say, groping around with my right hand to help extricate him.

"Mel!" It's Jackie's voice. "Snap out of it, girl. They're just changing your pressure dressing."

I open my eyes. "Jackie?" I see now that a nurse is adjusting a fist-sized bandage near my groin. "Where's the doc?"

"He'll be here around lunchtime."

I scan the room in disbelief. "He's not here?"

"Nope. Just me and the troops," she says, glancing at the nurse who tucks most of me under the covers. "How's the arm?"

I try moving it. No response.

"They'll be getting you up soon. How does everything else feel? How do *you* feel?"

"Not sure yet. Dopey." And subconsciously horny, apparently. And embarrassed and still sunburned and now packing a hefty gauze appendage in my nether region. That was quite the dream. Yummy. And ridiculous. Even while my body is struggling to recuperate from the surgery, my mind goes off on a sexual tangent—which I have no time for at the moment.

I'm starting to come around, to take notice of things. "Hey, can you get rid of these blankets? I think I can move my toes. All of them."

Jackie does it. We both stare at the toes on my bad left foot. Not only are they a healthy pink, they're wiggling. Not a rock star wiggle, more like a folky sway. But still, compared to their poor performance pre-op, this is monumental. I take it as a sign of greater things to come.

Jackie goes off to get something to eat and make Mel-progress phone calls while I validate the efficacy of the bedpan as only an invalid person can. I wiggle my toes a lot, willing—unsuccessfully—the movement farther up my leg. It's the least I can do, well, actually the most, for the three remaining hours of my flat-on-my-back confinement. I think healing thoughts for a while. I think present-in-the-moment thoughts. I think hungry thoughts because it's been a long time since the last banana or fresh tortilla. I spend an equal amount of time and energy avoiding thoughts of a successful outcome, homecoming and comeuppance for CCSVI non-believers. My dead arm is my biggest concern. Am I worse off than before? Have I made a mistake? Tempted fate?

Proprioception—my favourite game—takes up the remainder of my wait time. It involves me trying to guess where a specific body part is—what position it's in and which part might be touching which other part—without moving said parts. I refer to that body image map in my brain that was explained in the apotemnophilia article. Once I've guessed the position I move so that the sensation of movement tells me whether I'm right or not. When an area on my body map is working properly, my guess is right—affirmation. When an area on my body map is damaged, my guess is wrong—affirmation of a different kind: negative. My hand—no matter how many times I test it—just won't play fair. Wherever I pick it up or place it, it cheats. I call foul. I'd quit the game and walk off the playing field if I could, but I *am* the playing field. My hand, my *mano*, wants to be a spectator—a spectre—of itself. What if other body parts join in the mutiny?

I stare at the ceiling.

The nurses finally help me to sit up. It's no easy feat with this limp deadbeat arm hanging there and getting in the way. It's like a super-elongated breast hanging off my shoulder. It has sensation but isn't capable of general grasping, pushing, pulling or holding me up. I feel sorry for it and wish I could tuck it into a firm-support arm-bra...until I'm furious with it.

Finally, those same nurses get me standing. It feels different... better...despite the lingering sedation and the dead arm. They settle me into a wheelchair and roll me right into the shower with double the nurses. It's crowded and a lot of Spanish is flying around with the soap and water—particularly the word *mano*—as though I'm not here. But I am here, or at least coming back to here. And then I'm done and freshly bandaged and dressed and sitting up feeling pretty human. Jackie comes back with an ice-cold soda and a dry sandwich, which I inhale in thirty seconds flat. We wait for the doctor.

Waiting for the doctor means contemplating a plethora of things: finding out if he was able to get that little balloon to where it needed to be, if it could be successfully inflated and what to expect, assuming the little improvements I'm experiencing are not just a placebo effect.

The meeting doesn't go quite the way I had imagined it...*or* dreamt it, but there are a few similarities. The nurses bustle around, parking me next to Jackie at a small table, just as Dr. Falik arrives. He greets us, opens his laptop, asks me standard questions, makes notes, then lifts my unresponsive hand onto the table, stroking my arm as deliciously as he did in the dream. His dark eyes are still sparkly, his white coat is again half undone and his slick dark hair is still slick and dark. His aftershave is just as intense and pleasant, but there's a seriousness on his part. He assures me the paralysis is temporary, maybe a few days, but in the meantime there will be some tests to make sure there's been no permanent damage.

"There will be blood thinners daily," he explains, "to keep the newly expanded vein segments open." He pats my arm.

"So you really did it?"

Jackie gives me an odd look but remains quietly observant. I need to hear him say it.

"Yes, yes! You don't remember?" he asks.

"Just going in, nothing else."

"Well, you talked the whole time. And we had to do a lot of work. Five balloons. Five veins. Five hours. Much longer than usual. Here, I'll show you." He pulls his laptop over and opens a file—a long series of images with my name attached. I'm relieved and excited to know a lot of work has been done. I show him my pink wiggling toes.

He nods and smiles, then explains how the injected contrast dye revealed all the convolutions and bizarrely twisted veins between my heart and my brain—the azygos and jugular and others. He shows me the valves, blockages—stenoses—and the various positions of the different-sized balloons as he maneuvered them meticulously upward, inflated them, waited the allotted time and then continued little by little farther up and closer to my brain. It's fascinating, but objectivity is difficult. I see a shadow of the rest of my head—including teeth—in the images. And I can't stop examining my headshots even while he passes me the adjusted bill—incidental expenses like extra balloons, extra hours and additional tests. I glance over the paperwork, slip it into my purse and slide my credit card to Dr. Falik because apparently he doubles as a cashier.

"Was I moving around?" I ask, noticing all the different positions of my teeth.

"You were talking a great deal," Dr. Falik says, quietly laughing, relaxing now that the main points—medicine and money—have been covered.

"We had a conversation?"

"As I said, you were very talkative for most of the five hours."

"Five hours? Talkative?" I consider myself more internal than external, more introvert than extrovert, and I'm feeling even weirder about not being able to remember a single second of the conversation. "About what?"

"Well, you love Costa Rica and want to come back..."

I wait expectantly.

He goes on, gesturing with his hand. "Not for this medical stuff, you said, but for a cocktail party." He laughs quietly again. Jackie muffles a laugh, murmurs something about a phone call and exits pronto, leaving me one-on-one with the doc.

"Oh, my. Really?" I blush brighter than my lingering sunburn at the thoughts that may have erupted into words—my inside voice making a grand entrance in the operating theatre. To an attractive and captive audience. My legs get all stiff and I go into plank mode—in this case, due to the implications of the word *cocktail,* which is almost non-existent in my vocabulary, and the fact that the doc's name is, well, a bit of a trigger. I wonder if I uttered, "So, Falik, a cocktail?"

Dr. Falik continues. "And you mentioned your problem."

"My hand, you mean?"

"No, no," he reassures me. "Rather, it's your sexual *pepinillo*. Your orgasm dilemma."

"Oh, that..." I wave it off. "It doesn't matter now. I can't believe I even mentioned it."

"But you explained in such passionate detail, Señora, that we repeated your test. In fact, you insisted. You said it was urgent. Right before we took you in. It's detailed in your bill."

"Never mind that! I have bigger problems. Like MS! And this!" I flop my dead arm onto the table. "This!"

Dr. Falik is taken aback. "Señora, of course. As you say. We will do our best for—" His phone bleeps and anxious lines appear on his forehead as he answers. I remember that these specialists handle more than party balloons. He stands abruptly with his phone to his ear, pops my medical-souvenir CD out of his laptop and into my hand along with his business card. "If you have any questions," he says, then rattles off

Spanish instructions into his phone before heading for the door.

I can pick out only a couple of words, "bananas" and "satisfaction," not necessarily in that order. In my confusion, I pick up my lifeless arm and wave goodbye.

Looks like I'll be discharged whether all my parts are operational or not. Wait! I do *not* want to leave this freakin' hospital! Not like this! I try to tell the nurse, the one who speaks a little English, that I'm not ready to leave. Or go back to my hotel or back to the other MSers—the hopeful ones—looking like a failure. Looking worse than before, instead of better or even the same. It would be like wearing a < on my personalized dead-arm-band rather than an = or a >. And if I don't improve in my remaining week, how can I possibly go home to BC, to my financial-wizard friend Charlene, who magically and optimistically got my credit card limit exponentially raised for this life-altering endeavour?

"Jackie! Tell them! Explain!" I say to every empty corner of the room.

"Señora?" The nurse, laden with a stack of boxed prefilled syringes, hesitates in front of me. "I can show you this now?"

"No! Where is Jackie? She should be here!"

"Ah, *tu amiga.*" She backs toward the door. "A moment, then."

By the time the nurse shows up with Jackie, I've come to the realization that I can't share my anxiety with her either. I can't have my caregiver-friend give up on me before I do. I have a responsibility to keep her positive so that I can reap the symbiotic benefits. So I don't mention my narcissistic little upset. I still have hope, albeit fragile. Onward and upward, one step at a time.

The three of us get down to business—the business of belly shots, and I'm not talking on-the-bar navel tequila shooters with a follow-up bite of lime. I mean self-inflicted blood-thinner injections—prescribed daily for a month—directly into the abdomen. We get a demo, then I do the real thing with my one good hand—a straight jab. It's creepy and uncomfortable but not totally foreign to me. I've done this kind of thing before with other MS drugs. Jackie's not so good with it. She goes a little pale under her sunburn. I tell her to buck up as a massive bruise flowers from the injection site. Band-Aid time.

"Okay. All set," the nurse says, turning to leave. "They come for you now."

"So that's it?" I ask.

Jackie pipes up, "What about..."

"Everything at the hotel," the nurse reassures us, "Everything! All set over there! Nurse. Physio."

"Doctor, too?" I can't help but ask, wanting some concrete answers about my arm.

"Yes, of course."

"Okay," we both say, nonplussed.

Within minutes we're ensconced in our familiar van. Jinx and Moira are here, too. We're all a bit raw from lack of sleep or unnaturally induced stupors. Jinx is even more obnoxious, ignoring Moira and snuggling up to José, making me thankful for Jackie—again.

Moira's cheerier than before, her whining transformed into hopeful euphemisms about her significant improvements, which makes me feel cranky and shitty and wanting to hibernate and lick my wounds—more specifically, my arm. I lift it up to my mouth but don't want to attract attention to my appendage so I lay it back in my lap and keep watch over it like it's a newborn alien. I stroke it and murmur to it and think about those amputees with their phantom arms in the medical journal and those others, too, the apotemnophiliacs who want to amputate their perfectly good arms. I'm neither of those but I'm something. I want to be a luckier something than I am at the moment. I visualize the word *temporary* all the way to the hotel, our home away from home for another week—a week to begin reinventing my reality.

A lot of things happen during this week but because I'm obsessed with my dead arm, I can't help but associate each of the five events with a particular digit on my inanimate puppet-hand.

The first thing—and I'm not exactly pointing fingers, but I will bestow this episodic honour upon my index finger—is that Jackie tries to murder me. Up until now, Jackie has been a really good friend. I mean, besides our too-numerous-to-count buddy years, she took time off from work and even from Cam to help me get through this international medical adventure. Plus, she seemed kind of thrilled about the chance to witness first-hand the new, improved me and to see Costa Rica on my dime, borrowed or not.

Back in the room, we realize pretty quickly that I'll have to use Adele rather than my smaller, more versatile wheelchair because nobody can aim a wheelchair in a straight line with one arm. We go through everything that I need help with: standing, sitting, getting dressed and undressed, reaching the toilet paper and anything else in the bathroom, turning over in bed and much more. And I can't do any of it in the dark because I can't tell where my body is, so I'd fall down or keel over if I'm sitting.

We're too weary the first night for a heart-to-heart, so we have a reassuring hug and fall—literally—into bed exhausted. I wake up an hour later having to pee. IV fluids need somewhere to go and in a hurry.

I cajole Jackie awake, and she mutters a bit but doesn't complain. Hurrying has the same effect on me as sexy thoughts—I get stiff, all over, but I make it just in time with a whole lot of help. We opt for the wheelchair because Jackie can push me.

We're not so lucky the second time or the third. Every excursion demands extra effort, towels on the tile floor, clothing changes, wheeling me into the shower and hanging out there with me. It's not a pretty picture. I am in tears, and that makes me furious.

Jackie's attentiveness and empathy wane by my fourth and consecutively more difficult attempt to wake her. I don't mean to slap her. It's just that there's no time for cajoling, so when I jostle her and poke her and all she does is flip onto her back, I slap her. Maybe it's a little harder than I meant it to be, but it works. She's awake all right. Spitting mad and rubbing her cheek.

She manhandles me silently through the new routine and onto the toilet in record time. Then leaves me there to stew. For what feels like an hour. Well, I'll show her. I don't need anybody! With one heel braced against the toilet and the opposite knee levered under the counter, I almost get back into the wheelchair. Somewhere during the transfer from toilet seat to wheelchair, my good hand—the Slapper—starts to lose its grip on the counter. Really slowly. I'm buggered.

"Jackie!" I call. "Jackieeeeeeee!"

Finally, all muffled from the cozy bed, she answers, "What?"

"I slipped!" I say, which isn't quite true...yet.

I hear what sounds like "Tell someone who gives a shit."

"I'm bleeding!" I say, which also isn't true, but is very possible.

I hear her skitter into the doorway, but I can't see her because I'm all twisted around. Before I know it, she's got me under my arms, grunting, cursing, trying to lift me. I tell her my body doesn't work this way, but does she listen? Oh no. I slip out of her arms and drop in a sudden rush, hitting my forehead on the counter. Now I *am* bleeding. And Jackie's sorry. And we're both in tears but still can't quite manage to get me up. She wants to call for help. I won't let her. "Just leave me here," I say, and she responds predictably with "Fuck you, Mel."

Jackie lays a bath towel on the floor, maneuvers me onto it and drags me slowly to the bed while I clutch at the towel. She grumbles something about dead weight and body bags. I feel more like a fridge. Between her pulling and me pushing I finally end up in the bed.

Sympathetic facial expressions greet my forehead Band-Aid at breakfast the next morning. At least the bulging pressure bandage against my groin could be abandoned. Jackie and I apologize to each other after coffees and a cigarette.

൮◦

The second finger thing that happens—and I credit my pinky with this one because that's the finger that gets caught in an embarrassing situation—is that I meet two men. Guy #1 is sitting in the Villa Flora gardens on a bench with his shirt open at the neck, rolled trousers and a lopsided hat. He's got one arm across the back of the bench, looking like he's waiting for some *chica* to nestle up against him. I figure I'm that gal because it's a fun photo op and the guy's sculpted from smooth pewter-coloured metal.

With Jackie's help, I snuggle in next to him. Then Jackie aims her phone at us in various shots—me smiling into the guy's gun-metal eyes, me kissing the hard line of his cheek, me naughtily shoving the fingers of my dead, bad hand into his trouser pocket. Don't ever do that. It turns out there are jagged edges in hidden places that are not finger friendly or fit for exploration. It's a finger trap! My finger doesn't hurt when it's still but the second I try to pull out, it stings something fierce. My good hand tries to assist. Then Jackie tries with her good hands. A little drip of blood oozes down the creases of Guy #1's pants. Jackie drops my hand like a hot potato and marches off to find someone or something to help. Neither of us wants a replay of last night.

Enter Guy #2, preceded by a flimsy butterfly net. He emerges from a tangle of orchid vines and the gargantuan noir leaves of a Black Magic Colocasia. He's short and wide and swarthy, almost gnomish, with heavy eyebrows, a longish beard and turned-out toes.

"Hellooo," he says, in a smooth lilty voice.

I smile and try to look nonchalant, covering my trapped hand with my good one, but in my rush I lose my balance and tip into the lap of Guy #1. It can't be pretty. I try to push myself into an upright position, but it pinches my finger.

"Oh, dear," he says, approaching.

I mumble with my ear next to Guy #1's crotch.

Guy #2 bends at the waist and cocks his head slowly till we're face to face. "Are you all right?"

I try to look into Guy #2's inquisitive and incredibly unattractive face, but he's so close that his eyes have become one eye, making him comical and macabre. "Not exactly."

He leans back enough to examine my face, looking—I can only imagine—for signs of a stroke or a bullet entry. I guess the proximity of Adele explains away some of these options but also raises other possibilities. He grasps my shoulders. After a couple of overly cautious attempts to right me, he succeeds, and my trapped finger comes along with the rest of me, smearing blood here and there.

"Leo Moss," he says, offering his very wide stubby-fingered hand. Then, seeing the blood, he retracts it. "At your service."

"Thanks, Leo. Sorry," I say, wrapping my finger with the edge of my shirt. "Blood thinners."

Leo raises his shaggy brows. "Are you going to be all right?"

"It's too soon to tell."

He looks more than a little confused.

"Oh, my finger, you mean!"

"Well, and your slippage...a tad too much rum, perhaps? Anyway..."

I laugh wryly. "I wish that were it. And, yes, I'll be fine. My friend's coming back any minute now."

"Ah, a friend. Of course." He looks disappointed, which doesn't improve his looks in the least. "Glad to be of assistance."

Leo Moss touches my toes with his butterfly net, turns on his heel and disappears back into the foliage just as Jackie shows up with a pair of pliers and a spray bottle of Windex. She doesn't believe me when I tell her about Leo.

Two strange men—Easy Come and Easy Go.

⌁

The third thing isn't exactly a single event but more like a juncture, and it can only be attributed to my ring finger. The sexy-sounding vein in that finger, my *vena amoris*, is said to be directly connected to my heart, and I'm all about my circulatory system these days. I'm actually feeling terrific and energetic and on my way to feeling less MS-ey. My arm, though, is still unresponsive after multiple daily trips into San José for treatments using ultrasound and ultra-low-frequency magnetic fields and electrical microcurrents. Long-term prognosis: no permanent damage, possibly a pinched nerve. The ring finger is symbolic of weddings, so I decide to stay married to my immobile arm for better or worse, unlike the apotemnophiliacs.

⌁

The thumb's up next and it's not for a single event either but it deserves recognition for being so damn useful in a universal-language kind of way. Thumbs up is the best response to any and all questions relating to improved balance, improved vision and hearing, improved circulation in my feet, as well as any Spanish phrase I don't understand. It even works well, and I can't believe I'm saying this, for non-alcoholic drinks because liquor is on the no-go list until the blood thinners are finished.

~~~

The only finger left is the middle finger, and I'm saving that for Dr. Falik if he cancels our appointment for the third time. Everyone else on my team has been great—driver José, my parking-lot nurse Isabel, Carlos with his manipulations and Abby with her pool sessions and balance balls, though she pushed me to tears more than once. I've worked my butt off this week to ensure the very best overall outcome, but the unchanged status of my paralyzed arm deserves some kind of consultation.

~~~

It's our last evening here. The two of us enjoy a traditional meal in the dining room—fresh corn, avocado and the little tortillas alongside beans, rice and savoury chicken. Fruit and a soft local cheese for dessert. We make *Pura vida* toasts—me with my virgin daiquiris—to almost everything. We say goodbye to our coffee boys.

Jackie and I have survived each other, and I didn't die, and even most of my Band-Aids have been retired. We're packing when the phone rings. It's Dr. Falik, and he wants to meet with me at his office in the morning. We have just enough time on our way to the airport. He understands. He reassures me. Yes!

~~~

José gets us to Dr. Falik's downtown office with minutes to spare, but then we have to wait for the good doctor. When he arrives, he's as desirable as ever. He apologizes profusely, strokes my dead arm and tells me feeling *will* come back. Soon.

I have to believe him. He doesn't mention my blush-inducing cocktail-party wish.

"And, so...your improvements?" he asks.

I go through the list—standing, sitting, numbness, balance, vision, healthy flesh-coloured toes—many improvements but nothing substantial.

"We continue to hope..." he begins.

"Just hope?"

He corrects himself. "To *expect* continued improvement. Every case of MS is different. Every procedure. More gradual progress for you, perhaps. And your arm should be fine in a week...maybe two. Keep up your physio. Health must be your priority."

"Don't I know it!" Health is my big fat new goal now that the Liberation goal has been reached. There's something bothering me. "Dr. Falik, I do have one more question."

He closes my file, resting his hands on my brief Costa Rican medical history. "Of course."

Dr. Falik's phone rings, but I go on. "What about that other...?"

"I'm sorry, I must take this, but you can email me with any concerns." He rises from his chair, intent on his phone, but adds, "Good luck, Miss Melanie. Let us know of your progress." He gives me a quick dismissive smile and runs his fingers through his hair as he turns away to answer the call.

There's abrupt knocking on the thick door, voices outside.

The doctor ignores the added interruption and so do I. I lean forward, not wanting to interrupt his possibly life-saving call, but this is my last face-to-face chance to ask. "What about that other test? The orgasm test. I mean seeing as you have the results, I might as well..."

"¿*Qué?*" Dr. Falik asks impatiently, startled to see me still there.

The voices outside are muffled but sound vaguely familiar...Spanish, English...rising voices. It almost sounds like a scuffle.

I try again, louder this time, "The Sexual..."

"*Ay*, the orgasm," he says, looks askance, realizing he's talking into the phone. "Eh, *lo siento*, sorry. *Sí, sí, en un momento.*"

"*Or-gas-mo*! Yes!" I blurt out, just as José, Jackie and the receptionist tumble through the door.

The receptionist apologizes repeatedly while José pleads, "Come on! Go, now!" and Jackie chants, "We're going to miss the fucking plane!" while they try to steer me and my scooter toward the door.

Dr. Falik reaches impatiently for my chart, either to give me results or to throw it at me and my team members, but he loses his grip. When the pastel rainbow of papers slides out over the desk and across the shiny floor the three of us freeze, hold our breath.

Dr. Falik throws his hands up in the air, mutters a profanity and says, "Email, *por favor*. Now I go!" And he pushes past us all and rushes out the door.

Exhausted as I am on the long flight home, my brain is stuck in over-drive. I can't stop thinking about the trip, my future, my health, my dead arm. It's going to be a long slow haul. Heavy stuff, but still hopeful. Jackie's asleep beside me or pretending to be. So is the snoring uber-tanned ponytailed guy in the Costa Rica T-shirt on my left. I close my eyes, imagining good *Pura vida* things ahead.

I wake up groggily to the captain's voice announcing our Vancouver approach. And the guy next to me extricating my bad hand from between his legs. Now how did...? Never mind. Just smile, apologize like a good Canadian and buckle up.

Pura vida, indeed!

10
Flypaper for Freaks

Back on Canadian soil. All I can feel is exhausted. Jackie and I didn't sing on the flight back. In fact, we barely spoke.

I insist on driving through chilly Vancouver out to Horseshoe Bay, onto the ferry and off—all with my one good arm. Jackie fluctuates between silence and shotgun-brake conniptions. She half heartedly insists on getting me settled in at home and I wholeheartedly—on the outside at least—refuse her extended care. I breathe a sigh of relief when I drop her off, and I'm pretty sure she's doing the same. Our relationship needs to revert back to friendship before the frays and chafes of the past ten days tear a hole in it that can't be mended. It needs rest, and so do I.

I pull into my short narrow driveway. I feel that overwhelming sense of relief to be home. The dinged vinyl siding never looked so good. Even the unplugged Xmas lights looping along the low roofline seem to welcome me back. Here, at least, I can maneuver to the back door in private.

On a good day—physically speaking—I can get Adele out, off the scooter lift and into my place in seven minutes. Seeing as this is not a good day—due to exhaustion, post-flight dehydration and one dead arm—I'm going to have to rethink this. Strategize. Concentrate. I have my cellphone right here in my pocket in case things go sideways. I recite my new mantra—*Do not call Jackie. Do not call for help. Do not call Jackie. Do not call for help.*

I usually use Plan A, step/lean down the length of the van—with my cane—to the rear door of the van where Adele rests on her interior lift. All that moving and balancing terrifies me right now, so I opt for Plan B.

I get the sidedoor open and lean awkwardly all over the place. There are lots of handholds in the van but now there's no hand to hold them. I finally jiggle my travelling wheelchair's rear tires down to the ground. More cautious jostling, and I get all four wheels on the ground. I have to bash the bastard back and forth to unfold it one-handed so there's somewhere for me to sit.

I put my dead hand in my lap so it doesn't get caught in the wheel and roll myself to the back of the van backwards with my one reliable foot because one-handed wheeling would take me in a circular direction. It takes four tries to raise the van door. The lift is button-operated, but I still have to lean/stand to release the brake on the lowered scooter, roll it off the lift, engage the brake and transfer myself onto it. *Do not call Jackie. Do not call for help.* I do it—finally!—without crying but sweating buckshot despite the February chill. All I have to do now is motor the lift back in and shut that van door. Stand...balance...reach. Three times. Stand...balance...pull. Step back. Pull. Lean. And the final push—slam! I sit down hard on Adele, feeling somewhat self-satisfied. I didn't call or fall. I'm almost home free.

I ignore my suitcase, scoop my purse and attached house key out of the van, close it up and lock it. I can't desert my wheelchair out here in case it disappears in the night like my last one did. I have to think like MacGyver. I use my cane to hitch along my chair like a badly behaved pup trailer behind a semi truck. It's not particularly reliable, but we all make it to the door.

Now for the key. It's a bit tricky. I have to pull the door toward me in order to roll the tumblers in the lock. Simultaneously. In other words, it's a two-handed job. *Do not call for help. Do not call Jackie.* It takes more ingenuity. I insert the key and wrap my purse strap around the doorknob and my upper arm so I get some leverage. Seven strap adjustments later and I'm in! Only forty-five minutes!

I park my redundant equipment—the scooter and travel chair— settle into my indoor wheelchair, hit the can, crank the heat, drink a gallon of water and crawl into my own bed in my grubby travelling clothes, cradle my sorry-ass arm—and sleep.

〜⌐

Sixteen hours of shut-eye ought to be enough for any body. Even one like mine that's in recuperation mode, reorganize mode, positivity mode, relearn-to-walk mode. But, instead, I feel like I'm sleep deprived so I hit up my blood thinners, watch the new belly bruise flower and go back to bed.

Waking up this morning is a new experience. I feel like more than a fraction of a million bucks. The arm is still hanging limp, but as I organize myself I keep propping it into positions it should naturally find, which makes it a happier arm. I show it tough love, keep re-placing it when it flops to my side. It begins to feel needed again as I create a gargantuan list. It starts with the big things:

☐ Get better
☐ Get organized
☐ Be positive

Lists for me are like random sloppy brainstorming diagrams so this one, too, deteriorates to sublists:

☐ Eat well/less
☐ Quit smoking
☐ Make physio appts (3/week)
☐ Exercise at home
☐ Rest!!!
☐ Gym membership
☐ Job search
☐ $$$$$
☐ Bills
☐ Visa???
☐ Stop avoiding well-wishers
☐ Keep notes on health/progress?
☐ Sort receipts
☐ Groceries
☐ ~~Liquor~~
☐ Finish blood thinners
☐ Liquor

Then sublists become sub-sublists of itemized dates and times and necessities. It's a fractal thing.

I am determined to have a routine—at least until the injections are done—which will be some cause for celebration. Listing takes a long time. So does drawing two little round eyes above the naturally formed mouth on the unnaturally closed fist of my bad left hand, in that opening between the thumb and index knuckle. "*Pura vida*, doofus," I make the little face say, its lips unmoving, making itself into a ventriloquist's dummy ventriloquist. This is as playful as I can muster. The fun goes out of it pretty quick, though, as the droopy mouth won't cooperate any better than its hand-head. It looks too depressed to hang out with. Yikes. Getting the waterproof ink off proves too time-consuming, so I leave it on. I tuck it into my sweater like Napoleon so I don't have to make contact.

I feel weird. More buggered up and somehow better at the same time. More helpless and more driven to independence. I feel like a pendulum in constant altitudinal flux. I imagine being on a swing like a worry-free kid, but it makes me dizzy. I'm lost without my Costa Rican team. I have to take responsibility—dear gawd—for myself.

My plans and appointments require assistance, but I refuse to call Jackie. It's just too soon. I put her on my emergency-only list with my old buddy, John, and the ever-travelling psychically inclined financial wizard, Char. I call the HandyDART van—an excruciating admission of disability—and painstakingly arrange for transport, aboard Adele, to and from physio. I just can't trust my driving abilities yet. Taking the HandyDART, despite adding excessive travel time, means I won't be overtaxing my friendships. And it's not like I have anything more important to do with my time.

m⸺

I get to physio early, sit in the waiting area looking around at all the equipment, all the folks working on their potpourri of weaknesses—shoulders, backs, hips, knees, you name it. I feel like a voyeur, which is more socially acceptable than a temporary apotemnophiliac. My dead arm makes me feel like a freak more than the MS does. A freak that belongs here.

I leaf through a motivational magazine. One Dr. Wayne Dyer quote in a random sidebar insists: *The law of attraction is this: you don't attract what you want. You attract what you are.* I drop the magazine like a hot double-baked garlic-infused spud. FU, Dr. D. I am *not* flypaper for freaks.

My physiotherapist, Meg, is sweet, petite and looks about twenty but she's very confident and reassuring as far as my arm goes. The legs will have to wait. Do what you can at home for now, she tells me, and we'll work on that arm. She doesn't comment on my little ink-smudged fist-face, but her eyes dart to mine for signs of humour. We'll work up to the gym, she goes on. I realize she's part of my *new* team. Like the HandyDART. Huzzah!

I love the equipment—zappy little electrodes, pulleys and weights, hand pedals, stretchy bright latex bands. I leave with a ream of exercise pictographs, tired but happy. Okay, not happy, but more optimistic.

Over the next couple of weeks I repeat the trip a dozen more times. I've been exercising at home, too, so my legs feel a bit stronger and my balance slightly better, but there's no improvement in the arm. So much for optimism.

At physio one Thursday I'm using the hand-pedalling machine when I drop my glasses. They fall to my left, my bad side. I hang my limp arm down lower and lower hoping to drag them over to my right. I lean too far. So far that I can't sit up. My core strength is non-existent when I'm hot or tired or both. A struggle ensues...with myself. I'm red-faced and sweating and awkward and furious.

I hear a man's voice before a pair of shoes come into view.

"Oh, dear," he says. I turn my head to the side for a look. He's short and wide and verging on ugly, which makes him safe. He's wearing a safari coat. He bends at the waist and cocks his head slowly till we're face to face. "Are you all right?"

"Not really. Give me a hand, would you?"

He complies, tilts me back to upright, retrieves my glasses and disappears before I can thank him. A vaguely déjà vu moment, but I can't put my finger on it.

As I head out to the HandyDART, I overhear the receptionist on the phone. "Leo Moss? I'm sorry, but he just left."

I snap my fingers, sort of—the fingers on my bad hand—on putting two and two together. The Good Samaritan from Costa Rica strikes again. And my fingers move again, ever so slightly. I'm excited. And curious. Cure-ee-us.

I scoot outside to wait for the HandyDART and to find this Leo fellow to tell him I remember him and to thank him, you know, properly. An older BMW convertible, dirty, dinted, black, with the roof down, backs out of a distant parking spot and heads my way. It's him!

"Leo!" I call out. The fingers on my bad hand ineffectually wave to him from my lap. I raise my good hand for a better wave and call out his name just as the HandyDART pulls noisily up between us. Sigh.

The driver loads me and Adele, buckling us in. The whole time this is happening my bad hand is vibrating, making little lurching movements in my lap and opening and closing its little mouth like it's gasping for air.

"Gawd," I whisper to it, "what is going on with you? What's wrong?"

It shakes its knuckly little head.

I take a different approach. "What, I should ask, is right with you?"

"Lew," it mumbles.

"Excuse me?"

Its response is clearer this time. "Lee-oh."

"Leo? You remember?" I notice other passengers staring. I'm aware, suddenly, that I'm talking to my hand—and my hand is talking back! I cradle it and stroke it like a newborn to keep it quiet until we're out of the public eye.

When I get home, I refresh the eyes on my hand. I sit it on my knee. "So you can talk, eh?" I ask my hand. It just shrugs, but that's something at least. I congratulate it, thank it and the arm it's attached to for moving at all. I try to get it to tell me about its relatively amazing "birth" day, despite the fact that the only thing coming out of its mouth is a garbled attempt at the country-and-western ditty "How Do You Like Me Now?" The hand persists, repeating the song or at least the chorus for the rest of the afternoon. Physio Meg had encouraged me to use music to help stimulate stubborn body parts, so I go along with it. Practice pays off. By wine o'clock that little hand has a reasonably clear speech, albeit annoying as hell. It requires muscle and nerve cooperation, which is incredibly encouraging. So I ask it again about its ability to talk.

"Just to you," it says smugly.

"Lucky me," I say, questioning my sanity and envisioning an even more complicated social future. I slide it into my pocket. Out of sight, out of overtaxed mind. I have things to do.

I take my last dose of blood thinners with a quick right to the belly. Jab it in there like it's nothing, dispense with the last "sharp," dropping it into the little red sharps container like it's nothing, too. Bye-bye, injections. Hello, first glass of wine in weeks. Pouring ensues.

I email Dr. Falik while I cautiously sip:

> Hello, Dr. Falik,
>
> I just want to let you know that my left hand is able to move a bit. Fingers crossed (almost). I'm feeling really well and I'm keeping up the physio (and bananas). Thanks again for the great vein job. I appreciate your expertise.
>
> Sincerely,
> Melanie Farrell
>
> PS: Seeing as you went to the trouble of doing that Sexual Neuro Response testing, you might as well send me the results.

Then I proceed to look up Leo Moss on Facebook. But before I get to Destination Moss there's an auto-response:

Dr. B.N. Falik is away from his office until May 1. In case of emergency, please contact your general practitioner.

Hmmm. Waiting patiently isn't a bad idea. I mean, I have to rest my body and get it off the waning track and back onto the waxing track, which has dangerously slippery possibilities. But patience is one of the virtues I haven't had a handle on for, well, forever. It's not like I'm really interested in a sexually orgasmic encounter, anyway. Much.

I am interested, however, in a non-sexual encounter. With an oddly sweet short unattractive splay-footed man. A good Samaritan who has come to my rescue not once, but twice. A Johnny-on-the-spot who inadvertently and chimerically brought my hand back from its comatose state, which makes the possible encounter one involving gratitude. Yes, that's it. I really just want to thank him. Twice. And maybe shake his hand.

"More is better, right?" I ask my bad hand, parking it on my desk. "You'd feel better, wouldn't you, if there was a little hand-to-hand—"

"Combat?" asks my alarmed hand.

"No. Contact," I reassure it.

"A hand job?" asks my suspicious hand.

"No! Just a little shake."

My bad hand makes a scrunchy "eww" face.

I tell it, "No, not that! Hand-to-hand, a quick grasp, a warm...oh, never mind!" I pull my sleeve down over it to shut it up. It keeps humming. I try the Napoleon pose. When that doesn't work, I begin telling the apotemnophiliac fairy tale, "Once upon a time there was a very very bad hand..." Enough said.

I dig through hundreds of Leo Moss profiles on Facebook but can't find one that's a match for my Leo. I even google Leo Moss images. I know I would recognize him, especially if I tilt my head, but even a minimal vino refill doesn't make him appear.

I'll just have to resort to everyday common sense with dashes of hope, persistence and opportunity on the side. My physio appointment is the day after tomorrow.

There are other ways to get information about a person—from other people. I don't waste any time.

I talk to the physio receptionist, who's obviously healthified and body-aware—young, lithe, probably a yoga instructor on the side. Pretty. And don't forget smart. I sit up straighter. "There was a fellow here the other day. Leo something-or-other. Is he here today?"

"Uh, Leo..." she says as she taps away at her computer. "Not sure who you mean."

"He has a long beard," I say, stroking my chin. "He's kind of short,"

I add, not wanting to say *he's kind of ugly*. "Leo...Leo...umm...last name starts with an M..."

She looks at me blankly. "Nope. No idea."

"He kind of did me a favour. I just wanted to, you know, say thanks."

"Oh, yeah?" Blank stare.

"He's kind of...uh...odd," I say. "But super nice, right."

She shrugs. "Sorry."

I can feel my face losing its patience. I lean closer, raise one conspiratorial eyebrow. "Isn't there some way to...check?" I drop the last word like a small bomb.

She carries on typing. "Against the rules."

"Right. Sorry. Yeah, sure." I don't want to seem pushy or weirder than I already feel. "I'll just, uh, wait...for my appointment. Maybe he'll be in today."

I turn away, make a face and so does my bad hand. I bury my nosy nose in a magazine until Meg, my physio gal—who happens to be slightly older and rounder and nicer and chattier—comes to retrieve me from the waiting room. We're working on legs today, too, she tells me, not just my arm. Cool. As soon as she sits me on the bed and gets the electric-impulse pads a-buzzing on my bad leg, I replay my gumshoe routine.

"Hey, Meg. There was a fellow here the other day. Leo something-or-other. Is he here today?"

"Leo?" she says, adjusting the zappy impulses. "Not sure who you mean."

"He's kind of short," I say, still not wanting to say *he's kind of ugly*. I try again. "Leo...Leo...umm...last name starts with an M, I think...he's kind of, uh..."

"Leo! Yeah, Moss."

"I think that's it," I say, all nonchalant.

"Super guy. Really into butterflies."

"Bad knee or something? Shoulder? I can't remember what he said." I am halfway to lying through my teeth.

Meg looks confused, then laughs. "He's not a client. He's our equipment supplier."

"Oh. He's a gadget guy?" Disappointing. A travelling salesman.

"He does maintenance and stuff."

"So...he pops in every few months?"

"Whenever we need him." Meg cranks up the voltage until it makes my toes and the messed-up muscles in my leg twitch. "You have to try to lift your toes when you feel the pulsing. Not your leg. Just your foot."

I concentrate, and it seems to be working—a little.

"I'll be back in ten," she says. "Do as much as you can."

I work at it, but I'm also thinking—okay, fantasizing—about the strange little man and his equipment. His, uh, work. And I wonder what he's really like. And I wonder if he likes to hang out with crips. Or maybe he's a guy that needs to be needed. Maybe he's just a regular guy, but my hand's reaction to him tells me he's more. "He's a Magic Man," that old Heart classic, is playing in my head—a new earworm. My bad hand and I sing along quietly while I exercise my bad foot, which thankfully doesn't sing.

"It seemed like he knew me. He looked right through me," we sing.

And then this other voice chimes in, maybe a tenor, and my hand stops singing and starts kind of twitching to the tune. "Come on home, girl, he said with a smile."

Next thing you know, there's a safari jacket beside me and a guy named Leo Moss inside the jacket, singing along with me. "You don't have to love me yet."

We stop singing.

"You're upright today. How nice," he says. "Feeling better then?"

"Leo!" I say.

My good hand reaches out to him and my bad hand tries to follow. He's older than I'd thought and really kind of cutely repulsive—somewhere between a hedgehog and a hobbit. I pull back a bit and so does Leo. "I wanted..." My bad hand tries again, reaching more quickly as though the momentum will assure some success. "Just wanted to..." After another embarrassing withdrawal, my bad hand lurches forward at the very moment he steps toward me. My very bad hand shoots past his and wedges awkwardly in his crotch. "To say thank you!"

Leo gingerly removes my hand, saying cautiously, "My pleasure, I'm sure. Don't give it another thought." He places my hand in my lap before turning away.

But I really want to give it another thought, and now my bad hand has ruined everything! I slap my bad hand right across its little face. My arm! It's a naughty but moving appendage!

"Wait! Look!" I call, pulling the electrode pads off my leg. Meg hurries over and I tell her about my hand and suddenly less paralyzed arm, that the whole thing moved, and she pats it and congratulates me, but it's gone quiet again and refuses to do an encore. I shouldn't have slapped it.

I see Leo moving past the receptionist to the exit. I can't just let him leave. I'm Attracted with a capital *A* and so, obviously, is my hand. The fact that he's not interested in me makes him somehow more alluring. I push Meg aside and holler, "Anyone know how to get to Butterfly World?" It stops him in his tracks.

We've been sitting in Leo's old convertible—top down—outside the concrete home of Butterfly World for hours, wonderful hours, just talking and laughing and talking. It doesn't matter that we're in an empty gravel parking lot in the middle of nowhere or that the establishment is closed for another week. We imagine the butterflies inside, busy erupting from their cocoons, their life cycles adjusted for the coming tourist season. It doesn't matter that he had to dismantle my scooter—in record time—to fit into the trunk amidst his work-related wheels and belts and boxes. It doesn't even matter that I briefly thought him unattractive.

This charming and resourceful man produces a bag of nuts and dried apricots, a bar of dark chocolate and cool water from his various pockets. He looks the other way while I pee—perched on the running board—then offers me a tissue and quotes Chuang Tzu into the spring breeze grazing the parking lot: "I do not know whether I was then a man dreaming I was a butterfly, or whether I am now a butterfly dreaming I am a man."

He shares fascinating lepidopteran tidbits, random facts: that many butterflies can taste with their feet, that they can't fly if their body temperature drops below 86°, that they see red and green and yellow, that the sphinx moth—not a butterfly—in Madagascar has a twelve-inch proboscis.

I chime in, attempting to show my intelligence and interest. "And there's that butterfly that builds a tiny nest out of petals, a rainbow nest for every single egg."

"That's not a butterfly either. It's a bee," Leo gently corrects me. "An *Osmia avosetta*. But, yes, they use nectar to glue the petals together."

"Oh, right...the bee," I say and decide—on this subject, at least—that I'm a more intelligent listener than talker. I encourage him to tell me more, and he's happy to oblige.

When Leo talks about butterflies, he transforms into someone strangely compelling, an extraordinarily sensual creature emanating heat. I want to stroke his heavy eyebrows, run my finger down his short broad nose, nibble his dangly misshapen earlobe.

We talk about Costa Rica, our serendipitous meeting there, his trip—searching out morpho butterflies and glasswings. I tell him about my Liberation procedure and my bad hand—which only creeps over to the driver's side twice—and even how I'd become a sporadic apotemno-philiac.

"What does it mean, apo-temno-philia?" he asks.

I sound matter-of-fact. "The overwhelming desire to amputate a perfectly good limb."

"Or other parts of the body?" He leans toward me, all intense curiosity.

"I guess so. I only know about limbs."

He strokes my bad hand, turns it over, runs his fingers over the palm.

I like it. I lean closer. "It's better now, my hand. It's coming back."

"Good for you. *And* your hand." He closes it, looks into its little face, and kisses it on the mouth.

I can feel it all the way up my arm. It is delicious.

And he can tell. "It's perfectly understandable."

I smile and look into his eyes.

"That overwhelming desire..." he says, placing my hand in my lap and starting up the car.

"Do you have a naughty hand, too?" I joke.

He sighs. "Not exactly." Melancholy creeps in, settles around his eyes. "As Hans Christian Andersen put it, in the words of a butterfly, 'Just living is not enough. One must have sunshine, freedom, and...a little flower.'"

We're both quiet as he pulls out onto the busy highway. I think about the aloneness waiting for me at home. I try to come up with better things waiting for me. I come up with sweet felicity-all. When I break the silence, I surprise both of us. "I don't want to go home."

"What *do* you want, Miss Melanie?"

Everything comes out in a jumble. "I don't know, really. I want to go somewhere. Walk around. Be someone else. Fly..."

"Like a tourist?"

I shake my head, annoyed. "No."

"Like a butterfly?"

I shrug. "Maybe. I used to feel like that sometimes. Now I'm more like one of your specimens, mounted..." *Trigger-word alert!* My legs start to stiffen into plank position. I avert my eyes from Leo to concentrate on relaxing my legs, but my hand does a sudden crotch-lunge. It's all I can do to restrain it. I pinch its cheek, hard. "I mean pinned...to some chunk of cork or Styrofoam or whatever you use."

"Oh, I don't collect them."

"But I saw you with a net in Costa Rica."

"A rare occurrence. I try periodically but I can't make myself go through with it. I prefer the lens approach. I'm a harm-free hunter looking for killer shots." He passes me the last dried apricot.

My voice competes with a passing motorcycle. "And you're not attached?"

Leo's preoccupied with maneuvering us through a rush-hour intersection. "It's not everybody's cup of tea," he says.

"I guess not."

"It's a matter of personal ethics. A lack of desire. Even an inability to maintain a..." He swerves to avoid a cyclist.

Well, that's a disappointment. Or a challenge. "Does it bother you?"

"Bother me?"

"You know, not being able to...?"

He looks confused.

I get empathetic. "There are little blue pills for that. You know, right?"

Leo blinks. "Not *erection*, Miss Melanie. *Collection*. I can't maintain a collection for the life of me."

"Oh, Leo, I'm sorry. I..."

Leo interrupts. "Does the flap of a butterfly's wing in Costa Rica set off a hailstorm here on the West Coast?"

"Huh?"

"The butterfly effect. It's a metaphor. A famous one..."

"Oh, I knew that," I say, while my brain fumbles around to connect these two concepts with something happening between us now, something intelligent or fateful. When sensibilities fail, stop thinking, act natural, and do something.

There's a red light ahead. I wait for it. I lean over, pull his face closer until it's touching mine. I flutter my lashes against his. He hesitates briefly, then flutters back.

I release him when the driver behind us honks peevishly. We both look straight ahead. "The butterfly kiss," I say. "It's a metaphor. A pretty famous one."

"Flypaper for freaks," Leo mutters, shaking his head, but he's smiling.

I'm amazed that he's familiar with the expression. And I'm titillated. We have so much in common! I figure it's another sign, but I don't let on. I keep my cool. "Sticky attractions, you mean?"

"Can be." Leo nudges up the cuff of his sleeve to expose a forearm tattoo—the coiled strip of flypaper, several faded flies. "My first...before butterflies."

I get it. "So who's the fly here? You or me?"

"I'm not sure but flies...or caterpillars—as the Little Prince says— you must endure if you wish to get to know the butterflies."

Our eyes meet in the rearview mirror for a small quiet eternity. Leo breaks the silence. "I'd like to propose something."

I hesitate for three seconds. "Do you have stairs?"

Leo makes a quick U-turn. "Not a one."

I don't say a word about my domatophobia—fear of houses, other people's houses specifically. Stairs are obviously anxiety-inducing for a wheelchair aficionado but it's the awkward doorways, tiny bathrooms and cluttered floors that really put the spin on me. I breathe. I smile. Who knows where this will go or how?

We turn up a steep gravel driveway on the high side of semi-industrial Waterton Road. His place, when it comes into view at the top of the rise, is not what I expected. We come to a stop next to a garden of sorts—a hundred or more old tires of varying sizes bunched amid a maze of pathways, each tire petal-cut and filled with a razzle-dazzle of shrubs, spring blooms and bright new foliage. Each tire is a little ecosystem of hopeful flora standing up to the pervading odour of pulp and industry.

Next to the small sea of flourishing tires sits a converted shipping container—Leo's pristine olive-green container home, with a spacious deck and generous windows with cream-coloured awnings. It's simple, sensible and cute as hell. Nothing scary there.

But it's not alone. There are three more containers abandoned helter-skelter in the opposite corner of the property. They are butt-ugly, big, rusty, peeling rectangular boxes, but regardless, Leo's place, as a whole, makes for an odd sanctuary—relaxed, not stuffy. A shambhala for butterflies and one particular human.

"Wait right here," Leo says, hopping out of the car. Like I have any other choice. I wait for him to get my scooter, but he heads right in without me. Maybe he needs to pee. So do I. Maybe he's tidying up. I check my windblown hair in the mirror and look out over the mill, the massive booming ground and across the waves to Gabriola Island just as Leo reappears in the doorway pushing a shiny new wheelchair. "Just happen to have one, right out of the box," he says as he opens my door and gets the chair into the perfect position to receive me.

"Handy," I say, which makes my bad hand buzz and twitch. My

transfer into the chair is awkwardly slow. "How did you get so good at this?" I consider the possibility of a cripple fetish.

"My mother..." Leo begins. That's when my bad hand darts out to poke him hard in the belly. Leo gives a grunt but he doesn't lose his cool or his balance.

I pull my hand back and apologize, but I wish I hadn't asked. I consider the possibility of a mother fetish or an overly attentive man looking for a mother replacement.

I have an even worse thought. "Your mother, does she live with you?"

"No. It was a long time ago. Polio...among other things," he says, releasing my brakes but only some of my anxiety. No one wants to sandwich a new friend between slabs of disease—stale or otherwise.

We make our way up the winding pathway to his house. He points out butterfly-friendly highlights as we go—flat stones for basking, piles of decomposing leaves for hibernating, clumps of native grasses and stinging nettle farther back for larvae.

I've learned to expect the worst but hope for the best, so I'm doing both when Leo pushes me up a small wooden ramp, across the cedar deck and through the open door. Our conjoined silhouette precedes us across the worn plywood floor. I hesitate in the entrance, wanting to stay in the sunlight, the flowers. I swallow. The room is cramped. A bench strewn with tools and sketches on graph paper, an antique piano stool and overloaded shelves from floor to ceiling—boxes, bins, spools and parts.

"My lab," Leo says, as he squeezes past me and flicks a switch.

"Lab?"

"For my work...and inventions."

Dr. Frankenstein comes to mind, but when the inner door slides back and a warm rosy light flows over us, all my qualms disappear.

"*Entrée*, Miss Melanie."

Talk about rabbit holes! My bad hand breaks into a Lucy-in-the-Sky-with-Diamonds hum. I feel like Alice or maybe Georgia O'Keeffe. The walls are muralled with gargantuan flowers—butter yellow, soft peach and drooping salmon petals. Windows open at the top, and railings everywhere! The effect is more joyful than elegant, more delightful than grand. I feel kind of breathless, overwhelmed.

"Did you do these, Leo?"

He sighs. "Guilty."

"It's stunning. I feel so small. Inconsequential."

"But you are, indeed, part of the great sequence."

I attempt to look thoughtful but let the philosophy slide. Practicality reigns. The room is almost devoid of furniture. "Where do you cook? Sleep? Uh, wash your face?"

Leo slowly spins my chair, pointing out a tiny fridge, a tinier stovetop, counter and discreet cupboards. He pulls a cord high on the farthest wall, releasing a Murphy bed. It almost fills the room with its sumptuous leaf-green bedding.

"Slick," I say. "Everything's so compact." Like Leo, I think. "It suits you."

"It's the joy of less. I live small. Don't need more."

I'm envious of satisfied people but also skeptical. I have trouble believing. "Not even a bigger flower garden?"

Leo shrugs. "I've had much more and so very much less. This is enough. The key to life, Miss Melanie, is wanting what you have, not having what you want."

This tells me something, something important. I could learn a thing or two from this man. But I have more pressing concerns. "And your loo? You have one, right?"

"Of course I do. Do you...?"

"Yes, I do."

"Need help?"

"Oh. No. Thanks."

Leo slides open a pocketdoor next to the bed. I wheel myself in, relieved to find a small but adequate-for-a-wheelchair tiled bathroom. It's pretty cool, doubling as a shower.

When I come out, Leo's sitting cross-legged on the bed.

"Serious cocooning?" I ask.

"Oh, no. You're thinking of moths."

"Actually I'm thinking of people. Getting comfy."

Leo offers his hand. "Join me?"

Decision time. "Okay." Easier said than done.

I want to be all graceful but that doesn't work. I get on the bed but my legs don't follow me. It's my bad side. He has to come around and swing my legs in. He helps me arrange myself against the pillows and disappears into the corner kitchen, mumbling something about a picnic. He soon reappears with a wicker basket and resumes his pose. I love picnics and this one takes the cake—peppered salmon morsels, creamy cheese, sweet tomatoes, a Pinot Grigio. We nibble, sip and recapture the ease of the earlier afternoon. Between life and philosophy we inevitably come back again and again to butterflies.

Leo emulates an encased pupa that clicks its midsection to scare off predators and he moves aside his beard to show me the full effect of the tattoos on his chest, the ones that mimic the "eye spots" on a giant swallowtail's wings that, in turn, mimic the eyes of a predator. I ask about mating.

"Kind of like humans," he says. "They use sight." We look at each other. "They use pheromones." We both breathe deeply, lick our lips. "Then they...couple." Leo's gaze is mesmerizing.

"I've seen them together," I say. "How long do they...?"

"Maybe an hour. Sometimes overnight."

I put my good hand against the inked eye spots on Leo's bare chest.

He flexes his pecs. "I'd like to give you a gift, Miss Melanie."

Gifts demand compensation. "Oh, Leo, you don't need to..."

"But I'd like to. It's very special. I'd like to give you a butterfly..."

I shake my head. "I'm terrible with pets."

"I mean a butterfly orgasm."

"A what?"

"A butterfly..."

"I don't know. What exactly...?"

"Well, it's really called Venus Butterfly. A lovely, prolonged, almost tantric approach...simultaneous inner and outer stimulation. Think of wings. I could, uh, demonstrate."

"Demonstrate?"

"On you. Two erogenous zones. At once, with double the intensity."

"Sounds...interesting. It's usually one or the other." I can't deny that Leo's become more and more attractive. "Do you think that would count as one orgasm or two? I mean if it's simultaneous."

"Does it really matter?"

"It does. Quality over quantity," I say, thinking what a way to use up my last orgasm.

Leo looks relieved. "Well, if it's well done, it would be one, but a spectacular one. The cream of the crop, you might say." Leo winks.

"You're very confident. I mean with the whole timing thing."

"Almost a guarantee."

My good hand is still on his chest, caressing the outline of his tattoos when he leans over and butterfly-kisses me. My body stiffens into plank mode but Leo doesn't seem to mind.

"And what can I do for you, Leo Moss, besides the obvious?"

"Let me show you."

"Whenever you're ready then."

"Think butterflies. I'll start," he whispers, nuzzling my ear. "Skipper...now your turn."

Oh, it's a game! I think back over the *mariposa*-influenced afternoon. "Um, swallowtail?"

My bad hand lurches toward Leo's fly and with help from my good hand gets the button undone, then works the zipper down while our lips meet. Between kisses we murmur mouth to mouth.

"Admiral," says Leo.

"Lacewing?"

"Emperor."

"Wood nymph?"

My bad hand erratically searches around in Leo's unzipped pants, comes up empty, clenches and pouts oafishly under my chin. My body planks periodically, but I relax myself out of it.

Clothing disappears despite the cantankerous hand. Leo has to wrestle my shirt off. The rest is somewhat easier. As he stretches out on his back next to me, I kind of giggle, do a double take.

"Leo, you've got something stuck there. What is that?" I ask, pointing to his crotch. When I reach to pluck it off, it moves. "Leo! Kriste! It's a caterpillar!" I move away as best I can.

Leo cups the caterpillar and other pubic parts as well. "Mel, it's okay. I can explain."

"Explain? I don't mind bugs but I don't want to sleep with them!"

"It's not a bug." Leo says vehemently, obviously uncomfortable and still covering his privates. "It's a tattoo!"

"A tattoo..."

Leo nods.

I'm relieved it's not alive, but now I'm suspicious of the bigger picture. And I can't deny that I'm also curious. "Show me."

"No laughing."

I reassure him.

Leo slowly slides his hand away. "This is Mikey," he says, revealing his tiny, garishly striped penis—all yellow and black and white. I look up briefly to his eyes, which are clear and bright and honest. I don't laugh. I don't even crack a smile. I study it. My bad hand does, too. It's just like those butterfly life-cycle diagrams from grade school.

"Mikey's a...monarch?"

Leo smiles expectantly. "I just knew you would understand. Isn't he beautiful?"

"He's very, um, small."

"Oh, not for a monarch."

"No, I suppose not. But for a..."

"Man, you mean."

"It's just the surprise." I hurriedly add, "Not that it matters, of course."

"You said quality over quantity."

"Yes, but..."

"A micropenis works just fine. Einstein had one."

"Hence the name..."

"Mikey's the reason I wanted you to come. I mean one of the reasons. Here, I mean. Well, not just here. I mean the other way, too. In hopes that you could help me. Find relief. You see..."

"There's more to see?"

Leo micro-nods. "You *see*," Leo goes on, "when you explained that apotemnophilia I realized I could put a name to my relationship with my...penis. Because you helped me to do that, and you're so open and understanding that I saw right away you'd be the perfect person to assist me and..."

My bad hand imitates a car alarm that only I can hear. "Assist you with what, Leo? Amputate Mikey?"

"No, no! Not amputate. Metamorphosis is what I'm after. Mikey's tired of his prolonged caterpillar life." Leo lowers his voice to a whisper. "And I'm tired of Mikey. I've developed a deep-seated *aversion*...that apotemnophilia. And *he, Mikey*, wants to fly. Away. I just need the right *secretion*...for him to form a *chrysalis*. I've tried everything...thought maybe you'd have the magic potion."

I'm confused, and speechless.

"You seem put off," Leo points out.

"It's a lot to take in," I say. "Sorry."

Leo shrugs.

"I might help you," I say, "if I honestly thought I could. But, isn't it more complicated than that? Doesn't he have to shed his skin or something? And make some silky Velcro button to dangle from?" Wait a minute...how in hell did my mission get sidetracked by his mission? "You know, I've got my own problems. Orgasmic ones."

Leo turns away, swings his legs off the bed and slips on his shirt. "That bad, eh?"

I don't expect him to be truly interested, but I explain it to his back anyway, tell him about my last remaining orgasm, my desire to be done with it, my desire not to be done with it, which spills over into the bad bedfellows—disease and desire, which disintegrates into sniffling and finally balloons into full-blown bawling. I cry about every damn thing that's gone bad lately—my dwindled bank account and overblown credit, my overgrown right armpit hair, my difficulty with socks and shoes and buttons and zippers and bra hooks and knives and forks and jar lids and transporting hot liquids and anything else via wheelchair, and how my MS has affected friendships, my social life, my sex life and my overarching self-worth. Then I tell him how different it feels to be with him.

"To talk to, I mean...not different like weird or anything," I explain because I feel I need to. "Different like unusual."

Leo passes me a tissue and my shirt. I snuffle into them and then into Leo's shirt when he appears teary-eyed beside me, and then into his beard and his swallowtail-tattooed chest spots. He says, "Not a good day for resolutions," and I agree and then we just go at it. I mean sexually. I mean all over the place with secretions and hardening. I mean with gusto like we're frantic butterflies and there's no tomorrow.

Neither of us, sadly, can keep up the frenetic pace so we slow it down until it's dreamy and sensual to the nth degree. He moves my limbs about as though they were his own. Our seemingly symbiotic breath passes from mouth to mouth between us. We carry on until we can't.

When we are lying side by side, exhausted, not even touching, I ask, "Anything?"

"Too soon," he says. "Still drying. How about you?"

"Not quite. I was close though."

"That only counts in horseshoes."

"And curling," I add.

"And bocce."

We sigh. So does my bad hand. Mikey, thankfully, remains silent.

Leo sounds sleepy. "I guess you need a ride home."

"It's too late for the HandyDART. I could call a cab."

"Drive you tomorrow?"

"Tomorrow."

We drift off, avoiding reality for a few more hours.

11
Braking Point and Seizure

I feel like a million bucks, partly due to my post-procedure, albeit molasses-slow, anticlimactic progress. I'm stronger and my bad arm is back to where it was pre-procedure—except for my left hand's lingering mouthiness. After a few awkward encounters, Leo and I agreed not to see each other for a while. After six weeks, I rarely even ask about him at physio.

I've been busy observing. What with May Day, World Turtle Day, provincial Drink Water Week and National Speech & Hearing and Vision Awareness Month, I've had a lot on my mind—so much, in fact, that I missed Mental Health Week. I also have a lot to be thankful for. The disease hasn't cursed me with optic neuritis, tinnitus or slurred speech. Yet. Best to concentrate on the present. The future can be such a temperamental bitch.

Speaking of temperamental, it seems I'm still on the outs with Jackie. And Char's been weirdly distant—uncommunicative, in fact. She hasn't been responding to emails, texts or even phone messages even though she knows I rely on her financial wizardry. I know Char and Jackie talk to each other. They probably think I'm just not trying hard enough.

Money's becoming a big issue. I've avoided calls from Visa and Mastercard, and the interest keeps compounding. Okay, maybe I'm not quite feeling like a million bucks. Maybe half a mil. But at least with my left arm somewhat recovered I can drive myself a little more safely to physio. So I do.

The snooty receptionist isn't at her post when I arrive but Meg's there, as chipper as ever.

"We're going to change up your routine today, Mel."

"Change?" Ugh.

"More core. The ball," she says enthusiastically, leading me to a different area of the clinic.

Despite Meg's trustworthy spotting skills, in ten minutes I'm done for. We move to the more familiar eight-foot flat walking bridge. This I like. She adjusts the railings to my height, motions for me to step on.

"No zaps first?" I ask, pointing to my lower leg. She usually hooks me up to the electric muscle stimulator to prompt the muscles I need to step properly with a bent knee rather than a stiff-legged balance-challenging swing.

"Stims are all out of commission, Mel. Sorry."

"Too bad. Next time then." I step on and begin the slow trip to the end.

"Sure hope so," she says, sitting beside the bridge, ready to adjust my foot or knee if either slips out of alignment. "Waiting for a maintenance guy."

My ears perk up. "Oh? A new one?" My brain's working overtime trying to keep my body parts on track while imagining all kinds of terrible situations befalling Leo.

"Nope. Same one. He should be back soon."

"Back?" I ask. "He hurt his back?" I imagine him helping some other more attractive cripple out of his car and into his bed, only to wrench his back. Terribly.

"No, no. He's been away."

"Where would someone like that go?" I imagine him back in Costa Rica.

"Someone like what?"

"Oh, you know...unusual."

Meg shrugs. "South America somewhere."

"Wow." My brain's in overdrive, rescuing him from all sorts of imagined tragedies.

"You have to keep moving, Mel," she reminds me. "Two more minutes."

I snap to, put in my two minutes, thank Meg and scoot toward the exit.

A voice stops me. "Aren't you forgetting something?"

I turn to see the receptionist waving a sheet of paper.

"Me?" I ask.

"No one else here."

I look around the empty waiting room and then at her. She drops the paper, twists her hair into a rope and expertly creates a topknot with chopsticks. "Cash, debit or credit?" she asks.

"Oh. Right," I say, adding a mumbled apology. "You weren't here when I came in."

"Too bad that doesn't make it free, eh?"

I pull out my bank card, and she passes over the machine. I punch in my PIN, hit Enter and pass it back.

"Declined," she says.

"What? No way."

"Try again?"

"Yes, try again!"

We do. I check my PIN.

"Declined," she says again.

I mutter expletives, blush, give her my best-balance credit card—no PIN required. Most of my feel-good has dissipated. I feel like only a thousand bucks.

"Declined."

"That's not possible! Are you sure you...?"

"Yup."

"Try it again!"

Polite's gone out the window on both sides. She rolls her eyes. "Declined. Whatcha wanna do?"

"Jeez," I say, stuffing the stupid card into my stupid purse in front of the stupid receptionist. "I don't know. What are my options?"

"Cash?" she asks.

"I only have a twenty."

"That won't cover even half of it."

"Well, just bill me."

"Against policy."

"I can give you a cheque."

"We don't take cheques."

"I'll pay next time then! I'm here every week. Twice a week!"

"Hmm," she says, looking me over. "I'll have to get an okay for that. Wait here."

I feel like a hundred bucks. I don't wait. My bad hand flips her off as I exit. I'll show her! I'm gonna sort this shit out when I get home.

Good thing I have that twenty. My gas light's blinking empty at me. Half of that twenty will get me home.

~~

I line up both phones by my laptop and iPad ready to sort out my precarious financial existence. I check emails first out of habit. There's another message from Mastercard on my land line and two missed calls from a Visa number on my cell. Ignore. It seems my bank account is overdrawn. I call the bank to explain that my disability cheque will be here in a week and that I can't afford penalties on both ends. They know, they say, but no, I can't get a loan. No, I can't get overdraft protection. Manners and assistance disappear once the money's gone. It's a lose-lose situation.

I think through my short list of close friends in order of most available cash flow. Again, I try to connect with money wizard Charlene, leaving her texts, messages and emails at both her home and business. Then I tweet her, Skype her and even Facebook message her. I don't want to harass her but she's the one who set up my credit and my trip and other stuff. I still don't know how she did it, but it's been awesome. *She's* been awesome, and I want her to be awesome again.

I spend umpteen hours on hold in several different departments of my credit card company while I try to keep my phone-grabbing bad hand under control. It wants to throw my phone through the window. I also text my longtime friend John.

Hey, buddy. Long time, no see. You in town?

I finally get through to a real-life Visa person...in some other country. Gawd, I wish it was cheerful Delhi Patrick! This voice is crisp. No, I can't up my credit limit. No, my payments can't be lowered. No, I can't pay with my Aeroplan miles. I explain that my cheque will be here in a week, and I make sure I don't use the word disability because in credit-card land it's bound to get you flagged.

John, at least, texts me back right away.

still on the road. sales are a bitch. bring you a buffalo? lol

Sigh. I text back.

what's it worth? lol. have fun.

I call Jackie, who on a good week might be able to spot me a hundred. She even answers! And she sounds cheery! She asks about Char cuz she's being kinda weird. I ask about Char, too, for the same reason and more. Is she okay, I ask? She's always okay, Jackie says, isn't she? It's easier to conjecture about someone else's hypothetical problems when you can't do anything about your own. Then before I can ask her for a loan, Jackie asks about my post-procedure progress. I tell her it's slow but assure her things are improving. Good, she says, because that trip was tough. At least you didn't have to pay for it, I say. No, but she did have to miss work, so lost income. She wishes she hadn't put her savings into Cam's video store because Netflix is killing them, but she didn't know that a month ago when she bought a leather couch because it was on sale and just the right size and, oh, the colour! Damn! Can't wait to see it, I say, knowing I don't have the gas to get there. She says she saw a Help Wanted sign and thought of me. I tell her I'm not even close. Oh, she says. There's silence while she realizes our hopes for my miraculous recovery may not be fulfilled any time soon...or even at all. She says something always works out. See you soon, we lie.

I think through my short list of friends—the ones who aren't so close—and I try to remember who might owe me money. But the reality is that nobody owes me money, and I can't ask acquaintances, and even if I could it wouldn't help enough. My possessions include nothing of value, nothing marketable or saleable except my devaluating scooter and lift. I can't sell my MS-tainted kidney or my blood. My hair is too short to sell, and I can't even trade in my one gold filling because the dental work would cost me more than it's worth.

Char's car pulls up outside. Rushing to meet her at the door, I feel a massive flood of relief. She can fix anything to do with dollar signs!

"Char, you have no idea how glad I am to see you! Jackie and I were starting to..."

"Mel, we have to talk." She sways in the doorway.

"You want tea?"

"No. Thanks." She heads for the kitchen table, sits and clenches her hands in her lap. This is not the Char I know. She's dressed down—zero makeup, no jewelry. Uh-oh. Priority shift.

I roll up beside her, put my arm awkwardly around her. "What is it?"

She takes a deep breath. "Just listen, okay?"

"Okay," I say, nodding dumbly. I stop touching her but stay close. "You don't look...is it...?"

"Mel!"

"Sorry. I just..." That temperamental bitch, Future, is right here in the kitchen with her sister, Mortality.

"I'm not sick, Mel. It's worse than that."

I wonder what could be worse than sick. "Worse?"

Char rubs her temple. "Money trouble."

"Is it serious?"

"Oh, it's serious all right."

"But not cash-flow serious, right?"

"Our accounts have been frozen. All of them. Mine. Glen's. The business..." Her voice diminishes with each word, the last only a whisper. "Everything..."

I shiver. "Frozen! For how long?"

Char snaps, "However long it takes! Revenue Canada jumps in fast and then treads water while they watch you drown."

"But, what happened?"

"It's a long convoluted story."

"They must be wrong. You'd never...Glen would never...you're both so..."

Char shrugs, sighs and asks for a cigarette.

I've never known Char to smoke. "Is there anything I can do?"

She drags long and hard. "You, Mel? I can't imagine."

"No, no, of course not. I wish I could."

"Me, too. But I have to go." She stubs out the cigarette. "Auditor first thing in the morning. We'll talk soon."

"Sure. Of course. Any time."

Char gets up to leave and I pull her in for a real hug, tell her how tough and resilient she is. I'm filled with empathy, compassion and an underlying survivalist angst. I guess this is how secondary extinctions occur—financial ones. And my resources have been washed out by the ripple effect.

I don't want to ask. I don't want to ask. I'm going to have to get around to asking. My bad hand is poking me in the ribs. "So, I hope I didn't add to your problems, Char. You helped me so much! I couldn't have done it without you—Costa Rica, the procedure, everything!"

"Forget it. Glad I could help...when I *could* help. Good thing we set everything up in your name." She shrugs. "My mess would have happened anyway."

"Speaking of messes, I..."

"You just get better, Mel. Pay your bills on time. Get yourself that job. Pay your taxes." She smiles wryly. "You should have enough to do you for a while anyway."

"I should? But..."

"You'll be fine."

"Yeah...yeah, you too."

She shuts the door on her way out.

She leaves me with so many worries to shuffle that I don't know where to start. I feel kind of sick. Not like flu, more just exhausted and headachy and weak and...like I have MS. All systems slow. I watch schlock on TV, listen to the radio in the background, wallow at the computer, lurk on a couple of chat threads where people are in verbal combat, punch random half-baked words into Google search like *potato*, *lottery* and *butterflies*. Thinking about Leo going on yet another quest to find a rare species in South America, I realize that he's even weirder and more passionate about his mission than I gave him credit for. Maybe I can be that way, too. I mean passionate. And not about sex but about finding work. Like a real job. A real grown-up job I can be passionate about!

Tomorrow. Tomorrow, after I scoot the empties down to the bottle depot for gas money so that I can afford to look for a job while figuring out how to beat down my debt.

I get up bright and early, realign all my desktop communication devices, park my mega-mug of java within easy reach. I have a little problem with focus, feeling kind of split between websites with advice for debt management and the ones posting employment opportunities. I explore all my options. Amazing how time flies when you're having fun. And when you're not.

By the end of the week, I've learned a lot—that with my meagre income it would take me ten years to pay off my credit card debt. Even with a minimum-wage job it would take me seven years. And that's if I don't eat. I've learned that physiotherapy is considered a luxury and owning a vehicle is an oxymoronic asset that works against you. I've learned to turn the ringers off on both phones because it will only be the bank or the physio clinic or a credit card company. Mostly I've learned about anxiety, embarrassment, humility and desperation. Also, that bankruptcy is the only option. I have an appointment this afternoon with a financial adviser.

On the employment side of research I've learned that I need to forget about finding work and focus instead on an entrepreneurial enterprise. If I was located in a bigger city I could get myself a bunch of cats and charge petless apartment dwellers an hourly rate for café cuddles, but I don't have start-up capital. If I lived in Bangkok, I could practise Tata, professional face-slapping with all its rejuvenating skin benefits, but it takes two years of schooling and my bad hand might miss the cheeky target. If I hung my fedora in Orlando, I could really put my disability to good use by hiring myself out to an elite Disney World tour agency that caters to Manhattan mothers—nothing better than a fake relative in a wheelchair or scooter to get those folks to the front of the Pirates of the Caribbean lineup. Guide-dog imposters work too, but I don't have a dog. I'm obviously lacking in positive outside-the-box attitude.

I tear myself away from the computer long enough to ready myself for the meeting. I don't know what attire is appropriate for filing for bankruptcy. Do I want to look well-worn but not bag-lady pathetic, right down to the underwear—period panties and a fraying underwire bra? I can't, I just can't. I choose a plain skirt, a solid T-shirt and a light jacket so I look like I've been a productive somebody in the past. I avoid perfume, makeup, jewelry, any signs of superfluous spending or liquid assets. My old semi-precious ring stays home, but I wear my utilitarian London Drugs wristwatch because it demonstrates the ability to get to appointments and job interviews. Off I slowly go.

∿⁓

Wind excites me and makes me feel like I'm moving faster and with more purpose than I really am, especially when I'm scooting on Adele. Today the surprising gusts make me feel like my whole life is moving... moving in the right direction. My hair and my bad hand disagree with me all the way from my van into the old brick building and up to the sixth floor.

Elevators rock.

The receptionist is pleasant and dressed better than I'll ever be. I smooth my windblown hair and have a good look around. There are other people in the swank waiting room—a middle-aged couple, an older guy and a well-coiffed, pedicured woman my age. There's nobody under thirty. The young ones are all out accruing debt like there's no *mañana*. We all avoid eye contact.

I'm curious about that attractive woman. She goes into the inner sanctum ahead of me. She doesn't look broke. I read all the certificates on the wall and realize these financial advisers have clients at both ends of the money scale. I sit up straighter, read through a couple of pamphlets. It isn't long until the woman emerges chatting happily with an older woman in a navy business suit who could be an older, greyer version of TV's Ugly Betty. They're still chatting out by the main door when the receptionist ushers me into the office to wait. There's a clutter of paper and a dark rainbow of folders on the large desk. The top folder—forest green...the colour of money—is open. I peek only a little and everything's upside down, but I see a column of numbers on the top page. Biggish numbers with lots of zeros. I avert my eyes.

My adviser arrives—yup, it's Betty. She's nice enough—courteous, not condescending—but she has a reaction to my deodorant. She sneezes and gasps and then hurries to open the office door and windows, ignoring the papers that fly off her desk. She explains the bankruptcy process quickly, goes over my finances. I try to interrupt, just to point out that a couple of possibly important documents have escaped via the window, but there's no stopping her. A blank contract is retrieved from the carpet and passed to me along with my homework: affidavits from two reputable car dealers that my five-year-old vehicle has devalued to less than five grand and monthly budget worksheets, detailed down to every pod of laundry detergent. She also hands me my bill. My eyes start to water almost as much as Betty's.

Filing for bankruptcy costs money—regular payments for the nine months it takes to complete the process. It's like having a baby—expensive but supposedly gratifying. If I toe the line, do my homework and live without luxuries and a few necessities for the next nine months, I'll be free and clear of debt. Who needs a respectable four-point credit rating anyway? I'll never ever buy a house or another car or medical procedure or plane ticket. And the biggest and most immediate bonus of all is that the relentless collections phone calls will stop.

I watch her cut up my credit cards. In a rush, I sign away my privacy. I'm in a hurry. I want to get my deodorant the hell out of there before she codes blue. She sneezes and coughs and scoops up a small chaotic armful of paperwork. She scrutinizes me and chooses a red folder to shove it into. I clutch my scarlet folder under my jacket and make a rapid scooter exit. I'm on my final approach to the elevator when the lights on the sixth floor suddenly go out. Holy shit. It's not totally black, just dim and eerily quiet.

A few heads pop out of other office doorways. There's a flurry of reassurance. It's the wind, they say. I wait twenty minutes, watching over the balustrade as others calmly take the stairs to the exit. I go back to Betty's well-heeled receptionist. She's apologetic while we discuss my dilemma and the fact that the power outage is expected to last four or five hours. She assures me I'm not the only disabled person in the building—there's one on another floor—and that the fire department will arrive shortly. The fire department? Holy shit! She explains the firemen will get me out—no problem. No problem?

When the five firemen appear they're too wonderful for words. I mean all those moustaches and uniforms and, well, firemen. A little crowd has gathered. The moustaches explain to me how one of them will carry me down over his shoulder. I say no way. I point out that I'm no giant but I'm not a featherweight either. Plus I'm wearing a freakin' skirt. They check out my body and ask me what it can and can't do, then discuss alternatives among themselves—the pros and cons of the one-handed seat carry and the two-handed seat carry. They decide that six flights of stairs make those particular options too tricky.

They settle on the two-man fore-and-aft carry. Sounds sort of smexy but awkward. They explain as they go, first getting me up to standing at the top of the stairs. Then Moustache One snuggles up behind me and slides his arms in under mine and wraps them around my chest. Whether it's due to the anxiety of being picked up—physically—or the close proximity of these pec-tacular men, my body goes into plank mode. I have to convince it over and over to relax. The crowd is getting bigger and more curious and no wonder. I'm pretty curious myself. Moustache Two backs up to my front—it's very cozy between them. He leans down and picks up my legs and wraps them around his waist. Oh my! There's a bit of adjusting. And away we go with a moustached spotter before and behind us and another moustache brings up the rear carrying Adele. I look up when we get down to the fifth floor and wave to the crowd. They clap. My bad hand pinches Moustache Two on the butt. One of the spectators whistles before I get it under control. I apologize profusely to my moustaches and thank them. I try to be less heavy the rest of the way down.

I'm delivered out into the wind and onto Adele. The moustaches even escort me past the flashy red fire truck to my van and tuck me and my equipment in. Moustache One—my aft man—passes me my purse and my scarlet folder...just as a blast of wind hits. My folder and papers lift and scatter and all five moustaches scramble about to retrieve them. They stuff the works back into the folder, all apologetic. Never mind. I thank them some more as they wave me out onto the street. Best moustache ride ever!

I feel unexpectedly good, lighter, like I've escaped a fiery death sans the fire. I'm imagining this wind is lifting the burden of debt off my shoulders—one thousand-dollar bill after the other. I'm almost euphoric. I feel that I have a grasp on at least one aspect of my life, which makes me more hopeful about the other aspects.

I want to tell somebody how good I feel. Or show somebody how good I feel without actually explaining why. Or ask somebody for advice about car dealerships while I'm feeling so good. I get to thinking about my friends—Jackie and Char and John. Right now none of them seems to be the right somebody. It's that lull in long-term friendships when you just want to reach outside of your circle to someone who doesn't know or think they know your every weakness or flaw. Somebody with a different perspective. Somebody open. Somebody weird, but in a good way.

I swing by Leo's place while my bad hand waves gaily out the window. There's no sign of life at Leo's. Not even a butterfly. I tear one of my budget-homework sheets in half to scribble on and leave the note in his mailbox because I can reach it through the van window. HEY STRANGER, CALL ME? MEL. I add a friendly little heart. I try not to snoop but I can't help noticing there's only one other item in the box and it's junk mail. Either he's back from wherever and just temporarily out *or* the post office is holding his mail for him.

Next stop, the Ford dealership. If the estimate is over five grand, vehicle seizure is inevitable. Somebody'll just come and tow the sucker away. The lift equipment in the back for Adele—that I didn't mention to my financial adviser—is another complication, adding value, so I have to specify that's not included. Their estimate is still above five thousand. When I say I need it to be lower and I need it in writing, they get suspicious and usher me off the lot.

I try the Chevy dealership. They're not usually big on Fords, but their estimate is even higher. They like my low mileage. Since when does a wannabe seller have to dicker for a lower price? I try honesty, explain my real predicament—with authentic tears and sniffles on the side. They back away slowly, citing legal repercussions.

I decide my note sounded too lonely and vague, so I go by Leo's again, retrieve the first note and leave a new one: HI LEO, I REALLY

NEED SOME ADVICE. CALL ME, OKAY? MEL. I add my phone number this time.

I go home hot and hungry, exhausted and newly anxious. I can't imagine living without my vehicle, especially now that I can drive again. I hate the complicated HandyDART system—the time involved setting up pickups and drop-offs, the interminable waits, and it still costs money both ways. Not to mention the fact that you have to be sociable en route. I can't imagine living on thirty percent less groceries or making these cheap shoes last another nine months. I already want the bankruptcy to be over. If I was prone to migraines I'd suspect one was coming on. I take some Tylenol, give my head a shake. One thing at a time. Repeat.

I need sustenance, an energy boost to fend off this malaise. The choices are minimal. Everything in my fridge and cupboard suddenly has a price tag on it. I have a bowl of oatmeal for dinner. Well, half a bowl. I feel like crap. Fuzzy around the edges. MS exhaustion, more than likely. I carry on with determination, sort through what's left of my windblown paperwork and fill out my first monthly budget. Holy shit, living's expensive! And I have to knock almost two hundred bucks off the top for my financial adviser. My rent takes the biggest chunk of my income, but I can't find anything cheaper that's wheelchair friendly aside from subsidized housing, and there's a three-year wait for that. Groceries can be cut down. More beans and macaroni, less meat and fruit. Physio at seventy bucks a pop—I could just cry...again—has to be cut down from three times a week to once a month. But I still owe them for that last session. There goes physio. And there goes the overdue pedicure that keeps my toenails healthy because even my good hand isn't capable of rising to that particular occasion. And then there's wine.

Maybe my financial adviser can postpone my official filing for a month. I dig through the scarlet folder for Betty's business card. I find it but, funny thing, there are several other scuffed cards in there, too—the result of Betty's office windstorm or the blown-folder episode on the street, who knows?

I chalk it up to synchronicity because one of those cards is pretty interesting. It's got a little photo on the left—an attractive, sexy woman.

And I recognize her as the woman from the waiting room...with nice hair and, I imagine, babied feet. And it gives me an idea, an entrepreneurial one. A socially beneficial concept with a self-help twist. No overhead, no initial output, zero travel, work in my PJs and money in the bank.

The card reads:

STEAMY PHONE SEX
DIAL 1-600-HOT-TALK

But can I overcome my phonophobia for cash? You bet your sweet ass I can. Huzzah! Hope!

I sit in my wheelchair, stare through the window, daring to imagine a decently comfortable future with just the right tinge of indecency. I daydream in one-month increments and then one-year increments, conveniently forgetting about progressive MS and aging and my nine months in bankruptcy restraints. I daydream so hard that I start to feel funny...disconnected. I daydream so hard that I think I see Leo peering in the window. Leo? Peering in the window? A wave of fatigue rolls over me. I'm not sure what is real and what isn't. I can't seem to roll over to the door fast enough to find out. In fact, I can barely make it at all. I feel so weird—fuzzy around the edges and far away. So very weary...it takes me forever to get there. To open that door. "Leo?"

$\mathcal{m}\!\!\!\sim$

It's a stinging blow to my cheek—a full-handed slap—that opens my eyes, causes me to gasp, "Ouch! What the fuck?"

Leo's face is inches from mine. He's firing imbecilic questions at me. What's your name? What day is it? Who am I? How many fingers?

"Fuck off!" I say. "What's the matter with you?"

Leo pulls his phone out. "I'm calling an ambulance."

My cheek is still burning. "Why? For who?"

"For you!"

I grab his phone and say, "Melanie Farrell. Thursday, June third. And I have ten fingers."

He holds up three stubby fingers.

I say, "Three. What is *wrong* with you?"

"Me? You scared the hell out of me, Mel! It's a good thing you were sitting down."

I see it in his face, the flush, the panic, the concern. I figure maybe something did happen but I can't figure out what.

He asks for his phone back.

I pass his phone to my bad hand for safekeeping and ask Leo who the hell he's going to call.

He slows his words down to a soothing crawl. "Don't get excited, Mel. Nine one one would be a good idea."

"Nine one one? This isn't an emergency. I'm just bankrupt and disabled and unemployable and..."

"Has this ever happened before?"

"This what?"

Leo and my bad hand are in a phone tussle but he keeps talking. "The rolling eyes, the lolling head, the guttural moaning, the twitching..." He motions to my lap and the spreading stain there. "And you peed your pants."

I try to cover my damp lap. "Gawd, that sounds scary..."

"Very."

"How long?"

"A minute. Maybe less."

"Sounds like a..."

"Like a what, Mel?"

"Never mind. I'm fine. I was just so excited to see you!" I smile to reassure him.

"You know what happened."

"And I wanted to tell you about my day, my bad day."

"You need to see a doctor. This isn't normal."

"I left you a note. Did you get it? I wanted to ask you for help in sorting out my..."

He's like a spaniel with a throw toy. "We have to do *something*."

"Promise you won't call nine one one?"

Leo hesitates, sighs. "For now, Mel. But you know what happened, right? Even though you don't remember?"

I don't want to say it out loud because it will make it real and I don't want it to have happened because it's never happened to me before and I have trouble believing it really did happen because I don't remember a thing, plus now it scares me and obviously scares Leo, too. I don't know if this thing that just happened will be the beginning of my end or the end of my beginning, but I figure there's no getting around it. I'll have to bite the throw toy, too. I lock eyes with Leo.

"They're threatening me, my van…with vehicle seizure."

"Vehicle what?"

"You're not listening. Vehicle…seizure."

He nods. "There. You said it. And you know that's what happened. But we need to find out why. After that you can tell me everything else."

12
Stop, Drop and Roll with the Punches

I cajole Leo out of the 911 call and a visit to the ER and phoning Jackie or Char or John for support, but as much as I stubbornly reassure him that I'm fine, the more he insists on some kind of action. So we actively research seizures on the anxiety-compounding internet, which takes forever because there are more search results for dog and cat seizures than for the human variety.

I want Leo to leave so I can process the information in my own time, but I don't want him to leave because I'm worried that I have a brain tumour and I don't want to fall down and really hurt myself before painfully dying. I need a stall tactic until my wave of fear subsides, so I repeatedly demand all the creepy details of what happened that I don't remember. I wear us both out in the process. A decision is made. Leo stays the night, keeping his phone in his hand and an eye on me while I snore the night away with exuberance.

⌇⌁

First thing in the morning Leo hustles me into the clinic. It's a good thing he's here because my doctor points out the futility of trying to diagnose an unremembered "event" without a witness. I learn a lot of things, like how weird it is to have a third party present in the doctor's office—tipping the scale from one-on-one, making me the minority. I need testing at various locations—which I could have had done tidily if I'd just gone to the ER. I learn that the "event" may or may not be related to my MS, that one "event" isn't classified as epilepsy but more than one "event" is, and that epilepsy drugs are recommended despite non-diagnosis. Screw that! I'm also prohibited from driving for six months, which may be irrelevant if bankruptcy leads to vehicle seizure. There's that word again—seizure!

I take possession of some new vocabulary, too, like *grand mal, idiopathic, hemispheric* and *tonic-clonic,* which sounds like a bar drink or at least a pseudonym for a good, stiff hangover cure—Double Seizure with bacon and a cheese omelette, please! But tonic-clonic's really only the new word for *grand mal*, like *event* is the new word for *seizure*, which replaced the word *convulsion*, which took over for the word *spell*, which was a pinch-hitter way back when for *fit*.

We rule out causes and triggers like head trauma, fever, flashing lights, alcohol, coffee, hypoglycemia, menstrual cycling and sleep deprivation, which leaves stress. They both tell me I should relax, take it easy. What a grand mal freakin' idea!

All this doc-talk makes me feel sick and headachy—like there's really something wrong with me—until I recognize it as hunger pangs but in my head. I leave the clinic with a new team of medical pros and half a dozen appointments.

We pick up sushi—Leo's treat—on the way home, then eat at my kitchen table while I gulp tea and watch him sift through the list of appointments. The sushi revives me physically. Mentally, I still feel disconnected, like I'm watching from the sidelines as Leo mutters and scribbles my future onto a calendar.

I have trouble believing it really happened. I'm thinking about creating a Facebook Event—date, time and all the creepy details. I could invite my growing number of event fans, like doctors and technicians and…I catch Leo looking at me warily.

"Are you okay?" he asks for the umpteenth time.

"Fine," I say as I smile and change my imaginary Event privacy settings to private. "Just daydreaming."

"Well, then, you're all set here." He nudges the calendar toward me. "So, how are you going to manage?"

There's a sharp knock at the door and Jackie pokes her head in, calling, "Mel? Are you all right?"

"I am now," I answer back. "Come on in. Join the party."

"Party?" Jackie talks her way into the kitchen. "I tried calling but you weren't answering your phone." She stops abruptly when she sees Leo. "Oh. Hello."

Leo stands up and extends his hand while I find my manners. "Jackie, Leo. Leo, Jackie."

Jackie reluctantly takes Leo's hand. "Leo who?"

"Moss," he answers, pulling himself up to his full five feet.

Jackie's poised for fight or flight.

"He's a friend, Jackie. Geez," I say, pointing her to a chair opposite Leo. I don't mind being neutral territory between the two, considering the bad start.

Jackie's eyes flit from Leo to me to Leo, then down to the papers on the table. "And what's all this? He's not selling you something, is he?"

"I'll tell you everything but not from the beginning. I had an event yesterday...a neurological *event*."

Jackie looks blank.

I can say it out loud now. "A seizure."

Her demeanour changes immediately. "Oh, Mel. Are you okay?"

"I'm fine. Just need a few tests. That's what the paperwork's about. Now pour yourself some tea."

"Why didn't you call me?"

"Leo just happened to be looking in the window. He saw the whole thing."

"Luckily," Leo adds.

Jackie's voice oozes suspicion. "Looking in the window?"

"First things first, Jackie. Tea."

"Listen," says Leo, "maybe I should go and let you two talk..."

"No," Jackie and I say simultaneously but for different reasons.

I add, "Can you stay just a little longer?"

And Leo does and Jackie pours tea. When I get it through Jackie's head that I really don't remember what happened, aside from the before and after, Leo takes over. He recounts my event, answering Jackie's darting questions as best he can. Jackie is as disturbed as Leo was when I regained consciousness. She chastises Leo for not taking me to the ER. I chastise her for chastising Leo. Leo stays admirably calm. He doesn't chastise anybody, merely defends himself with logic and the fact that I refused to go to Emergency or even call it an emergency, which irritates Jackie even more.

Next, there's organizing to be done—who's going to get me to which appointment. Leo points out that he's necessary as a witness for certain appointments. Jackie counters, alluding to our lengthy friendship, her observations about the deteriorating state of my MS, and her stellar and stalwart performance as my caregiver in Costa Rica. I choke on my tea. They ignore me entirely so I retreat to the bathroom, leaving Jackie and Leo to pore over my calendar like a couple of generals strategizing over a map in the war room.

I barely get the door closed when Leo calls out, "Are you okay?"

Two minutes later—while I'm trying to one-handedly pull up my pants—Jackie inquires, "Are you okay?"

I reassure them one at a time, "Fine, thanks!" And I wonder if I'll have to keep answering that question for the rest of my life.

When I reappear at the table, they fill me in. Some kind of unpleasant but necessary truce has been established and my appointments have been divided equally between them, starting tomorrow with Jackie and the required lab work.

They're still discussing who will keep an eye on me, check in on me by phone—make contact, contact, contact—as they clean up teacups and put on their coats. After the standard reassurances, they leave together—a united front in the face of adversity—still discussing their battle plan. I hear their car doors slam and their engines start up.

They forgot to shut the door on their way out. I hear the toot-toot of a horn, and then the distinct crunch of metal. I approach the door with trepidation. I can't tell who hit what, but Leo's old Mercedes and Jackie's little Toyota are doing some overly intimate touching. I sneak the door shut ever so quietly—oh shit, oh shit, oh shit—and then I lock it and go about my business. My business of worrying. Eventually they leave. I know nothing and saw even less.

But I'm kind of scared to do much of anything in case it might trigger another seizure, but of course I can't do nothing because there's stress in that, too. I keep thinking I feel that wavy faraway feeling that I felt just before I zoned out, but it must be my imagination. I feel sharp little pains on the right side of my head, but maybe I'm just projecting. I keep my phone with me in case I need to call 911 or my friends call to check up on me. And they do, relentlessly—in the beginning, at least.

Besides listening—over the next few weeks—to Jackie's snipes and Leo's sighs about each other's driving abilities, insurance deductibles, personal appearance, manners, sincerity and character in general, I sleep a lot. And I graciously accept the help I need, mostly transportation and pep talks. I even lend Leo my van while his Mercedes is in for repairs.

I also research online and worry for the time it takes to get through all the appointments—blood work, EEG, EKG, CT and MRI—and the various preparations for said appointments and specialist visits in between. I make some interesting temporary fashion statements during this time—accessorizing with a heart monitor rather than a purse, gooey multicoloured electrodes attached to my scalp, no perfume, no makeup, no deodorant, no jewelry, easily accessible shapeless attire. It's not a pretty picture, and it's certainly not the time to run into Bastardo in the hospital hallway—who's scared to ask me anything—and his new younger girlfriend who can't help but ask what's happening with my hair. Aside from that, it's uneventful. One post-CT neurologist remarks on something "funny" in my right hemisphere, but he can't be sure. With MS, nobody can. A black hole is a black hole. And a seizure is a seizure. My newest team can't agree on the cause. The epilepsy specialist says mine is not MS-related and the MS specialist says it's not epilepsy-related. Both agree it's not related to the Liberation procedure. We chalk it up to a stress-related isolated anomaly.

I reap totally impractical and unexpected benefits. Jackie brings me a pound of neon Post-it notes. Leo brings me a fly swatter shaped like a butterfly. Jackie gifts me with a second-hand mother-in-law plant. Leo, a gift certificate from Pinky's Tattoo Parlour—non-refundable. Jackie, an ugly pair of oversized striped mittens. It goes on and on, but Leo wins the day. When he's done with my van, he returns it along with the two very low estimates I need for the bankruptcy folks in order to keep possession of my vehicle. And even though I can't drive it right now, just knowing I have a vehicle makes me feel better. My scooter works fine for my cloak-and-dagger trips to the food bank. At least there's more in my fridge—sometimes—than relish.

Aside from the anxiety and poverty and quasi depression and medical appointments and extended periods of crawling in and out of bed, things are as peachy as they're ever going to be. I think about my life. I examine my hands, thinking about all the things they've done, places they've been. I think about the millions of places they'll never go. I look mortality in the eye. I feel like the non-walking near-dead. Despair sets in. It dawns on me that my bad hand hasn't spoken a word since the seizure. Not one bloody word! Holy hell, maybe it's dead...or gone back to being normal...wait, that's almost the same thing! I give it a squeeze. Nothing.

"Are you dead?" I ask it. I give it a good hard pinch, then a little whack with the butterfly-shaped fly swatter.

It mumbles a bit through colourless lips. "Can't see," it slurs.

"Oh, right," I say, uncapping a fine-tip permanent marker and drawing on its eyes. "Better?"

It gives me a good long stare. Then it raises itself up and with gusto it slaps me, not once but twice, screaming, "Carpe diem, dumb-ass! You're not dead! Now seize the fucking day!"

I'm forced to agree. Using the neon Post-it notes, I reprioritize my survival. Top of the list is an appointment at Pinky's Tattoo Parlour to give this brilliant dick of a hand the permanent face it deserves.

13
Link, Synch and Bare All

"This is going to hurt me more than it's going to hurt you," I tell my bad hand on the HandyDART ride down to Pinky's. The driver ignores me once I give him the address. I figure he's used to unconventional behaviour. My bad hand makes suspicious little slits of its temporary but soon-to-be-permanent eyes. I pop an extra Ativan and two more painkillers.

"Don't be a dick," I say to the hand. That gets the driver's attention. He's eyeballing me in the rearview mirror.

"You got a problem, lady? I can drop you right here."

I wonder if the chair-lift at the back of the van has emergency ejection capabilities. "No, no, I just..." My bad hand shoots up in the air, and I wrestle it into my lap. "I'm just practising my ventriloquism..." I say to the driver, "for a puppet show. A puppet show, you know, for kids."

The driver rolls his eyes and mutters under his breath. My bad hand dances around in his line of vision, then plummets at rocket speed into my belly. I let out a little grunt.

The driver's not buying it. "For kids, huh? And your little puppet there, his name is Dick, right?"

"As a matter of fact, it is," I reply, my face the epitome of kewpie-doll innocence while I tighten my chokehold on Dick until he calms down. "How did you know?"

The driver shakes his cynical head. "A wild guess. Hey, what's the point of being a ventriloquist if your puppet doesn't talk?"

"So you couldn't hear him?"

"Not a peep. You have to project," the driver's saying.

"Project?" I ask in confusion, thinking about Char and her futuristic horoscopic projections.

"Your voice...project your voice."

Dick raises himself up till we're almost eye to eye and states that he no longer wants to have his facial features indelibly tattooed.

"Did you hear that?" I ask the driver. And to Dick, I whisper, "I thought you were excited. Carpe diem and all that."

Dick shouts, "A hand can change its mind, can't it?"

I look expectantly at the driver's eyes in the rearview mirror, and he looks expectantly back.

"Louder," I order Dick, who screams, "I DON'T WANT TO GO!" He tries to pinch the driver's shoulder. I haul him back and sit on him.

The driver shakes his head and turns up his radio, saying, "You better work on that, lady."

When Dick stops squirming, I allow him back in my lap. He sighs, then has a moment of panic. "I'm scared," he says, pressing his little face to my breast.

"Listen," I say, stroking his knuckled crown, "this is for your own good. And mine. I've only been right-handed for a couple of years. I can't put liner on my own eyes, never mind your tiny ones."

Dick yawns. "I'm getting sleepy."

"Perfect. So am I. See? There's nothing to worry about. You might snooze through the whole thing."

"I want an epidural."

"Oh, for gawd's sake. You're not having a baby. And you don't have a spine."

"Psychotropics then?"

"Psycho what?"

"Cannabinoids. Weed. Pot. It works for MS pain as well as..."

I study Dick. "Maybe later. How did you get so..."

"Knowledgeable?"

"Yeah, that."

"Well, I've been reading...studying...over your shoulder, so to speak...while you've been wallowing in your loathsome sea of self-pity and—"

"Never mind. We're almost there. That Ativan is kicking in...and for you and me, highs are like houses. *Mi casa es su casa.*"

"Buzz, buzzzzzz," is Dick's final comment.

"This it?" asks the puzzled driver, pulling up in front of Pinky's, a well-worn ranch house in an old section of town. There's a neon sign flashing "OPEN" in the window. "I thought you were going to a kid's birthday party."

I assure him this is the right address.

m—

My fears and Dick's are pretty much unfounded. Pinky herself meets us at the door. She's Rubenesque and even hotter than Kat Von D. She settles me into a reclining chair of swanky black leather in her funky "parlour" off the kitchen, which puts me at ease immediately, while I show her my attempt at eyes and lips for Dick.

"You want a male or female?" Pinky asks.

I grin, thinking, wow, I haven't thought a sexy thought in forever. "Well, it depends."

She pats Dick. "I mean your hand." She's serious about her art.

I rein in my grin. "His name's Dick."

Pinky raises an eyebrow but when I don't elucidate, she says, "Let's go with that," and proceeds to draw the eyes and lips accordingly.

The needles are uncomfortable but not exactly painful. Dick spasms at the first few pricks. Next thing you know, it's all over. Pinky cleans up Dick's blotchy, red, new and improved face, then applies a liberal dose of lotion and covers him up with plastic wrap and adhesive tape. Perfect. She gives me lotion and instructions for aftercare. Dick is to remain covered for the first twenty-four hours.

I thank Pinky and wait outside for the HandyDART, which is predictably an hour and a half late—same driver.

"Jeezus, what happened to your puppet? Didn't go over too well?" the driver asks as he loads me and my bandaged hand into the back. "Birthday boy bite you?"

"I got a tattoo. My first," I say rather proudly.

"Used to be goody bags," he says. "Kids these days!"

I don't bother to explain.

m—

By the time I get home, the drugs are wearing off. Dick, however, sleeps on. I tuck him into one of Jackie's regifted ugly striped mittens for good measure.

I think about that flicker of arousal I experienced at Pinky's. I think about the last time—months ago, now—that I had an orgasm. I think about the last fun-but-unfulfilling sex with Leo and the future possibilities of the same—or better? But Leo's become my caregiver, which is not sexy and which sets the two of us on vastly uneven ground. Plus he didn't apply for the position but was tossed abruptly into it. He's driving me crazy, taking his assumed responsibility too seriously. I don't want to think about this, so I go back to thinking about Pinky. And sex in general. And orgasms. Or rather the lack of them. I should follow up on Dr. Falik's test results. Just for the hell of it. And the hope.

I email Dr. Falik's office and get a response right away. This time it's in Spanish and it's really long. I copy and paste it into Babelfish, which does a poor job of translating at the best of times. Babel, indeed. There's a lot of medical jargon—a whole theoretical paper, none of which relates personally to me. At the very bottom of the email is a notice saying Dr. Falik is out of the office. It doesn't say when he'll be back. I reply that my MS improvements seem to be fading and that I would like my test results. I get back the same automated reply. I'd call him but due to the bankruptcy and unpaid bills the phone company's restricted my calls to local.

Speaking of phones, it's time to get started on my new business venture: 1-800-SEX-TALK. While Dick's recovering, it's the perfect uninterrupted 24-hour time slot. After that I intend to sit Dick down for a serious chat about decorum and expectations and just who the hell is the boss around here. And come to think of it, I'm going to set things straight with Leo. Tell him that I don't need a babysitter and that he needs to give me some space. I have no intention of enabling his possible dependency on my dependency. That's just icky...and sad. Jackie's interest in my "event" has taken a very normal back seat to her boyfriend, the video store and her own life.

There are difficulties in starting up a business without cash flow. First off, I don't have the funds to purchase a 1-800 number. Or a second cellphone. Or a domain name. Or a supply of Red Bull or that new hyper-caffeinated chocolate. Stamina and new-enterprise adrenaline will have to see me through. I have no backup plan, so giving up is not an option. I pin up the svelte phone-sex business card from the bankruptcy office for inspiration. I have to DIY this operation. First a name... with call letters out of my existing phone number—498-366-7639—that mean PHONE SEX.

I search dictionaries and Scrabble sites for seven-letter words with the right combination of letters, but there are thousands. Adding the area code might help, so I look up ten-letter Scrabble words starting with P, Q, R or S. There are still too many. I look up ten-letter words just starting with S. There are 2,200. Then I punch different combinations into Google. Then I play on paper. What I come up with isn't particularly hot or memorable or easy, but it will have to do until I can afford better. 1-4YU-FON-SMEX.

I research the phone sex genre, make a long list of dos and don'ts, a short list of what I need for marketing, a shorter list of acts and attitudes beyond kink I won't tolerate, and a name for my sex-talking character—a name that's easy to spell and remember, that isn't too sophisticated (like Devon) or sickly sweet (like Candy) or easily misunderstood (like Kim) or common (like Sarah). I pick Ginger—a spicy throwback, both relatable and desirable for the older gentleman or even gentlewoman who shies away from internet porn.

Then I put my existing technology to work—an ancient laptop, an iPad and the smartphone I bought with money I used like it was mine. I ask Google a lot of how-to questions, keeping legality and netiquette in mind.

I peek under the mitten to check on Dick. The bandage is intact but he's burning up. I take two Tylenol. It's too soon to panic and call Pinky, so I tuck him into the mitten and get back to work.

I couldn't explain for the life of me how I do it. But I drag and drop, download and upload, link and synch and HTML myself silly until I have a velvet-curtained website with an age-legal adult-content permission button, a sizzling blurb, a payment button and, in a large bold font, the call characters:

1-4YU-FON-SMEX

By four in the morning, I, Ginger, can take calls on my phone or iPad, and only be connected after agreement and incremental—ten to sixty minutes—prepayment. I try calling my-Ginger-self to make sure it works before it goes live, but I realize I can't afford to talk sex with myself.

Dick's still slightly feverish and now he's getting itchy. I'm too damn tired to think the worst about botched face jobs or infections or rashes. I have my own appearance to worry about. Never mind that the callers won't be able to see me. My research emphasizes the importance of playing the part, and Mae West backs that attitude up with a quote: "An ounce of performance is worth pounds of promises."

I dress appropriately despite the ridiculous amount of time it takes. I practise my "Hello there!" Ginger voice and enthusiastic moaning in a variety of pitches. I can't maneuver in heels any more, but I do pull on some ancient thigh-high black stockings, my slightly tattered scarlet underwire and matching panties, groaning and gasping convincingly through every step. I put on lipstick and fluff up my hair. In honour of Mae, I top it off with my back-of-the-closet knee-length mink coat—the one I bought second-hand long before it was politically incorrect and at a time when I could walk, strut, even run if I had to.

Getting dressed with gusto is hard work. I arrange myself in front of the computer and wait and yawn and wait. I rest my head on the keyboard for just a minute, then startle awake to the ring of my cellphone. Where am I? I shake off my stupor. Action!

"Well, hello there," I say, all sensual and husky.

There's a hesitation, then a male voice says, "So sorry. Wrong number."

"No, wait!" I blurt.

Too late. He's gone. My only caller, and it's already 5:00 a.m. Sigh.

The phone rings again. I simplify it this time but try to sound inviting. "Hello?"

"Mel?" asks the same voice.

Oh, shit. "Um, who's calling?"

"It's Leo. Are you okay?"

"Oh, for gawd's sake, Leo. You're checking up on me at five in the morning? I'm just fine!" Reminder to self—check call display.

"I'm glad all's well. Sorry about the early call but I'm catching the first ferry...just letting you know I'll be away...heading off—"

"Perfect," I say.

"...off to Ecuador and then Bolivia."

"Nice!" I say, examining my website, smoothing my mink.

"I'll be gone a couple of weeks at the most."

"Well, thanks for calling. Have fun, eh?"

Leo hesitates. "You'll be all right then?"

"Yes. Of course I will. I managed just fine before..."

His silence means hurt feelings.

I sigh. "Don't worry, okay? Really." I can at least be civil. "What are you doing down there anyway?"

"*Diaethria neglecta.*"

My back goes up. "I've been neglecting you? That's a bit much!" I say, thinking *people and their bloody expectations!*

"*Diaethria neglecta* is a butterfly, Mel. A real beauty..." And off he goes, describing how the number 88 appears on its wings, how it favours urine-soaked ground and high Andean altitudes. And he does it with that inimitable contagious Leo passion.

I soften. This is someone I could have possibly learned to maybe nearly love. "Listen, Leo, I'm thrilled for you and I really want to thank you for stepping in and for being such a good friend at the drop of a—"

Leo tries dry humour. "Body?"

I don't laugh. "Yes, a body. But I'm fine now."

"And you have Jackie if you need..."

"I do. But never mind that. Just go. Have a great trip, then come home and tell me all about it. Okay?"

"There's something I want to discuss with you. I was wondering if you'd consider..."

Awkward. Personal. "Oh, shit. My phone's dying, Leo," I lie.

"Oh, well then...we can talk when I get back."

"Absolutely. And we can keep in touch. I can't make long-distance calls, Leo. Maybe email?"

"I won't have much access."

"Right."

"Right." Leo hesitates again. "Well then, take care of yourself, Miss Melanie."

"You too, Leo. Have fun," I say, relieved to say goodbye and get back to my survival project, wondering only briefly what was left unsaid, vowing to spend some quality time with him when he returns.

ᵐ⌇

I adjust my ring tones—a train whistle for unknown callers and a piano minuet for my few existing friends and contacts. I reset my call display options, think about what *was* said between me and Leo. I realize that if I can't make long-distance calls, neither can some of my prospective clients. I need to scale down and join the shop-local movement, like the 100-Mile Diet, only for phone sex.

I make up ten business posters with tear-off tabs saying CALL GINGER @ 4YU-FON-SMEX, print them out and cut the little tabs one-handed. This is so old school. It's already light so I have to hurry. No time to change. I arm myself with a stapler and head out on my scooter to tack up my latest marketing attempts on a couple of community bulletin boards and on a post next to the suburban mailboxes within scooter range but outside my immediate neighbourhood. Streets are still deserted this time of day, so there are few witnesses.

When I get home, I collapse on the bed, tuck my phone into my bra, pull the mink over us and sleep the sleep of the exhausted but hopeful, crippled but determined, broke but eager entrepreneur.

ᵐ⌇

A train whistle blows. I look around in dream-world terror, try to jump out of the way, screaming, until I comprehend that it's my new ring tone. My business ring tone!

"Hello," I mumble, still hoarse from fear. The phone clock reads 10:19 a.m.

A quiet male voice asks if this is Ginger.

I tell him to hold, clear my throat, sip my water, consider turning on the light, think better of it, check my PayPal account—yup, there's a payment for ten minutes, though PayPal has gouged me for service charges. I get into a more comfortable position under the mink coat, take a deep breath and purr, "Well, hello there, stranger. What can I do for you on this lonely, uh, morning?"

It takes four minutes for him to tell me what he wants—front porch and back porch, me to point out that this isn't a renovation company, him to think I'm joking, me to get it, him to tell me never mind just the back porch bend over, me to tell him just a minute honey and describe how I'm stroking, licking and squeezing him softly and firmly here and there first before I bend over, him sliding his apparently gargantuan member in and out of Ginger/me half a dozen times, me to agree and to urge him on to the finish line with appreciative and well-practised moans.

I'm kind of disappointed. It was so boring...and easy. I could do a few dozen of these calls a day. I tell him what a pleasure it's been and to ring me up again. He says to wait, that he's got five minutes left. Oh. Talk to me, he says. He likes my voice and he's on his coffee break.

I prefer questions to answers so after a minimum of small talk I turn the tables. *This* is work. "Let's talk about what you like...for next time. What's your favourite room to have sex in?" I ask.

He tells me he's in the lunchroom, alone.

"No, I mean when you're not at work."

I imagine him imagining.

"The kitchen?" I prompt. "All those shiny counters? Or maybe in the shower? Lots of lather. Squeaky clean... How about the bedroom?"

He says he'll think about it but his supervisor's calling him so he's got to go.

"Do you have a name, stranger? For next time?"

Harold, he tells me. Call him Harold. The line goes dead.

I'm wide awake. Even Dick is bumping around. It's the perfect time to talk...during Dick's big reveal.

In the brightly lit bathroom I slip the mitten off Dick, peel off the bandage and plunge that gooey face into the warm running water. Dick splutters while I clean things up. Aside from the lingering pinkness and a bit of peeling, he looks good. Really good. Bright-eyed and bushy-tailed even. I hold Dick tightly in my right hand and look into those newly tattooed eyes.

"We need to talk," I say, rubbing more of Pinky's lotion ever so gently into Dick's tender face. "It's about your behaviour..."

"Show me, first. In the mirror. I want to see," says Dick.

"When we're done."

Dick retorts, "*We* implies that we're *both* going to talk, not that you're going to talk and I'm going to listen."

"You're right," I say, but my tone signifies otherwise. "But this is about your groping and pinching. It's about trust!"

The train whistle blows between my breasts. I pull the mitten quickly over Dick so I can concentrate. I answer huskily, "Hello there, stranger..."

And so it begins...

∿⟋⟍

It's a slow summer business start-up—three calls the first week, two calls the second. Folks must be barbecuing or at the beach. I boost my marketing strategy by thumbtacking up twice as many posters. Calls double, so I repeat my blitz, even resorting to a discounted July special. It pays off over the next month with new callers and some repeat customers, which tells me my acting is improving. Sometimes it's enlightening and educational, other times tedious, tawdry and laborious—like the majority of ordinary positions...I mean jobs.

Routines are relative. I sleep when I can—in spurts—mostly during the day, eat what I can afford, borrow or find, exercise once in a while and steer a dry ship. In other words, no vino. While the routine's not ideal for my health, there are benefits, like only smoking what I can bum on the way to the food bank.

I made peace with Dick. He loves his new face so much he's always taking selfies. We had to make a deal—good behaviour equals selfie time. The better his behaviour, the more often I remove the mitten.

He surprises me one afternoon when I'm reaching for the mitten to quell his fidgeting. Dick rebels, dragging his knuckles, refusing to be muzzled.

"Time to get lost, Dick!"

"Give me a job, something to do!" he squawks as we tussle. "I just need to be useful!"

"What can you do?" I say in exasperation. "Your fine motor skills are shot. You're unreliable."

"I'm learning to adapt. You should try it sometime."

"Oh, for fuck sakes, that's all I..."

"I want my own laptop," he says, trying to wriggle free.

"Can't afford it." I tighten my grasp.

Dick's middle finger escapes, pointing to my smartphone.

We're in a stranglehold at a crossroads.

"It's the perfect size," he points out.

"You need working fingers to run that puppy."

"I have knuckles on my head. I can learn."

"What am I supposed to use?"

"You've got the iPad and the laptop. Seems fair."

"Fine," I say, tiring of the battle.

"Fine," he fires back.

I know he'll fail.

That isn't what happens.

In fact, he's a quick learner in his awkward but persistent closed-fist-ed way and becomes incredibly handy. Everyone needs to be needed, I guess, including Dick. And he looks pretty cute, nose to smartphone screen, translating foreign idioms from my clients, like Helmut's favourite *Schwangerschaftsverhütungsmittel*—condom—which is unnecessary for phone sex but fun to say. Dick is pretty good at researching slang on the fly. Like Paul One's favourite: panty-smashing. Or P.E.P.S.I.—Please Enter Penis Slowly Inside—which is what William likes to hear me beg. Or Joe's surefire woody-maker: polishing mirrors—minge to minge—with my chimerical girlfriend.

I also have tea with Jackie periodically. She's still smitten with Cam and she's relieved that I'm eventless, as in seizure-free, and she makes it very clear how unsurprised she is that Leo has disappeared from the picture. Dick, thankfully, has zero attraction to Jackie, so he behaves when she's around.

I keep in touch with John by text, but I haven't seen him face to face for months. Charlene's taken Glen and the schnauzers and moved into her sister's basement in Winnipeg. She still sends me weekly horoscopes but that's about it.

None of my buddies has a clue about my new business and I don't intend to tell them, at least until I have something to show for my efforts. Being a non-miraculous recipient of the Liberation procedure is failure enough and I can read it between their lines regardless of which form of communication we use.

While I really expected there would be some kind of contact with Leo, it hasn't happened, though that's fine with me. His place looks the same the day I recklessly get behind the wheel for a medically illegal but beneficial air-conditioned drive and inch halfway up the driveway until I have a clear view of it. There are butterflies in his blooming garden. And on his old Mercedes where we ate apricots.

Dick's really the one who keeps me sane. He's my left-hand man, the one who gives me regular pep talks and also acts—according to him—as my business manager. He's really just my assistant but he's a pretty awesome one. He keeps his mouth shut when I'm involved with a client but doesn't hesitate to give a thumbs-down if one of them is nasty or obviously underage and needs to be downright blocked. It's only happened twice. I mean it's a business and I'm on the phone for sex and I'm perfectly capable of chatting, panting and moaning through the pearl necklaces and rim jobs and impossible acrobatics—my morphable telephone body can do anything—but I have my limits. And so does Dick.

There are times, too, when both Dick and I have to work hard and fast, especially on the special effects. Caro—my first female—is turned on by the sound of my KitchenAid mixer, especially the whisk attachment. Ernie likes to listen to me pee, which means Dick pouring water into the toilet from an impressive height while I giggle and sigh on speaker phone. Shy Paul Two—I have to keep my Pauls straight—gets wood, as he puts it, the size of a banyan tree when I snap my bamboo back-scratcher across my palm—the inside of Dick's head.

My growing list of clients includes a few favourites. Surprisingly, Harold, my very first customer, is one of them. He's opened up. He still calls from the lunchroom and like everyone else he's still lonely but now he's a humorist in progress. "Have you got hearing aids?" he asks me one night after our steamy fruitful five minutes, then adds, "From your job?" I don't get it until he says, "From unprotected phone sex?" I laugh, not because I'm paid to, but because he's trying so hard to be relaxed and entertaining. Another night he tells me that sex is like math. You add the bed, subtract the clothes, divide the legs and pray you don't multiply. It's something I first heard in grade school but, hey, he's trying.

Caro's right up there with Harold. Not only does she love kitchen gadgets, she's all about the pleasures of food and its preparation. She goes crazy for my zesty sexed-up recipes—all that kneading and greasing and melting and peeling. My Chicken in Mourning recipe is her all-time favourite. She's a sensual soul, a real sweetheart, a sweetheart with sizzle—and also with Parkinson's. Once an aspiring chef, she can no longer cook for herself.

Shy Paul Two, the big-wood guy, doesn't actually *say* "big wood." He sings it, thanks to Ginger's encouragement. His words were getting lost behind his stutter. Well, not exactly a stutter, more like a series of grunts. It's some kind of breath control issue I don't really understand but we muddle through it.

Christopher and Bertrand both live at the assisted-living place just past the Starbucks on the outskirts of town. Bertrand is a war vet. Christopher's severely arthritic and can't always remember who or what he is.

When I think about it, I begin to see a couple of patterns. One is that business goes up at the end of the month when disability cheques come in and then peters off mid-month. The other pattern has to do with demographics, and the variables have nothing to do with race or religion. The majority of my clientele seem to be disabled—physically or socially. It's a niche market. This is definitely a way to be part of somebody else's "team" while being personally "productive." It's a win-win situation. It's even possible eventually to make a modest living while I help a few vulnerable marginalized people with their health—sexually, physically and mentally. Dick even finds studies that bolster my intent. Ginger helps folks counteract the effects of social isolation—like increased stress, inflammation and decreased immune function. Plus orgasms stimulate your brain, help reduce stress and insomnia, improve mood and alleviate some types of pain.

I think again about that expression "flypaper for freaks," and I admit that I don't mind so much now being one. It has its limitations, for sure, but it also has certain freedoms. And then I think about Leo.

Thinking makes me antsy, especially in hot weather. The heat makes my MS body lethargic so my brain tries to make up for that. Dick's half-asleep. The phone is mid-August silent. And I'm only in my second trimester of bankruptcy. Plus I can't legally drive for another fifty-seven days. Limbo blows.

I sit in my van with the air conditioning on high. And since the motor's running anyway, I figure I'll just drive around the block, which makes me feel like such a badass and benefits my thermostat-impaired body to boot. It feels so damn good I put on my sunglasses and drive a little farther and then figure I might as well cruise out past Leo's place. I actually pull over by his mailbox for a minute, then advance on up for a look-see. The curtains are all drawn in his container home and, even with the scrubby grass so overgrown, it's as charmingly quirky as ever. There's a smallish shiny windmill up and back of it that I'd never noticed before. It's barely spinning. I sit there like the windmill, barely breathing, just to watch his butterflies, especially the monarchs. There is a lone monarch on the roof of his car and even a pair mating on the curve of a sun-soaked rock. It's so damn peaceful.

I give my head a shake and hit the gas, drive home wishing for a storm or something, anything to shake things up, to break through the doldrums. I pick up my mail, carry it in my teeth as I wheel into the house, spritz myself with water, park my chair in front of the electric fan and sort through the junk mail.

I'm left with two letters, one from Dr. Falik in Costa Rica and one from some lawyer here in town. Dick lazily nudges the one with the pretty foreign stamps. After tearing it open with my teeth, I scan the single page for a numeral. And there it is. Omigod, omigod, omigod! I don't have one orgasm left...I have *sixteen*!

That is sixteen ineffable shuddery satisfying Orgasms with a capital *O* to enjoy at my discretion! Or lack of it! I want to share the news! I think about Leo. He's the only one who knows that my orgasms had whittled themselves down to one. But, hell, why complicate a good thing with conversation, not to mention his awkward absence. I'm so ecstatic that I'm verging on orgasmic right now.

I slide my fingers under my light summer dress and up my thigh ever so lightly, initiating a delicious shiver. Even my panties are no barrier for insistent fingers. Dick tries to get in on the act.

"Dick! Not cool," I scold. "You're my business manager now. Office etiquette and all that."

Dick backs off to observe from arm's length, which is somehow less weird. My fingers search out that sweet spot that is mine and mine alone. The one that used to be a sliver to the left of my pink jellybean but has shifted over to the right. Circles—nice, but...I look around for something with a little more buzz than just fingers, something within reach. Dick gestures helpfully to the toy box in my bedroom. Too far, I tell him. He nudges his smartphone. Of course! The Vibe app I haven't touched in months! I find the app, ramp up the speed from "Heaven" to "Woohoo" and slip it between my already tingly thighs. Now this is better...and better still. Oh, my. This orgasm is a locomotive in need of a runaway track. A train whistle blasts between my legs. Holy hell, here I go...

Oh, yum. Ohhhh, freakin' yummmnnmmm
mmmmmmnmmm mmmmmmmmmmm
mmmmmmmmmmm
mmmmmmmmm

mmmmnmmmmmmm
mmmnmmmmmm
mmmmnmmm

mnmmmm

mmmm

mmm

mm

m

What a lovely, crucial, exhilarating thing, an orgasm...this orgasm. As the train whistle blows again I realize it wasn't an orgasmic aural response I'd heard earlier but a phone call. A missed call. A work call. No thank you, not then—are you kidding me?—and *certainly* not now. Not yet. I rescue the phone, give it a sanitary wipe and hit the mute button. At least till I return to earth and get my bearings.

I love you, Dr. Falik. And you, electric fan. And you, smartphone. And even you, Dick. Oh, and sweet messed-up mother of a body, I love you right now most of all.

14
Wreckoning

Dick keeps pointing to the second letter, the one still lying on the kitchen table. When I fumble trying to open it, Dick assists with positioning so I can peel away enough paper to extract the letter inside.

What now? It's addressed to me. There's my name below the lawyer's address at the top of the page. I sit up a little straighter as I spot *a letter is being held...and upon documented proof of your identity*, which raises my hackles. But what follows is a line that detonates my iceberg heart: *Leo Moss, now deceased...*I read those four words over and over. I read them fast and I read them slow. They're always the same. Finally I read the whole letter.

> Dear Ms. Farrell,
> This is to advise you that a letter is being held in trust for you and, upon documented proof of your identity, we will turn it over to you. We regret to inform you in this manner; however, Leo Moss, now deceased, left specific instructions regarding this missive.
>
> Please contact us to set up an appointment.

Wait, what dirty bloody scam is this? What malevolent spoof? Some local shyster, maybe. And Leo—what an asshole for getting me involved in some shit I don't want or need or have the energy for. I'll go over to his house right now and straighten him out. No, I can't. It's too hot. I'm a thousand degrees mad but at least my heart is beating again, thumping away like a crazy-ass fool, and I have a searing pain in my head. Wait, he's not home. He's in Bolivia or Ecuador or somewhere chasing butterflies... no, it's been weeks since he went. He must be home by now.

He must be...he must. Be, Leo. Just be. I'll call him. No, I'll text him. No, I'll call this lawyer. No, it's too late in the day. No, I'll...I'll...

I dial Leo's number. The chills hit me when I hear *This number is no longer in service.* It's an inevitable feeling that we've all imagined having. I redial just to check. Same outcome. I don't know what to do. I mean I really don't know what to do...so I dial another number, one with a live voice. "Jackie?" I say into the phone. "Something's happened to Leo."

She starts in, "Oh, what now, the little..."

"No, Jackie, listen. Leo's dead. Leo is dead, Jackie." Saying it out loud makes it real and sad and disturbing and terrible and unbearable. I just start sobbing. No, sobbing sounds somewhat controlled and there's nothing controlled about this bawling shattered mess that is me. And is still me when Jackie lets herself in a half-hour later.

"Mel, Jeezus," she says, putting her arms around me, patting my back. "I don't know what to say. I'm so sorry."

"You didn't even like him," I sob. "And now he's dead. Done. Finished."

"Time for tea," she says, plunking the box of tissues in my lap and heading for the kitchen, the kettle, all the busyness that is her forte. "So what happened? He wasn't sick, was he?" she asks as she not only makes tea but also rinses dishes, sweeps the floor, tidies the counter.

"I don't know," I say, somewhat composed now except for residual sniffles. "That's the worst part. I just got this letter." I wave it at her but she carries on.

"Letter from who?"

"Some lawyer."

"Well, what exactly does it say?"

"Not much."

She reads the letter. "So this lawyer's got a letter for you. Weird. What do you think it is, a love letter? Geez..."

"Not likely. The last time I talked to him I wasn't very..." Shit, that brings back the tears.

"Nice?" Jackie finishes my sentence with an accusation. Then her face gets that stricken look. "You don't think...he wouldn't, would he? I mean would he take his own life? What exactly did you say to him?"

"I don't know! Nothing. Almost nothing. Is that worse than a bad something? Anyway, I don't think he would ever...I mean we were just..."

"Friends?"

I ignore the sting in Jackie's voice. "He's not the kind of person..."

"But you never *really* know about people."

I shake my head as my tears amp back up. "No, he was one of those satisfied people...satisfied and content with his life."

Jackie ignores my tears, sets a steaming cup of tea in front of me and finally sits down. "Let me see that again," she says, reaching for the letter.

"You don't have to," she says, after re-examining it, "you know, *do* anything."

"How can I not?"

"What, you're feeling guilty? Obligated because you were bitchy? It's a little late for evening up the scales, isn't it?"

"It's more than that! And why are you sticking up for him? You couldn't stand the guy."

"We barely knew Mr. Leo whatever-his-name-was."

"You have no idea."

"Then tell me."

"It's hard to explain."

Jackie's not the most patient listener. "Try," she snaps.

"Leo was different."

"No kidding. And?"

"Don't be mean."

She sighs. "You're right. I'm sorry."

I try to explain my unusual relationship with Leo. I edit as I go. Even now some things are private. I can't ever make Jackie understand the connection of differentness between Leo and me—our flypaper-for-freaks affinity—or how there had been so much more than a spark between us. So I tell Jackie about the shift from awkward new lover and friend to awkward caregiver after the seizure, how he wanted too little and then too much, and how I really don't know if any of what I just said is how it really was. And Leo isn't here to ask. And why didn't I ask him before? When it might have mattered... "And I don't even know what happened...how it happened...how he died...or even where. He's just...gone."

Without a word, Jackie lets me finish, which is unusual. "So," she says after a moment of silence, "make the appointment. They'll have some answers. And I'll take you. Okay?"

"Okay," I say. It's all I can muster.

We hug, and I assure her I'll be all right while she cleans up our teacups.

"Oh, I almost forgot," Jackie says, pulling a letter out of her pocket. "It was on the porch. You must have dropped it on the way in. From your landlord?"

"Open it."

She opens it cautiously like there might be another emotional bomb inside. She winces. "Looks like your rent's going up another hundred bucks."

"Perfect," I say.

Jackie leaves but we don't say good night because saying good anything doesn't seem right.

I make sure my phone is off and go to bed, trying like hell to think about nothing.

⌀

Days of misery follow—crying jags and bouts of dry-eyed fury, sleepless hours filled with endlessly circling thoughts of guilt and blame, attempts to moan and groan and talk sex on business calls, refusal to take business calls, macaroni binges, dirty hair and generally exacerbated MS symptoms. I feel like shit, like the soft underbelly of some doomed species. And I have to go it alone because Dick seems to be in silent shock. I slip the mitten over him to let him grieve in peace. It occurs to me that I should have concentrated harder on staying Alone with a capital A. That I should have kept my guard up, that feelings are dangerous, both physically and mentally.

I'm pissed off at the lawyer, who won't answer my questions or discuss a damn thing over the phone. Nothing until I show up with two pieces of ID in hand. So by the time appointment day arrives, I've stopped crying but I'm ready to either kill someone or roll my chair in front of a bus.

ᵐ╼

Palaver day arrives in its own good time and it's pouring rain. I wear something with pockets so I have somewhere to park Dick should he wake up. Jackie shows up late to chauffeur me and my scooter to the offices of Wilmer & Wilmer. They're kind of hard to find. The offices turn out to be a couple of dingy windows above the Janitor's Supply Depot in a faceless building in the older part of town. The only entrance leads into a crowded space full of cleaning supplies.

"Stairs around the back," says the older man behind the bleach-scented counter.

"No elevator?" I ask, already suspecting the answer.

"Nope," he replies. "You have an appointment up there?"

"I do."

He turns to the phone on the wall behind him and dials. "Hey, Bert, there's somebody down here to see you... No can do. Got a scooter... No, like a motorized wheelchair kind of thing..." He turns back to us. "He'll be right down."

Bert—Mr. Wilbur—an exact copy of the counter clerk, soon appears at the front door with a damp file folder poking out of his worn jacket. "Sorry about that," he says, slipping out the file and offering his hand to Jackie. "Ms. Farrell?"

A train whistle blasts in my purse. It takes me a minute to find and turn off my phone. "That would be me," I pipe up, trying to ignore his automatic assumption that able-bodied Jackie is the only person here capable of a legal conversation.

Bert covers his surprise, asks me for ID. I show him my underused driver's licence and my overused medical card. "This won't take long," he says, ushering us to the back corner of the store. He opens the folder on top of an oversized bin of rubber gloves. "Here's the letter, Ms. Farrell, the one that Mr. Moss left in trust for you and..."

"Wait, wait a minute, I have questions!"

Jackie jumps in too. "She certainly does."

"Oh?"

"First of all," I say, "what *happened* to Leo? I mean how did he..."

"Oh, my," Bert responds. "You don't know? I assumed you were aware of the circumstances. You were friends, no?"

"Yes," says Jackie.

"No," I say. "I mean yes but more than just..."

"How *did* it happen?" Jackie interrupts, afraid I'll go off on an emotional tangent.

Bert puts on a compassionate face. "We know very little. A bus crash in Bolivia, in the mountains I believe. It took the embassy in La Paz quite some time to track me down. They didn't contact you? They assured me...well, anyway...my sympathies, Ms. Farrell. Really, I thought you would know. It's been some time..."

"How much time? When?" I ask, wondering if I had had any sign, any unusual feeling that particular day or night.

Bert shuffles through the folder, comes up with a gold-stamped letter. "Sixteenth of June, Mr. Moss was deceased."

"That's two months ago!"

"Exactly," Bert says, checking his watch. "There were many fatalities, according to the embassy. The death certificate is here as well, but it's in Spanish."

Jackie rubs my shoulder to give me something to think about other than the disastrous scenario she's imagining that I'm imagining. She sees I'm losing my composure so she takes over. "About the letter."

"Yes," Bert says, "Mr. Moss—"

I interrupt. "Did you know Leo? I mean outside of business."

"No, not personally. Mr. Moss came in—"

I interrupt again. "Did he seem happy?"

"He didn't seem unhappy. It was just business. Mr. Moss came in mid-May to notarize his will."

"I thought it was a letter," I say. "I was hoping..."

"There is a letter, Ms. Farrell. A letter, a will involving property...a home. It's out on Waterton Road."

"I know the place, but what does that have to do with me?"

"His property along with his possessions and a life insurance policy are all bequeathed to a single beneficiary—you, Ms. Melanie Farrell."

I'm baffled. "Me? Why me?"

"What exactly does that mean? I mean does it mean...money?" Jackie asks.

Bert rifles through the file. "Life insurance—a hundred and twenty-five thousand."

"Jeez," says Jackie. "And no next of kin? No family?"

"That's my understanding."

"And there's property, too?"

"Yes, as I—"

I butt in, "Can I have the letter, please?"

Bert hands over the whole folder. "It's all yours, Ms. Farrell. If you're in need of legal advice in the future—and you will be—I'd be happy to assist. There'll be paperwork..."

"Shouldn't we have a look at all that now?" Jackie's practical mind wants to know.

"Not now, Jackie," I say.

"That's it then?" says Jackie.

This time Bert turns his full attention to me. "At your leisure. And as I said, Ms. Farrell, if I can be of service..." We shake hands and the three of us head back up the haz-mat aisle to the front door.

◠◡ᵓ

Once Adele is stowed and we're back in the van, Jackie asks, "Don't you want to know what's in there?"

"Yes and no." I'm confused and overwhelmed and dripping wet.

Jackie sighs in exasperation.

I probe around in the closed folder until I feel Leo's sealed letter between my fingers. It's thin, a minimum of paper. And I feel something else inside—a key. "Can we go to Leo's?" I feel right in doing this. Like Leo is guiding me...not pushing or pulling, just offering an invisible hand while I wade through this bewildering and unexpected grief with all its pragmatic details.

"If you say so," she says, shrugging.

The sun erupts as we pull off Waterton into Leo's heavily puddled driveway a few minutes later. The property seems bigger, emptier. There's an air of exhaustion now that even the sky's done weeping. Wild

grasses—bleached and bending—spill up against the chain-link fenc-
ing and the cutaway bluff at the back of the property. Smaller clumps
scattered about look like a mob of blond comb-overs from the heavy
rain. The shipping containers in the far corner, like some child giant's
dirty building blocks. But the tire gardens—while unkempt—still offer
late blooms—the skim of a bright wet rainbow palette. Moisture begins
to waft upward as the August sun holds hot and steady now in the sky.
Everything needs tending.

Jackie wrinkles her nose. "This is it? I can smell the mill." Her
voice oozes judgment. "It looks so…"

I go on the defensive for Leo's sake. "So unconventional?"

"I was going to say weird."

I realize I have a stake in this now, too. "But perfectly weird."

"No surprise really."

"Oh, it's full of surprises." I gesture to a pair of monarchs sipping
from a puddle and a flurry of tiny pale blue wings hovering around the
saturated blooms.

"Might not all be good surprises."

I can't disagree. "Might not. Can you get my scooter out?"

"To do what?"

"Breathe. I just want to breathe."

Jackie mutters something as she exits. While she's extricating my
scooter I open the letter. The key I'd felt, which looks like a house key,
is taped to the top of the standard sheet of paper with a few scant words
handwritten below.

> The key to happiness
> is not having what you want
> but wanting what you have.
> Sincerely,
> Leo M.

The rather impersonal letter is both a disappointment and a relief. I mean I don't know what I expected or why I'd expected more. But
Leo's note has a calming effect regardless of the intent.

Jackie brings Adele around and I climb on. I lead Jackie along a few of the curvy little garden paths. We end up on the cedar deck overlooking the tire gardens. I look away when Jackie tries the doorknob.

"Bit of a white elephant. Do you think this place will actually appeal to someone?" Jackie asks.

"Someone with a use for it or a vision. Someone like Leo..."

"Can you imagine?"

I ignore the barb. "I feel like we need to do something. Something special for him. You know, a send-off," I say.

"Like what? A funeral?"

"I was thinking more along the lines of an upbeat mini-celebration of life."

"You want me to sing?"

"I think he'd appreciate a song or a toast...maybe something symbolic. I guess a song will have to do."

"Wait," says Jackie, "I've got the perfect toast in my bag." She heads for the van, pulls a brown paper bag out of her gargantuan purse and waves it victoriously in the air, yelling, "Tequila!"

"*Mundo perfecto.* And grab my lipstick, *por favor.*"

I scoot down into the gardens and meet Jackie at one of the basking stones, now dry and warm to the touch.

She twists the paper bag around the bottle and unscrews the cap. She passes me my lipstick, and I bend down to draw a heart on the stone's smooth surface for Leo and a much smaller heart inside that for Leo's micropenis, Mikey. I do it because in death such an important body part deserves recognition like my own Dick would.

"Song choice?" she asks.

"'Magic Man.' You know..."

Jackie nods. "The one by Heart."

"Leo and I sang it together one time...at physio. It's right maybe because he kept rescuing me. Maybe because he was different..."

"I guess he was all right. Kind of a cool different guy, I suppose, in the end, huh?"

"Different...in the best way."

Together we grasp the brown-bagged bottle and say, "To Leo!"

above the stone heart and after a brief tussle over who drinks first, we each take a fiery hit. We follow with a very poor rendition of the song, mostly hummed to fill the space of forgotten words. But we do remember the important ones: *It seemed like he knew me, he looked right through me,* and *Try, try, try to understand, I'm a magic man.*

Jackie offers me the bottle again.

"Nope, that's enough for me. Let's go," I say.

Jackie looks back at Leo's final home. "Too bad we can't get into his house."

"Yeah, too bad," I say, fondling Leo's key and heading back to the van. I have to do things in my own time, and this isn't it.

⁓⁓

But home, when we arrive, doesn't feel right or I don't feel right in it. Jackie asks if I want company while I go through the papers but I decline.

"Are you okay?" she asks. "You're awfully quiet."

"No worries, Jackie. Really. Just a lot to think about."

"Call me?"

"Of course, but give me a day or two to let all this sink in."

Jackie studies me. "Sure, Mel." She heads out.

I call after her, "Jackie?"

She turns back to me.

"Thank you."

She smiles a gracious little smile, which is more than enough.

⁓⁓

There's so much to take in, to sort out, I can't think straight so I think crooked. And looping through it all is Leo's presence and his absence too. But thinking isn't doing. It's time to do something. I flick Dick with my finger. He burrows further into my lap so at least I know he's not dead. I check my phone—four missed calls. All phone-sex calls. At least my clients can cancel their PayPal payment if they don't get through to me.

I sort through the legal paperwork. It all looks legit. I call Bert Wilmer, the lawyer, who explains to me how long things might take—

transfer of ownership, a month, and the life insurance, probably ninety days. He also assures me that he can handle it all for me for a minimal fee.

"What's a minimal fee?" I ask, and Bert tells me it'll be a grand or two if I pay up front. I explain I can't pay until the life insurance money arrives.

He'd prefer to be paid before he does the legwork.

"Legwork?" I query.

Loose ends, Bert explains, but he says after taking my situation into consideration he'll make an exception for me.

I tell him to go ahead.

He says luckily he kept copies of everything.

"Everything?" I ask.

"Except the letter," he assures me. "That's a private matter."

The whole money thing freaks me out every time I think about it. It's bound to relieve my current situation, but it comes with responsibilities and demands and the deceptive trap of sudden excess. How to do the right thing. The smart thing. My fear of abruptly having too much may prove to be more extreme than the bag-lady syndrome I've been experiencing in my current situation. My current situation...

Shitballs!

I call Bert again in a panic. "I'm in trouble! Please tell me you haven't done anything! Started proceedings or mailed or faxed or sent anything out yet!"

He sounds annoyed. "Who is this? Who's calling?"

I try to calm down. "It's Melanie Farrell. You haven't..."

"Who?"

"Melanie Farrell...about Leo Moss's..."

"Oh yes, of course."

"You haven't done anything yet, have you?"

"These things take time, Ms. Farrell. What's the problem?" he asks. "The *immediate* problem?"

I tell him about my whole sad present state of bankruptcy, which means if *any* supplementary funds come my way in the current tax year, I'll be gouged by Canada Revenue.

"I see. And when do you expect your discharge?"

"January first. A hundred and thirty-seven long lean days from now."

"Oh, boy," is his reply.

I ignore the comment and go on to explain how dire my straits are. I ask if it's possible to access Leo's bank accounts unofficially.

"Unofficially?"

"Like not on paper."

"You mean illegally."

"Nothing sinister. Just for a wee bit of cash...to tide me over until January." I hear papers shuffling on the other end.

"There's only the one account. Eighteen dollars and fifty-seven cents," he tells me.

I think how that would buy me another bag of oatmeal, a kilo of rice, six cans of beans if they're on sale and three bananas.

"Hardly worth opening up that *illegal* can of worms, Ms. Farrell."

"You're right. Forget it."

"Done," says Bert.

"Wait. I guess the life insurance works the same way. I can't get just a smidge on the sly? Some sooner and the rest later or, like, I don't know—split payments?"

He's firm. "No. It's all or nothing. You have to (a) cash it out and cut your losses or (b) tough it out and wait for that cheque. Like a nest egg." He offers to wait until the new year to process everything. Looks like it's going to be a few more months of slim pickings. I thank him before hanging up.

I have another terrible thought. And then a bundle of them.

I call Bert again. "Same goes for the property?" I ask.

"These calls are costing you, Ms. Farrell."

"Just to clarify, we can't change the ownership papers now either, right?"

"I thought we'd covered that."

"Not specifically," I counter.

"Is there anything else?"

"Well, actually, yes. When January rolls around, what should I do?

I mean do you have any advice about all this? What to do with it? All that money and property in a smart way? It's kind of...scary."

"We're not talking millions of dollars here. You have more than three months to figure that out. Even then there's usually no rush, but in your case..."

"Yes?"

"It's not really my place..."

"Look, Bert, I need advice."

He sighs. "My accountant would tell you to sell. To save yourself from a pile of headaches. Sell the property and, except for what you absolutely need to live, invest everything."

"I don't know much about investing."

"Then avoid high risk. Go safe with your bank or whatever. Retirement savings. That way your future's still covered. Nice and tidy."

When I picture a nice and tidy future, all I can think of to say is "Sounds sensible."

"Very," says Bert.

"But you're not an accountant and neither am I. What would you do? Personally?" I hear Bert settle in, maybe put his feet up on his desk.

"Portholes, Ms. Farrell. Travel. I'd sell everything and book a non-stop cruise ship. Or a series of them, a few months at a time. Every continent. Ever-changing views, day trips if you're in the mood, a variety of onboard entertainment, non-stop activities, an accommodating crew at your service..."

I relax enough to laugh a little. "Sounds exhausting! I'm not really into cruises, not the best traveller. Short trips only. My wheelchair... Thanks for the idea though!"

"Sure. Any time," he says. And I know he means it, seeing as he knows I'm the one who will eventually be paying.

$\mathcal{m}$

Curling up for a couple of hours of shut-eye before peak phone-sex hours seems like the best way to avoid overthinking. It doesn't work. I try to steer away from what really matters and concentrate on matter in general and how matter has volume and mass. How boiling or freezing or condensation effects change. How a man turns to dust. How a stack of dollar bills becomes a whole raft of question marks. Like a lot of diseases, there's a broad spectrum of what I could do or be or have. Decisions don't come with guarantees. Before I reach my melting point, I reach for my phone and dial Jackie's number.

"Serious question," I warn her after hellos. "What would you do if you were me?"

"You mean about the money?"

"Yes, that, but the property too. You've seen it."

"Is that even a question? Find yourself a good real estate agent and get as much as you can for it."

"It's such an odd set-up. It might take years. Who'd even be interested?"

"It's semi-industrial down there. The area hasn't been developed but it will. Soon. Might be perfect for some kind of big warehouse."

"Yeah, you're right, Jack."

"Don't get wrapped up in the Leo-ness of it, Mel."

I frown at the phone. "I'm hardly the sentimental type."

"I hear it in your voice. Never mind the past or what might have been. You need to look ahead. You have options now!"

"That's the problem." I don't mean for it to come out that way.

"Do something for you. Just for you!" I hear Cameron's voice in the background. "Hang on a sec," she tells me.

Just for me...there was a time when impulse ruled. When I would have dropped thirty grand on an Orgasmatron—a pleasure implant used initially for back pain that induces side-effect orgasms. That's a lot of money and it might not even work with my failing sympathetic nervous system. Plus, losing Leo like that pretty much pulverizes desire.

Jackie's back. "Cam says see it as an opportunity. He says invest. Like in a business."

"A business like his?"

"Well, like *ours*. I'm a partner, remember."

I refrain from pointing out that as eclectic and fascinating as their little business may be, it's a fucking video store. "But is that what *you* would do?"

She lowers her voice. "Honestly? No. Get out of the rental market and buy yourself a condo or better still a house before prices get any crazier."

"I can't exactly look after a house now, Jackie. And I'm better off with less room, not more."

"Maybe we should *all* go in on a house."

We both laugh away the obvious nightmare that would be.

"Of all of us," I remind her, "you're the most practical. Or used to be. The rock. Don't you have any practical advice?"

"My parents would say work hard at something—anything—no matter your circumstances. Maybe in your case it's your health."

"Yeah, there's always that." When I hear Cam chiming in again, I thank Jackie and say goodbye.

Working on my health could mean throwing the whole wad at my MS symptoms—for more foreign Liberation treatments or a series of stem-cell therapies or a truckload of trendy supplements or pricey new pharmaceuticals. And likely none would live up to their promise—for me, at least. Except maybe physio.

I could try using some big bucks to wedge myself into a research study for one of the new technology-based therapies that result in bike-riding parkinsonians and tap-dancing MSers. They use laser light or sound waves—the most mouth-watering—a Portable Neuromodulation Stimulator (PoNS), which painlessly stimulates the tongue with electrical pulses. It's supposed to help increase the plasticity of the brain and form new neural pathways to recover lost function. But there's no escaping that MS is incurable and progressive. I choose to leave tricks like tap dancing to others and live with my physical idiosyncrasies. But live better.

The question is how.

If only I'd had the guts, focus, tenacity—and, let's face it, talent—to write that book. But I'd have had to start a lot sooner, when I had the energy. When I could still bang out forty words a minute. Now, one-handedly pecking out thousands and thousands of words— no matter how brilliant—would take me more than the rest of my life. Long-term anything takes commitment.

I think about doing short-term things. Very small sensible things like a new bed with a memory foam mattress, a new pair of shoes for my demanding feet, a steak and fresh veggies or sushi—twice a week—once the money's in my hand.

Then I think about doing nothing at all. It's unbearable.

I email Char. Subject line: Still up? Need advice.

She answers: Can't sleep. Signed up for my daily horoscopes yet? All kinds of stellar advice!

I reply: Time difference sucks. Call me?

She actually does, and I tell her everything, blurting out the whole Leo story from start to ultimate finish. "So what do I do? I ask, adding, "Gawd, it's good to hear your voice!"

"You sound totally overwhelmed, Mel. Slow down. Breathe."

"I am."

"Centre your breath...relax your body...I can hear the tension in you. I wish you'd try yoga or even mindfulness meditation."

I rustle around a bit, slow down my words. "That isn't really the kind of advice I'm looking for." And then I launch in. "It's the money, Char. What to do with it. I need to be smart."

"I say do something marvellous for yourself first. Something to make you feel alive. Something extravagant like a retreat. A week of silence at a Quebec monastery to clear your head, cut back on the information overload... "

"Sounds perfect—for you. For me and my physical situation, not so much."

"You need to think outside the box. You're not just your MS. You're more than that!"

I keep my voice even. "I know that. However, it's a factor. A big one. I'm thinking about long-term living."

"Want to sign up for that settlement on Mars?"

"Char...seriously." I'm starting to sense a hint of resentment.

"Okay," she says. "In your situation..."

"Keep in mind it's not a million bucks."

"It may not be a million but it *could* be..."

"I'm not talking about business deals, Char! *Or* investing in your nirvana business! You're not exactly..."

Char takes a deep breath. "Negativity is *so* toxic, Mel." She takes another breath. "Do you want to hear me out," she breathes, "or don't you?"

I hesitate long enough to decide that I do. "Sure. Of course I do," I say, adding, "Sorry."

"Okay. We looked into this in Hawaii. You could have that million to work with if you get, say, half a dozen people to put in money, all equal shares, and you set up a co-op and build something that works for *you*. You have a say in every design decision, tailor-made for *your* needs."

"It sounds like a lot of work."

"You should have seen this gorgeous one outside of Hilo. They had their own individualized living quarters, smallish, but shared a big kitchen and gardens on a decent acreage."

"Sounds like a commune. Not sure I'm ready to drink the Kool-Aid."

"Oh, Mel. It *is* communal living but modern...upscale...you'd have privacy but other like-minded people around..."

"That could be problematic, finding like-minded people."

"But people, connections, are critical. A healthy amount of interaction keeps you from being isolated, from becoming a hermit, especially in your...physical situation."

"A cranky lonely bitchy cripple, you mean?"

"If you're not careful." She laughs to soften the warning. "It's scientifically proven that community improves your quality of life. And not one of those people could have lived that comfortably on their own. Not even the couples. All together they're able to have some luxuries, their own wine cellar and a movie room and even a sauna and hot tub. They built a Zen garden and a labyrinth. A beautiful view. Flora and fauna. All the benefits. It was really beautiful!"

"So who keeps it that way? They pay somebody? See, this is a problem. If I put everything into a luxury abode and fees for upkeep, there's nothing left over for daily living."

"They actually share the chores so there's only a small monthly fee. Quite reasonable."

"Now it sounds like a condo. But not only with fees—with chores!"

"It was just an example, Mel. There are lots of them right here. Victoria, Bowen Island, anywhere you want. Even right in Nanaimo. And not all of them have mandatory chores. They come in all shapes and sizes. If none of them are the right fit for you, consider building your own the way you want it."

"Sounds lovely but it seems to me that even mature adults think they know what they want until they have it."

"Well, you asked for my advice and I gave it." She breathes deeply, adding, "Freely."

"You're right, you did. And I do appreciate it, Char. Really!" Best to leave it on that note. "Look at the time!" It's almost 3:00 a.m. Char's time. We say good night, promise to keep in better touch.

᷈᷈

I'm too pent up to sleep. I think about what I think I need or what I think I want. I think about Leo. I think about the status quo and sticking to what I know—not counting what I can no longer do—and I think about doing what I don't know. I think tangentially about my phone-sex business and how it's both known and unknown territory but how at least it's mine. And my clients, well, maybe I'm doing a little good and if not—no harm, no foul. As a matter of fact, I should plan a little customer appreciation week to make up for my recent absences.

I keep thinking through Jackie's and Char's suggestions. I wish I could discuss all this with Leo, share my thoughts with him or ask for his advice. I miss that man. And I still don't have a clear sense of what my best options would be, moving forward.

The train whistle blows. Well, shit. I check my PayPal account—payment confirmed—and pick up the call with my best smoky voice. "Ginger speaking. Have I got a proposition for you on this lonely evening! A ten-minute freebie next week if you participate in my...poll... before we get to the naughty stuff! Just answer this one easy question. What would you do if you won the lottery? Say, a quarter of a million? Honest answers only. Are you in?"

᷈᷈

By the end of the week I have some interesting results. It's okay that my data leans heavily toward disabilities because (a) that's how my clientele is skewed and (b) unbeknownst to them, in my real life I'm skewed, too.

Paul One would spend a year or two fucking his brains out in Amsterdam while Christopher and Bertrand both want to live in Florida in a sex-positive retirement village.

Caro would move to Italy and live in a tiny row of attached trulli houses so she could have a private chef and learn more about authentic Italian cuisine. Marion's always wanted to live in a floathouse in Tofino. Paul Two wants to learn to be a proper stand-up comic—is there a school for that?—but mostly he wants a better assisted-living arrangement, one that feels like home. Ernie wants to live on peanut butter cups while he flies a hot air balloon or maybe a glider every day until the money's gone and then he'll decide to be gone too. Call #307, #311 and #312 all want simple life improvements—better food or better help or better activities at their respective retirement homes—and say how nice it would be to leave something for the grandkids.

They all—even the wannabe travellers—mention some kind of community. I don't want to need community; I just need to have it there when I want it. My poll has me more confused than ever. What is wrong with people? What is wrong with me?

15
Thinking Inside the Box

Kübler-Ross may have been right about the five stages of grief—denial, anger, bargaining, depression and acceptance—but for Dick and me it isn't so much a series of stages but a daily, sometimes hourly mash-up of all five. Times two because Dick and I are rarely on the same emotional page at any given time. I've never experienced grieving like this—the overwhelming suddenness of it as opposed to, say, an elderly relative's eventual death after a long illness. Or even my own MS diagnosis and gradual loss of function where you do your grieving over the extended period leading up to your final demise rather than Leo's abrupt end. This is like a barefoot walk on sharp uneven stones—all cuts and bruises.

It's a rocky month. Oh hell, more than a month. As well as counting down days—fifty-seven until I can drive again and a hundred days till the new year—I do the stuff that I have to do. Because it's what keeps me going, I take care of business, but it's like my smex-talk is on autopilot. I fill out and send in my pathetic monthly budget statement to Ugly Betty. I do too much thinking, and thinking takes effort. So does everyday dealing with my body.

Because of that damn mind-body connection my MS body reacts to grief too. It's exhausted and slow and stiff, uncooperative and weirdly hesitant as though the muscles simply forget how to organize themselves at the oddest times—one night getting into bed, one morning trying to stand in order to transfer from the shower seat to the wheelchair. It took six attempts. And Dick just doesn't want to unclench.

There is a new symptom, too. I've taken to calling them Grabbers. A Grabber is like a random pinprick accompanied by an electric shock. They vary in degrees of discomfort, from itchy tickles to yelp-inducing leg spasms. Most days there are only a few.

To avoid thinking or doing or avoiding the Grabbers, I sleep a lot—whenever and wherever I can. The mitten isn't always enough to put an adequate damper on twitchy tight-fisted Dick. I resort to forcibly unclenching his head and wedging the extended fingers and open palm between my knees or under my bum or most often between my cheek and pillow. It's like he's possessed, even then. I can feel him tightening, buzzing with effort, trying to draw himself into a ball.

We have a couple of cautionary mishaps—a painful collapse in the shower, two small knife wounds on Dick's chin. I spend a lot of time looking out the window and staring into space. So does Dick when he's not staring at me. Everything is on hold. I feel myself slipping more and more into a dusty blackness despite the onset of fall—usually my favourite time of year.

I give Dick an affectionate little rub. "Maybe you can pick out a new mitten...or a svelte leather glove from the thrift store for the cooler weather."

Dick nuzzles into my neck. It seems a good sign that he's getting over the shock or at least coming to terms.

◠◠◦

I wake up mid-afternoon on day minus 89 to a feisty blind-rattling October wind. Just the sound of it is invigorating enough to shake off the dark particles of despair and demand action, even if it's only cerebral. I lie there listening...and thinking. Clarity isn't a particularly familiar experience for me but suddenly..."Dick."

No response.

I give him a poke, then a pinch. "Dick, I've got an idea. And it's a better idea than anybody else's idea. It's brilliant!"

He snuffles and turns over.

"Dick, c'mon. It's a crazy big idea, and I need *your* help."

"What?" he mumbles skeptically.

"I need you to do some research."

"I'm tired of looking up sex terms."

"Nothing sexy, I promise. I know what to do! We're going to have a home! Not a co-op or a commune or anywhere that I have to give up control or share control. I can't control my body so I'm bloody well going to keep whatever control I can. It'll mean building...construction..."

Dick opens one eye.

"And recycling..."

He opens the other eye.

"And...and...going green...and living smaller but better! And even offering a service. Another service..."

"You're going to build a green brothel?" he asks, yawning.

"Nope. A small, uh, facility...a home...for assisted but independent living. And for us. You know, for us and people like us."

Negativity rears its ugly noggin. "Too complicated. Too expensive. Too much work. Ridiculous, in fact."

"Maybe. But we have—will soon have—a little chunk of property, thanks to Leo. We could live there—save on rent—in his cool little olive-green container house surrounded by flowers and butterflies and..."

"I'm not sharing that minuscule space with a bunch of people. We'd be like sardines...with wheelchairs!"

"No, no. Picture this: all those empty shipping containers converted into small units—wheelchair-friendly units that are affordable or, even better, subsidized."

"A growing demographic," Dick adds, thoughtfully.

"Community with privacy."

Dick shakes his little head. "It won't work. The lot's not big enough from what I remember."

"Challenging, yes, but the deed, the title says 1.7 acres."

Dick shakes his little head with stubborn vehemence. "Doomed to fail."

"But interesting, no?"

"So many hurdles."

"That's nothing new. Are you in?"

"Even if you did the conversions, you'd never get it okayed by the health authority. They have rules. A lot of them."

"Give me some credit, Dick. I happen to know from research for my own housing situation that it's easier to own a facility than it is to get into one, even a shitty one."

Dick looks nonplussed.

"And who," I go on, "knows better about what works and what

doesn't for disabled folks than one of them...me? Those containers are the perfect size—compact, manageable, private, kinda cool."

"There are codes! Specifications for that shit! Rules!"

"Rules that don't always fekking make sense!"

I can see Dick's little wheels spinning as he slides from stink-eye to think-eye. "You'll need a lot of help," he says.

"Starting with you." I move to sitting and peek through the blinds. It's a fantastic blue-sky day. A gust of wind sweeps a flurry of chaff from the cedars and a flock of spinning seeds from the maple trees. Everything is in motion, including me. It's a definite yes day! The first one in a long time!

"I need you, Dick. I need you to research everything! From the overall design to foundations and insulation. And cost..."

"Material, labour," Dick adds.

"And floor plans. And plumbing."

"And electrical. And zoning! What about zoning? And permits..."

"And power and water..."

"What about solar power?" he asks.

"I dunno, maybe," I say, beginning to see that Dick has his own green agenda and that I may have to make some concessions. "Okay, sure."

"We'd need to go there...to Leo's. Really check the place out."

"I know. I've been avoiding it, but I think I'm ready."

He gets right back to planning. "You'd need more help than just me. Professionals."

"One thing at a time. C'mon, let's do this." I give him a tug. "We have 89 days to plan. I'll get on the blower, call in the reserves—the only ones I have."

Dick corrects me. "Ninety counting New Year's Day. I'll start on that research. What are you waiting for? Let's go."

Dick jumps into his research after I text my old buddy John:

Long time no see. Where U @?

John texts back. *Atlin had snow. Home in a couple.*

I wonder what the hell he's doing up in Atlin. *Call me then. ASAP*, I text, hoping it's days not weeks till I hear from him. He doesn't respond.

m—

Thanksgiving is coming up, and I have a lot to be thankful for. Friends are one of those things.

I email Char, letting her know that I miss her by asking how she is and asking if she'll ever move back here or possibly return for a visit—like for Thanksgiving next week. I also tell her that I'm putting together a plan but that I'm keeping it under wraps until everything's gelled.

She emails me back pretty quick to say that a move back to the Island is unlikely, and no to Thanksgiving travel but that she and Glen will definitely be in town for a few days at Xmas. She's intrigued about my secret project but doesn't press for details. Instead, she uses her psychic skills to do a personalized reading for me from Manitoba—a blind reading, unclouded by project details or bias:

> Weak, transient effect: Discontinuity is the antithesis of balance. Expect a blossoming of transcendence the likes of which the infinite has never seen. Domestic change squares off against accident-prone Uranus in your wellness zone. This includes dealing with groups of people. Advocate new policies at this time to reconstruct the solution to what's holding you back from an astonishing future.

The message is clear as a bell. Go ahead and put together an assisted-living facility. If I don't I will be ass-chomped by the future, or struck by a meteorite, or both.

I interrupt Dick's research to tell him our project is a one-with-the-universe go! He nods, wipes the sweat off his upper lip but keeps his eyes on the smartphone screen. He's working away in split-screen multi-task mode.

"How can you do all this without me even knowing?" I ask.

"Alien hand syndrome," Dick responds, without looking up.

"Huh?"

"Sensory deficits." Dick looks up to my blank stare. "Apraxia... disassociation...of me. Pretty classic."

"Classic? You made that up. It's not a real thing." I have flashbacks of Dick's crotch lunges.

"Indeed, it is," Dick says, pulling up a wiki page and pointing to the screen.

I scan the wiki science page for alien hand syndrome, but I can't comprehend yet another addition to my medi-physical profile, so I stop trying. "Whatever," is all I can come up with in response.

How many kinds of differentness can one person handle?

I email Char, *Thanks, perfect,* and *All will be revealed soon.* ☺

The next call is to Jackie, but I hesitate. If anyone—besides Dick—is going to be negative, it'll be her. My finger hovers over the call button. If Jackie finds out that she's less in the know than Char, she'll be miffed. And if Jackie knows less than John, who's rarely in town, and if she's also the last to find out, well, she'll go ballistic. Though Char's new distant prairie residence has eased the rivalry in our female-friend triad, equality is still the standard. I decide to text Jackie to avoid conversation and also to cover my ass. I text, *New plan. Top secret. Tell you soon.*☺ She texts back, *Weirdo. OK.*

Dick and I spend the next two days poring over inspirational photos and specs and design ideas and fun diagrams and troubleshooting sites—all for shipping-container homes. It's amazing how time flies when you're in the midst of a cerebral squall.

I get a text from John on Friday night. *Pizza? Canucks tonight.*

I don't give a fly about hockey or pizza—especially tonight. Friday nights usually mean business calls, and I'm not prepared to faux-orgasmically moan Yes, yes, yes in front of John or even behind him. I text back, *Where are you?* fearing he's already on his way here.

Home, he texts. *Hawaiian or Meat-lovers?*

Shit! No can't. Hot date. Sorry, I type in, which is only sort of lying as I hope to be a hot phone-sex date for a few folks. Plus it makes me sound like I have a normal social life.

His text just reads, *K*.

I type back, *Wait! Tomorrow? Need your help!*

He doesn't respond so I phone him and apologize profusely for turning down his pizza offer and tell him how much I've missed him. Then I tell him in reverse chronological order about Leo's will and the property—where John says, "Seriously?"—and Leo bloody dying, and my not being allowed to drive, and all my medical tests, and the seizure—where John says, "Seriously?"—and the bankruptcy, and the side effects and non-miraculous results of the Costa Rican Liberation procedure and the trip itself. Then I ask him if he can take a look at Leo's property with me tomorrow.

John responds in typical John fashion. "Sure, what time?"

"Don't you want to know why?"

"I figure you'll tell me, Mel, when you're ready."

"I have a plan. Of course, it depends on feasibility. I need your advice."

"I haven't even seen this property yet."

"But I want you to see it with my big idea in mind. You have a certain kind of perspective. An open mind. A practical one. You won't just dismiss my plans or talk me out of it...unless you have good reason."

"Okay, okay," he says, laughing. "What's your big idea?"

I proceed to lay out my vision over the phone. When I'm done, there's only silence. "John? Are you there?"

"Yeah...yeah, I'm here. Sounds like a plan."

"But?"

"Just sounds like a lot of work for you. And a lot of headaches... Why not just sell?"

"You haven't even seen the place."

"True, but why not just get yourself into a place that'll work for you right now...and even down the road?"

I quell my inner rant and go with reason. "Look, I'm considering all the options but I'm nowhere near ready for assisted living in some institutionalized seniors complex where the more money you have, the more they charge and the more assistance you need, the more they charge. And condos, honestly, condos I could afford aren't built to accommodate wheelchair disabilities. Narrow spaces, no walk-in showers, those massive fire doors, fees and meetings..."

"What about a co-op then? They're catching on up north. Lots of community thinking. Plus, pooling your money with like-minded people gives you clout."

"Cooperation involves trust."

"That's why I specifically suggested like-minded people."

"Like-minded people rarely stay like-minded. John, not *everyone* is cut out for that kind of thing."

"You could learn."

"Being sociable...communal dinners. Ugh."

"There are different degrees of community. You could..."

"For fuck sakes! To start with, you need like minds, then you need like finances! I've never even made it to the middle of middle class. A bit of money, and that's all it is these days, doesn't suddenly give you equality or make you like-minded. Other people like me, people with disabilities, rarely have that bit of money to make those like-minded middle-class choices! Why not offer something outside the like-minded middle-class box for a few of us? And there would still be that sense of community you're talking about! And there's Leo. He deserves to have some influence!" Funny how admitting something out loud makes a person realize it's true.

"Wow. Sorry, Mel. I didn't mean to..."

I catch my breath, refusing a reciprocal apology. "Will you look at it? Come look at it with an open mind? See if it's even possible?"

"You know I will," he assures me, and not only do I believe him, I believe myself.

"So noon tomorrow okay? I might have a late night. Oh, and you'll have to drive me out there in my van cuz of the driving ban. I want to take Adele."

"Adele?"

"Adele. My scooter. My walking's not so good these days. Say yes?"

He agrees and I tell him I want to hear all about what he's been up to, but it's getting late and I have to get spiffed up and ready for my date.

He says, "Some things never change." I can hear the smile behind his voice, which is just like old times.

John's a pretty awesome friend, but I've seen less and less of him over the last few years. I put the blame squarely on John but maybe it's partly me—the self-absorption and social separation MS demands. I'll try harder.

⌒

When I hear John's pickup on day minus 75, I give Dick a little pep talk about behaviour and keeping quiet.

He reminds me that no one hears him anyway.

"No grabbing either," I warn.

"I have no interest," he says. "I'm strictly on reconnaissance."

"All righty then."

I scoot out to my van where John's peering through the back window at my spiffy scooter lift. Never mind hellos, it's straight to machinery. "This all new?" he asks.

"Fairly new. I don't use it all the time but my walks are getting shorter and shorter. It comes in handy. Here, I'll show you."

"Just tell me what to do," he says. "I've never..."

I smile. "A mobility-equipment virgin. Even better."

I meet him at the passenger door so I can explain how—once I get my butt on the seat—he has to release the brakes on the scooter, move it out of the way and, because it's my bad side, lift my legs one at a time into the van. I sense his discomfort. He's being way too cautious with me, so I assure him that I won't break and tell him to just get the damn things in the car. John's more comfortable when I verbally guide him through the lift extrication, the scooter loading and getting the lift back into the interior docking position with everything secured.

"All set?" he asks.

"All set. You're a natural."

He gives me a pat and a smile as he slides into the driver's seat. There's no mention of yesterday's somewhat bumpy conversation.

I explain where Leo's place is and on the drive I finally ask him what he's been up to since we talked last. He's not much of a talker, especially when things aren't going well, so I have to urge him to take me verbally along the highways he travelled out in Alberta and in northern BC. He skips over the details of his dual layoffs—one a corporate take-over and the other nonpayment for six weeks of work.

"So then what?" I ask.

"Then I ended up in Atlin...thirty-five miles out actually, working old mine tailings."

"What kind of tailings?"

"Gold."

"Is there money in it?"

"Won't know till we go back in the spring. Shit work but I needed something. And I really didn't want to come home yet...without something to show, you know."

It's my turn to pat John's knee. "I know exactly. None of us are living quite the way we imagined our futures, eh?"

"Too true."

"Jackie's tied up in this Cameron guy's video store. It's basically on life-support. Even Char and Glen with all their money smarts couldn't keep it all together. We're all in the same boat."

"Except your ship's come into port. You, of all people."

I ignore that last comment. "We'll see. Money...stuff...it doesn't make anybody happy."

"It helps," says John.

I can't argue with that in theory, just hope it's true.

m⁓⁻

We pull into Leo's leaf-strewn driveway, crushing blackberry vines that have grown across the drive as we ascend. I've been here in the spring and summer but never the fall. The container house comes into view. It all looks less hopeful suddenly, more derelict than quaint. I squelch the second thoughts.

John parks in front of Leo's place next to the dusty old Mercedes, looks around, gets out and heads for the back of the van. He extracts Adele and delivers her to me without a single prompt.

He scans the parcel of land. "Almost two acres, you said?"

"One point seven."

"Interesting." He takes a deep breath, unbothered by the sick-sweet smell of wood pulp from the mill.

"That's it? Where's that open mind you promised?"

"No, I mean *really interesting*. I wish I'd met the guy."

"Pretty sure he'd have liked you."

"Outside first?" he asks, producing a pen and a little notebook.

"Sure," I say with studied nonchalance, happy to avoid the interior and its Leo-ness a little longer.

It's a rough go in the scooter but thankfully it's a dry mudless day. As well as the general slope up to the back of the property, it's scrubby, rocky and challenging for Adele. John has to push me out of dips or over obstacles half a dozen times, sometimes deserting me to have a closer look at something or other. He notices things about the property I hadn't. The chain-link fence—mostly obscured by blackberry brambles and a few scruffy alders—runs along the sides and cutaway bluff at the back of the large lot, prompting John to sketch the general shape of the property. He draws in Leo's container house, positioned off-centre at an odd angle but one that gives the main windows a view of the dryland to the east, the booming grounds next to the mill and a deep blue channel of ocean cutting between here and Gabriola Island. John measures Leo's house (ten by forty feet) and makes a note of the other unused containers and a hodgepodge pile of steel in the south corner.

He's fascinated by the oddly elegant windmill in the west corner—the lattice of its steel tower and the trio of spinning blades forty feet up. Dick has been quietly observant but even he gets excited and stretches up for a closer look, which is funny because it's so far out of reach. The windmill—wind turbine, Dick whispers in my ear—is erected atop another container, one that's half-buried in the rear bank of earth. It has an oversized and padlocked door.

"Key's in the house?" John asks.

"No idea." I take a deep breath. Time to face the inevitable. "But, let's find out."

I follow John through the pathways between the near-fallow tire gardens and pass him the key that had been in Leo's letter. John slides it into the lock and swings open the door.

I feel better and worse in the dark and chill, the dust and cobwebs and quiet of Leo's tidy little workshop—privileged to have crossed paths with that sweet odd man, melancholy about his death and his unfinished projects, our missed opportunity and of course lucky...luckier than I can comprehend to be his beneficiary. I just hope this luck is the good variety.

John pokes around in the dimness until he finds a light switch.

I can't believe it. "Still power!"

He grabs a set of keys off a hook by the door. "I'll be back," he promises, leaving me alone to enter Leo's inner sanctum.

I scoot in and open the curtains on the large central window. Those marvellous flowers covering the walls—the ones he painted himself—are both welcoming and an offer of solace, so much so that I don't ever want to leave. I can see my way clearly to living here and I know that Leo would be glad about it. I can picture his handwritten words, *The key to life is wanting what you have.* And I get it—in this moment anyway. Not only the wanting what you have but *enjoying* and *using* what you have. I try not to think about the rest of the project until I get John's take on it.

Dick gives me a sharp poke, frustrated with being stuck inside and not out exploring with John. I ignore him and look past the bright floral loveliness to the practical. Aside from the layer of dust it's clean and tidy, his Murphy bed folded into the wall, his tiny kitchen spotless. Clutter is non-existent. The fully tiled bathroom at the back of the unit is inhabited by a few spiders but bright and cheerful. I open a few drawers and cupboards and his small closet, but thorough examination requires time to ponder and time to pay attention to the detritus of Leo's life. A life clipped short.

I leaf through the papers he left on the table—a pre-travel list, a couple of receipts, a small cheque made out to Leo from the hydro company and a stunning butterfly photo labelled *Diaethria neglecta*, the butterfly that drew Leo south. So strange that the first syllable is pronounced die and the word *neglecta* was the trigger for a misunderstanding the last time I heard his singsong voice.

John bursts in full of news like a twelve-year-old kid. "The guy was smart as a tack!" he says. "As resourceful as a honey badger, as—"

"So you found something?"

"A shitload of somethings! You're self-sufficient, Mel. That locked container is a shop loaded with tools, even an arc welder, and you've got septic—also built from a container—and you've got wind power that even feeds back into the grid, and there's solar power, panels up on the roof and—"

"So you figure I could live here. Which is awesome. But what about my big idea?"

John sits down at the tiny table and pulls out his notebook and pen. Darting from page to page, diagram to notation, he takes me through a loose plan of how to make it work.

"You really think so?"

"It'll take a fair chunk of change but, yes," he says. "You'll have to get plans drawn up and permits. That'll take a bit of time."

"I can't do anything till the new year. No funds till then."

"Right. Well, anyway, the permit might be seven hundred, maybe eight, and the plans can be pretty basic, probably cost about the same... maybe less. But in the new year like you say."

A little Dick voice whispers, "Eight hundred dollars. Don't waste it on rent. Do it now."

"Unless I moved in here now," I say to John, as if I'd already thought it through. "I'd save that much on rent. I'd have that at the end of the month but that'll only cover one or the other—plan or permit."

Dick shoots up to my ear, gives it a scratch and discreetly whispers, "Damage deposit."

It takes me a minute to twig to Dick's prompt. "I just realized...I'll get my damage deposit back. That's another eight right there."

"That'd get you started. And you might find a builder who'll do their own plans. But, those permits...there are legal issues and paperwork—declarations, authorizations, proof of ownership. Leo's obviously not here to sign. And you're not legit until January."

"Yes, January." Sad but true. I have to wait, twiddle my one good thumb. Or...*buck up or fuck up, Mel!* "Unless, John..."

"Unless?"

"Unless I *am* Leo."

"You'd do that?"

"You bet I would. On paper, at least. I have nothing to lose. I mean I have nothing now, and I had less than nothing before that. What could go wrong? I'll take my chances. It's only for a couple of months."

"You're sure? It's not exactly legal. You'll need documentation."

"I saw a file marked LEGAL in that bottom drawer. Would you mind?" I direct John, moving Adele out of his way in the tiny quarters. Dick and I hold our breath.

"Yup," he says, extracting papers.

"Allrighty then..."

John scratches his head. "You'll need a contractor, someone to organize, keep things on track. I might know someone who'd be willing to work with 'Leo,' no questions asked. And I happen to know he's between jobs at the moment so..."

"Really? Who?"

"Me," he says, aiming his thumb at his chest. He's dead serious. "You can think about it."

It takes thirty seconds of Dick nudging me to decide. "Yes! Trouble is I can't pay you anything until January."

"Oh, I can hang on till then."

"But, John, how?"

He studies a spider scuttling along the edge of the ceiling. "I'm staying at Mum's. It's just temporary. I help her out around the place."

"Of course, yes."

"Yardwork, whatever. Take her to the casino for her weekly."

"Your mum's a gambler?"

John taps my shoulder with his notepad and all its pertinent notations. "Aren't we all?"

I have to agree, especially now.

"Anyway," he adds, "I'll head back to Atlin in the spring once we're squared up. So you see it kind of works out."

Dick pipes up in my ear, "Indeed it does!"

"Like it was meant to be," I tell John. "And there's nobody better."

"We can work out the details when you get sorted."

"Of course. Get me the paperwork for the permits, and I'll get started. And listen, this has to be fair and square...for you, I mean. I don't want *anything else*," I say—meaning my MS—"to get in the way of our friendship."

He gets it. "Neither do I," he says with sincerity.

The view through the window holds such promise I dare to imagine a future. The vision, *my* vision. "Oh my gawd, John! It's really going to happen!" I quell Dick's excited agitations in my lap, adding, "And I'll be here every day to help."

"You won't have to."

"Oh, but I do! I want to. I do have to!"

"Maybe that's not such a good idea, Mel."

"What do you mean? You don't think I'm capable? Of helping?"

"It's not that."

"You think I'd be a hindrance...that I'd slow things down..."

"No, it's not that at all. Now, don't take this the wrong way..."

I cross my arms, ready to take a stand. "What?"

"You have a way of complicating things."

"What the fuck, John? What does that mean, complicate things? It's my project!"

"It is. Absolutely! But we...you...need things done quickly. In a way that's efficient. Straightforward, no sidetracks, no overthinking, no squabbles over petty details."

"Am I really that difficult?"

He sidesteps my question. "There's another reason. You can't be here acting like you own the place!"

"But I do! Almost."

"The less you're on the job site, the better. It's best if you're not here at all."

"But..."

"At the beginning, at least. Anyway, you'd need a scooter with four-wheel drive to get around here once construction starts. And there's plenty for you to do on your end."

"True, but..."

"You're the boss, Mel, but if you let me do my job as your general contractor, it'll go faster and smoother all round. Agree?"

Giving up control isn't easy, even when you know deep down that it's the right thing to do. I try to keep the pout out of my voice. "Fine."

"And don't forget you're the one paying me. My time is your money."

"I hate it when you're so sensible!" I shake off the argument—for now—and get back to business. "Payment—a reasonable amount in a reasonable time frame."

"We'll work it out. I'll need cash for up north come April. If not, I know where to find you," he says, smiling.

I smile too and we shake on it and Dick lays himself atop our handshake so John covers Dick with his other hand for a double-shake before we separate, lock up Leo's house and shop-talk our way into the van and all the way home. I offer to write up a contract between us.

"Sure, if you want," he says, "but I trust you, Mel."

This is rhythm 'n blues to my heart. It twangs all the way home— the one I can't now wait to vacate.

We carry on our discussion over tea at my kitchen table, sketching out rough ideas, possibilities of what might work, taking into account Leo's existing structure. I leave it in John's capable hands.

Leo would approve, I'm sure, as I imagine the finished project— sort of arrow-shaped with two adjacent but offset containers on each side, flaring toward the road below and the water beyond. The perfect scenario to allow for a bit of privacy, large windows and, obviously, a view.

16
Hits and Misses

On day minus 74 I give my landlady notice that I'll be leaving November 15. It's already five days shy of a one-month legal notice. She's nonplussed and demands rent for another full month. Not only do I need that rent money right now, I want out. I pull the good tenant card, then the broke card. She eventually agrees, even to the whole damage deposit reimbursement when I pull the trump card—my worsening disability.

Now that it's official and I can't be talked out of the move, I call Jackie to explain my big plan in minute detail.

Her response is everything I expected, but when she finally hears me out—really listens—she surprises me by saying, "I'm not good with heavy equipment and I don't have a lot of time, but what else can I do to help?"

Where do I start?

Dick nudges me, pointing to the Housing Code page in his Favourites and scrolling to the section on Accessibility Requirements—everything you need to know about interior design, height and clearance measurements. I read a bit to Jackie before Dick flips to a link on the Rick Hansen Foundation page, finally landing at a 102-page PDF of the *Building Access Handbook*. "It's all very specific, Jackie. Can you have a look? And help with the interiors?" I admit to having lost the ability to make lists. "I'll email you some links."

"That I can do!"

"Fantastic! I'll send photos of the interior of Leo's house, to give you a sense of how his place works."

"It would be easier just to go over there."

"Sure, yes, of course. Why didn't I think of that? Check out the handrails. They run along all the interior walls. Absolutely essential! Absolutely the perfect time! And this move, Jackie...I feel like I'm going home." I wait for reassurance or deflection or even a negative jibe. It doesn't come. "So, will you help?"

She says, "Don't I always?"

"I'll take that as a yes. Drop me off some boxes if and when you think of it."

"Aye aye, Commander."

"Don't..."

"Kidding, kidding! Boxes at the top of my list."

"I love you, Jack."

"And me, you, weirdo."

Then I email Char and give her an optimistic, fearless but brief outline of my plan. I tell her Jackie will keep her posted. She emails back, *Your sun energy's high now! You go girl! Xo*

Between research and anxiety, I begin to cull my stuff—bagging up clothing for the thrift store. I get rid of anything I can't manage one-handed—zippered jeans and jackets, anything with buttons smaller than an inch in diameter, boots and shoes that I can no longer pull on or—even worse—pull off. Clothes with no "give." Even old favourites I'd hung on to for decades. Two bags later, I'm left with a very comfortable but extremely pared-down wardrobe. It's okay. And so am I. Priorities. Next, the kitchen!

On day minus 63 John shows up with his drafted plans. I can't wait to see my concept!

We unroll the paper and John smooths it out with pride. I don't see anything like what I'd imagined. "John?"

He runs his fingers along a pencil line. "Nice, eh?"

"John, this isn't even my place. Where," I ask, "are *my* plans?"

"Right here." He pats the paper, frowning. "This is it. See? This rectangle is Leo's existing unit and here's the other three. Right here."

I see the rectangles. "But you've got them in a square."

"Isn't it great? It's a squared O. See how they create a little court-yard in the centre?"

"But that's not what I wanted. Not even close. I want them situated like an arrowhead..." I draw out my very clear vision with my finger. John doesn't respond so I carry on, "Two on each side, slightly offset, with the point...the arrow tip...to the back bank, and flaring, or whatever, toward the ocean."

"You want an arrow? That's not what you said at all. You said to go ahead..."

"No, like the crotch of a tree. You know? Like a V, a flock of geese..." My hands are describing what my words can't get across.

"...with what's best, you said. What's cheapest..."

"It's the view, John."

He scratches his head. "I did a lot of research. It's better...and easier for the layout and function of the plumbing..."

"But..."

"And the wiring..."

"What about the view?"

"And the heating. Like I said, I did a lot of research. Even talked to a builder in the States. This way, Mel, you get a little courtyard, protected from the weather, totally roofed, if you want..."

"I don't want a little courtyard, John. I want a view and so will everyone else. People like us, like me, who can't get out on the water...we want to look out at it."

"But..."

"But nothing."

"Okay, I get it. Whatever you say. You're the boss."

Ouch. "It's just that I have a vision." I draw my idea—wobbly lines—over his idea.

"I said okay. I'll redo it."

"It's not just my vision. It's Leo's too."

John rolls up the plans, tight-lipped. "How do you know that, Mel?"

I try humour because I don't have an honest answer.

"I better get going," he says. "New plans and all. Lots to do."

"John, I'm sorry. It was a misunderstanding. Your plan's a good one...it's great...but..."

"You need to be clear."

"I was totally clear! What I mean is I will be. Totally clear. I promise." I squeeze his arm to bolster the promise.

He's almost out the door when he remembers his other news. It's an offer of a little Bobcat that'll handle the digs for foundation and water lines. I remind John that I can't pay for the machine until January. He tells me no, it's an offer...free use of the machine. He called in a favour, he says, plus he told the guy about me so it's a freebie.

"Told him what?"

"About you. Your MS. And your plan. I had to..."

"Are you out of your mind? There's this little business of fraud!"

"That's just short term."

"Does the deal need a signature?"

"He's no bureaucrat, Mel, just a guy with a spare machine. And I said you were Leo's sister..."

"Jeezus, how many people can I be?" I wonder briefly if the power of suggestion—or inference—can induce multiple personalities.

"You can pull this off. You're...multi-talented."

I accidentally slip into my Ginger voice. "You have no idea, honey."

John ignores my tone. "I told them Leo's left you in charge."

Back to business. "Well, that part's true."

"And that, together, you and Leo are setting up this assisted-living place."

"Still almost true."

"People seem more receptive. Financially. Because of your situation."

"Especially with able-bodied you, pitching *my* idea. Well done."

"Is that sarcasm?"

I give him a wry smile. "Not this time. I can't afford it."

"You're right."

"So, carry on. With whatever works. By the way, John," I add, giving him a reassuring little hug, "you're awesome."

John sloughs it off and tells me he'll start prepping the site. He's excited, eager to get started. More awesome! My disability cheque comes tomorrow, so he'll apply for the permit then—with my Leo signature. He warns me the fee isn't refundable even if the application fails. Gulp.

If you think it'll fly, do it, I tell him.

And fly it does. Smooth as anything. Anything realistic.

A perfectly drafted plan of *my* vision appears on my doorstep.

On day minus 61 John texts me, *Bobcat fire.*

I picture inferno and text back, *Want me to come? Call 911?!!!????*

He texts, *it seating up job!*

I text, *English please!!!* I picture smoking tires and decimation. I text *JOHN!! ARE YOU OKAY?*

When he doesn't answer, I pull on my coat and get my scooter out to the van. I feel sick. It takes me forever to load it and even longer to get myself in. I'm sweating. I feel sicker. Could this bring on a seizure? I'm an illegal driver. But it's an emergency. I text again before I pull onto the road, *ARE YOU OKAY?!?!?*

All good! Nothing. Never mind! He texts back like nothing happened, like I just peed myself for nothing. He doesn't even give me a consolation reply.

An hour later, after a change of clothes, I text John, *PLEASE don't wreck the gardens!*

He texts, *Gardens?*

On day minus 60, minus 59 and minus 56 Jackie drops boxes off for the move and I ask her to keep Char in the loop. She's been in regular contact, Jackie assures me.

John doesn't tell me about getting express replacement parts for the burnt machine or about using Leo's old Mercedes as reimbursement.

Day minus 56 is also the day the forms for the concrete slabs are finished. I ask John how he's paying for supplies. An account for you at the Build-All Depot, he says, easy peasy, plus Char's uncle's golf buddy's son-in-law runs the place. I ask what the balance is now. He doesn't know offhand but promises a mitt full of bills next time he sees me.

He doesn't tell me about trouble with the building inspector or his trip to Emerg for a slashed thumb.

m—ε

On day minus 55 and minus 54 Jackie takes a load to the thrift store and delivers the first of my boxes to Leo's place. I can't get used to calling it anything else. She offers to clean out Leo's clothes but I decline the offer. She tells me the job site is looking good but I overhear her telling Cam what a mess it is. I want to see!

John doesn't tell me about the problems with the arc welder, the compactor or his pickup truck.

m—ε

From day minus 53 to day minus 52 heavy rains shut down the job site and soak Jackie and my packed boxes. We're both cranky and pessimistic and why-are-we(me)-doing-this apathetic. So we spend her day off going through her list of appliances and bathroom fixtures x 3. We double-check stovetops with front-access controls and special-order little fridges and sinks and stacked mini-washer/dryers. We triple-check easily operable bathroom fixtures—high toilets, fold-down shower seats, pedestal sinks and a shitload of grab bars. We pick out tile for the three bathrooms—floors and walls. We make a separate list for paint and ceiling fans and low cabinets with some roll-out drawers and a work area with knee clearance.

Jackie wonders how I've been managing without any specialized adaptations. I managed fine, I tell her...on the good days. We agree that Leo's will be easier for me now, neither of us mentioning my inevitably deteriorating physical future. Now is more than enough.

John doesn't tell me that he had to hire a plumber who worked through the night with him to get the underground pipe and drainage system set up before the concrete arrives.

m—ε

On day minus 49 they do the pour. I don't get to see that either. John tells me it will need time to cure but he's lined up the container move. It's pricey. A few grand, he says. He tells me not to worry, that they'll bill me.

"We still need credit at Home-Pro. We need to order the interior stuff."

"Done. At contractor's rate." John explains that Char's hubby's stepbrother's cousin's ex has something to do with the company.

"So, Char's been busy too? Aid from afar?"

John shrugs. "Friends, eh..."

I call Jackie and tell her to go ahead and put the whole order in. She tells me she already did.

"You talked to Char?"

"Yup. Her hubby's stepbrother's cousin's ex..."

"Never mind. I get it."

◦◦◦

On day minus 47, while Jackie stays behind to do a thorough clean of my apartment, I say goodbye to my old rental and move to Leo's.

After a mucky trip up the driveway, I finally get a first-hand look at the three fresh rectangles of cement in their oh-so-perfect spots, and I'm so tickled that I don't comment on the ruined tire gardens. I wave John over, telling him I trust his judgment and to just carry on. Now that I'm living here, there isn't much John *can't* tell me. But it seems that now that I'm here, he wants to discuss everything.

He leads me into the nearest container, where he's chalked out a basic floor plan. After nitpicking through decisions about window placement and wall and ceiling vents for airflow, he launches into R-ratings and losing interior inches and closed-cell something or other.

"I've got to unpack, John. I'm soaked."

"The insulation is critical in these things," he tells me. "It's not just winter cold or summer heat you have to worry about. There's condensation, corrosion, mould."

"Well, pick the best choice."

"The spray foam is the most expensive but framing, batting, you lose the most space."

"Go with batting. What's a couple of inches?"

"You'd lose space on the floor, ceiling and the walls. Cubically, it's a big difference. And condensation can be..."

"So, go with spray foam."

"It's triple the price."

"Shit." I resort to my go-to response: "What did Leo do?"

"Spray foam."

"Okay."

"Okay, what?"

"Do that. We know it works."

"Oh, it works, all right. But there's one more thing."

I brace myself and my diminishing inheritance. "What?"

"The outside bottoms need insulation. If I had a crew, we could jack them up to spray underneath ahead of the move but it would take time, rental equipment. Or we do it while the crane's here."

"Okay."

"It'll be cheaper than getting them to come out twice...for two moves...all the strapping. The stuff dries almost instantly so..."

Sheesh, I guess John even has moments of insecurity. "I said okay. Good call." I'm dying to get into Leo's where it's warm and dry and there's a comfy place to pee.

$$\mathsf{m}\!\!\curvearrowright\!\!\bullet$$

Once inside, I put my small bag of groceries away and get to work on the small mountain of damp boxes, trying to feel like it's home—my home. It's weird. And good. I think. When I have time to think. I empty Leo's clothes and personals into the same boxes that were used to move my clothes and personals—in the tiny space. I can't get the Murphy bed all the way down because of the boxes and the necessity of space to wobble or roll, so I spend my first night—well, really my second if you count my one-nighter here with Leo in the spring—on a ridiculous slant. Leo's very much still around, especially when I lie down, clinging to the foot of the tipped-up bed—his scent, his art, his calm quirkiness. He'd get a chuckle out of this.

$$\mathsf{m}\!\!\curvearrowright\!\!\bullet$$

On day minus 43, I can legally drive so I wrestle a couple of bags of Leo's clothes out to the van, but now I can't seem to operate my feet.

Too much sitting? Too much stress? Having to lift my leg/foot onto the brake makes for a dicey drive so, fine, I'll be a passenger for a little longer until I sort that out with practice or exercise or rest or something. I could use some help! At least I can scoot Adele down to the corner store for emergency supplies.

On day minus 38 a massive crane truck pulls into the yard—another ten grand minimum out of my nest egg. I hope to hell that lawyer is on task.

John's already had the three containers sandblasted and he's cut out the doors and windows and torn out the filthy original plywood flooring in order to lighten the load.

It takes ten and a half hours to swing, tilt, insulate and nudge the containers into position, but it works. I have all four units together in one place, and I can envision their future as a single entity.

On day minus 35 John shows up with a small crew: a buddy to work on the outside, paint, install windows and solar panels; and two younger guys to start on the interiors, electrical, plumbing, framing and flooring. They'll all work together on the finishing. Sounds good.

John looks a bit sheepish when he confesses he's promised them a bonus if they wait for that early January payday. Fine, good, I say, almost beyond caring.

I feel optimistic enough to fill out the Health Authority application for my Private Assisted Living Facility. All along I've been imagining three other high-functioning disabled people like me. I've completely overlooked the Assisted part. I actually have to have a caregiver here—living here—which would cut a third of my income and add another expense. And even worse, I've had all three new units finished with low counters and belly-button-high mirrors and switches, which don't work all that well for an able-bodied person. Dick and I have a major blame battle about which of us overlooked this gargantuan detail. I win but we both feel bad by the time it's over. And I have to admit I could sure as hell use some help myself on the bad days...plus there's the driving dilemma—we really need a care aide who can drive.

We get back to work. Dick puts an ad on Craigslist and I post on the Island Job-Op for someone qualified and caring. I can afford the ads because I actually made a whopping phone-sex profit of $146 this month. That's one helluva big bag of oatmeal, a case of beans and a few goodies on the side. Onward and upward.

The application is daunting, the rules even more so. I hate rules! I think about Leo and flypaper for freaks and alien hand syndrome and differentness. *Buck up or fuck up*, I remind myself and Dick, too, who is happy to assist me in shredding the application to smithereens. Fly under the regulatory radar, we must!

We skip caregiver for now and jump to the next crucial component. We post ads looking for disabled folks who are able to live independently with minimal assistance and who are looking for a comfortable non-institutional setting. Call for appointment.

ɱ⸺

The next three weeks are a blur of rain-or-shine activity—Jackie and John and his crew in and out and round about. It's messy and noisy and nerve-wracking and exhausting and expensive and fekking wonderful. I don't even complain when John and his boys string up bloody Xmas lights.

ɱ⸺

On day minus 16 I think about orgasms—mine, not my clients'—for the first time since the roller-coaster day I learned the details of Leo's death. Sixteen is the number of orgasms that Dr. Falik's test results said I had left. I ogle the hard-hat boys trudging in and out with materials, then with coffee. They're not unattractive but I can't even begin to get excited about them. I'm unresponsive to titillation at the moment. Sigh. I have too much to do anyway. Next year, I think, I'll enjoy each and every one of those orgasms, even if it kills me.

ɱ⸺

On day minus 15, a week before Xmas, I get a daytime train-whistle call, which is unusual—the time, I mean. It's one of my faves, Shy Paul

Two. He's stuttering/grunting more than usual. I try to calm him down, soothe him so we can get him to the finish line before his dime runs out.

"Sing it, darlin'," I remind him with my honeyed voice. "C'mon baby, I do love a crooner."

That's when Paul starts to cry, and it's that really tormented out-of-control crying.

"Oh, sweetie," I say, not sure what to say.

"I h-h-hate m-my la-la-la-life, G-g-g-ginger! I d-d-don't know what to d-d-do!" he screeches into the phone, along with a stream of curses.

I calm him down a little and try to find out where he is and does he need help and can I call someone for him.

Paul erratically belts out bits of his out-of-tune story through heart-wrenching sobs—fucking cerebral palsy, only twenty-four, fucking wheelchair, hates his fucking facility, bunch of old farts, no privacy, stupid caseworker. He goes on and on.

When he finally stops to catch his breath, I say slowly and more calmly than my impulsive offer deserves, "Paul, listen...I might know another place that would work for you."

"I don't need the psych ward," he warbles.

"I just mean a place to go look at. A place you might want to live."

Paul's sobs lose considerable momentum.

I keep my voice gentle, calm, firm, articulating each word. "I have this friend, Melanie, who's got a new assisted-living place that just might work for you. It's actually an *independent* living place. Not too much assistance. Could you manage that?"

Paul grunts a big affirmative yes.

"Okay. Well, Melanie will have to decide. It's small...just a couple of others. You'd have your own space. It's not quite finished, but she'll be there tomorrow." I hear only snuffling so I go on. "Can you get there tomorrow? Meet Melanie for an interview, have a look around?"

"W-w-where?"

I give him the address, warn him again about the not-quite-finished state of things, adding, "Afternoons are best for her. She's in a wheelchair sometimes too." I hold my breath.

He pauses long enough for me to wonder if I've gone too far and lost him. "Ginger?"

I exhale. "I'm here."

"Would you tell her...would you give me a..."

I see where he's going, head him off at the pass. "I'll tell her to expect you, Paul."

"Can you tell her I'm polite? And tidy?" he grunts/stutters. "And smart? And..."

"Oh, she'll be able to see all that for herself," I say, hoping all that stuff is somewhat true, adding, "And your honesty, of course," which I pose as a statement not a question.

"And you won't tell her about this? How I know you?"

It's a sad and abrupt reminder that both of us are socially forced to be embarrassed about something perfectly normal. "Sure, okay, but I doubt she'd care."

"Cool," he says. "And, Ginger?"

"Yes?"

"My name's not Paul. It's Randy. Randy Paul."

"No worries, Randy," I'm quick to generously reassure him.

Randy Paul hangs up and all I can do is hope he's okay while I think about names we're given and names we lay claim to.

〜◦

On day minus 14 the HandyDART pulls up the driveway at noon. The driver unloads a motorized chair containing a ponytailed young man, wearing shades and a studded black leather jacket. I breathe a sigh of relief.

I go out in my scooter to meet him while the driver returns to the van.

I straighten out my personas, offering my hand. "Ginger told me a friend might be by today. I'm Mel."

"Randy," he says, using his whole body to urge out his speech. Randy pumps my hand jerkily. "C-can I s-see it?"

I lead the way to #1, the farthest unit, explaining that it won't be ready till January.

Randy looks disappointed. "I'm d-desperate."

My Ginger-self wants so badly to say, Sing it, Randy Paul, sing it! "We'll have a deck soon but come have a peek inside. They're still working."

The door's open and the smell of paint and sealant is overwhelming. I call in, and it's John who appears.

"This is Randy, John. Would you mind giving him a tour around the paint cans? There's more mess than room. I'll be at home, #3. Come knock on my door when you're done."

I wait ten minutes for the knock. There it is. I invite Randy in but he prefers to stay outside so he can keep an eye on the HandyDART. He gets pretty jerky, probably anxious. He's uncomfortable looking me in the eye but when he does, I like what I see—intelligence, curiosity and a feisty spirit. He might keep things interesting around here. Dick seems to agree, rubbing my ear.

"I n-need a p-p-place before C-c-c-christmas!" he blurts out.

"That's less than a week, Randy! I don't think...how much assistance do you actually...there will be one care aide for everyone, and I haven't hired one yet. And we haven't discussed—"

"Don't c-c-care. I'll m-m-manage."

"I'm interviewing three tomorrow though." I lie brightly.

"I can p-p-pay rent. S-social s-s-s-s..."

No beating around the bush. I like that. I think about trust and gut feelings and I make a decision. "Okay, I'll see what I can do. Give me your number. We'll sort out the details. And we'll get to work here... finish up your #1 first."

He gives me a printed card with his name and number on it and away he goes.

Huh, I think, I'd better find that care aide ASAP. I head back over to #1 to beg and bully John into finishing Randy Paul's unit early.

"Interesting kid," John says, scratching his head with his silicone-smeared fingers. "I'll do my best." He calls after me as I'm leaving, "Hey, Mel, who's Ginger?" I scoot-skedaddle Adele out of there before I could possibly have heard him.

〰〜

On day minus 13 Dick and I go through the responses to our care-aide want ad. I carry out phone interviews with five candidates. The first two—a disillusioned dog walker and a retired kindergarten teacher—attest to their life experience but have no relevant qualifications. The third is qualified but she's a Christian on a mission and the fourth wants a pay hike before she even starts. The last one's the worst. She's prickly, arrogant and has a voice like a retching crow. Dick puts the kibosh on her mid-squawk with a press of his knuckle. It's disheartening to say the least. We refresh the ads and hope for the best.

Next we tackle the three dozen applications from disabled people looking for a new home. Holy hell. There's so much responsibility in picking and choosing. Decisions take energy. It makes me so suddenly weary...and even wearier when I look out over the muddy lot, the mangled tire garden and the still-growing pile of building debris—packing crates, cardboard, wood ends. "Maybe we should just wait for spring, clean things up first, take our time."

Dick looks me in the eye. "We can't afford to."

"Nah, we'll be okay once the bankruptcy's done and the life insurance comes through."

"Have you checked your so-called books, lately?"

"Oh, I have it all in my head. It's right here," I say, pointing to my cranium. "And here." I pat the messy stack of bills cluttering the desk.

"It doesn't look that great on the spreadsheets."

"What spreadsheets?"

"Here," Dick says, using his chin to open up a file on his little screen. "You have a lot of people still to pay. Not to mention..."

I can't bear to look. Money matters are as overwhelming as playing god to potential tenants.

Dick's frustrated with me. I can tell when he starts yelling, "Buck up or fuck up!"

"Can we even afford a care aide?"

Dick raises his little eyebrows. "If we cut back a bit on the vision, sure. Alternating days. Split shifts. Or shorter days. Five or six hours. They can still cover two mealtimes if folks—"

"Clients."

"If they need help with, say, showers or—"

"Shopping."

"Appointments."

"Gardening."

Dick frowns. "Gardening?"

"Well, yeah. I mean everybody's going to want to be part of making it all nice here, right? And keeping it that way. We have a lot of work to do!"

"Your expectations," Dick points out, "are totally..."

"Optimistic?"

"Something like that."

"It's called independent *living*, Dick."

"Okay then, let's just get this place lived in—occupied."

"You're right. Let's." Having a vision is as problematic and slippery as it is ambitious.

He's relieved to get me back on task, adding, "And let the care aides and gardeners fall where they may."

"But where to begin? Appointment after appointment? It's just too much to—"

"Cattle call," says Dick.

"Funny. Why don't we just have a drive-thru interview window? Then nobody gets their feet dirty...or their wheels."

"You know, that's not a bad idea."

"I'm kidding. Anyway, the driveway couldn't take it. It's already a mucky mess."

Dick thinks for a minute. "No worries. Here's what we'll do..."

m⁓

On day minus 12—the winter solstice—there's a weak but optimistic sun in the pale sky. Dick and I are totally prepared, bundled up against the chill with a charged-up Adele, her basket full of clipboards, pens, application questionnaires—rudimentary basics like age, gender, pets, what condition have you got, what help do you need, can you afford the rent, are you honest? John's set up a PRIVATE, DO NOT ENTER sign down on the road. Only those who make it through the first round will have the opportunity to ascend the driveway to see the place and to get a John-guided tour of the nearly finished unit #1.

Dick and I head down the driveway well before the designated noon start time, zigzagging around the worst mud and biggest puddles. It's a good thing. Not even halfway down and we're just about rammed by a mid-size Ford. The guy peering over the wheel looks to be a hundred plus. I'm waving him back down the driveway, yelling, "No! No! Back down!" and "Didn't you read the Do Not Enter sign?" when a big old Suburban rages up behind him. I continue to yell at them to back down, refusing to converse with the woman leaning out her window as I scoot past, pointing down to the main road—my destination—to get myself safely out of their way and to prevent any other early birds from entering the driveway.

We deal with the first two, turning them away. What we're offering is neither short-term care nor all-inclusive. Disabled, yes, but independent and willing to commit to the community long term.

We're just handing our questionnaire through the window of a Chevy van to the next potential tenant as three other vehicles line up behind. After that it's a steady stream of contestants, mostly with their aides or family advocates. Apparently, this kind of news travels faster than an STD in an old folks' home.

"I'm not exactly an empath," I confess to Dick between a concussed boxer and a young single mother with no disabilities about to produce a second offspring, "but this is hard. I feel terrible...so many people with no *right* place, no affordable comfortable place to call home. It's...*indecent*."

"You have to be tough. You can't afford to go soft now!" Dick says. "No frauds. No fakers. Nobody too well or too unwell. We're set up for mobility issues, not every other kind of disability."

I sit up straighter on Adele. "I haven't forgotten *or* gone soft, Dick. Give me some credit! That's why I gave the blind guy a pass. He doesn't need low counters or ramps."

"It wasn't his four pit bulls?"

"It was a combination, okay?"

"He wasn't even blind."

"He wasn't? But his friend said…"

"Your radar's slipping. Never mind. Just hold tight to your vision! No impulsive decisions. Notification to follow."

"Yup," I say, thinking, wow, I'm pretty lucky to just have MS. Also, thanks to Leo, I'm not desperately looking for a place to live.

m—s

"I feel like a border guard," I say to Dick two hours later. We've just sent the fourteenth vehicle up the driveway and wasted half an hour arguing with a slurry guy wearing a plaster leg cast and whiskey aftershave, followed by a woman with emphysema who sounds like she should be on a ventilator.

Dick responds by nudging me on to the next car. Two elderly couples wave a flurry of canes enthusiastically.

We don't shut down till the sun disappears. No lunch. Cold fingers and most other body parts. Not enough pee breaks—wish I'd worn some protection, something disposable, stylish, leak-proof, odour-guarded.

We have thirty-one applicants from the sixty-something vehicles. The day's a blur. We should have had them attach photos to their applications like the judges do on TV talent shows. Photos would help me remember who's who.

"How do we decide?" I ask Dick later, after culling the number by half. Paperwork for the remaining sixteen candidates covers the table. "I'm running out of steam. I can't even think straight."

"Lottery," he says with conviction.

"Lottery? That's ridiculous."

"It's no worse or weirder than the hoops and whims of the government system."

I have to agree.

Dick taps his knuckled head repeatedly. "Do you have a better idea?"

"Not at the moment."

It's well past ten. I see Jackie arriving and lugging her vacuum over to #1. What a trooper. I don't dare ask her for another single thing, even her opinion.

"Let's do it!" I say.

Dick and I agree—no backpedalling. Pull one name each and take what we get, luck of the draw. We fold up all the names and stuff them into a paper grocery bag and shake.

I pull a name and come up with Dawn. We match her name to her questionnaire. Dawn Barrington, age thirty-two, who is recovering from a stroke and suffers from jargon aphasia. She has weakness and is mostly confined to her chair but, aside from regular physio, needs little daily help. And she's improving...slowly.

"What's jargon aphasia? Is that a joke?"

"She can't speak," he says, "except in platitudes."

"Platitudes?"

"Stock terms, phrases, simple meaningless..."

"I know what it means! But we can only manage high functioning..."

He's getting frustrated with me. "It's just the inability to make the brain and mouth work together to communicate her thoughts."

"Oh," I say, adding, "She's so young for a stroke!" to balance my meanness with empathy. "I don't remember her. Do you?"

"Big smile, big, uh...low-cut shirt."

"Okay, Dawn's in. Now, your turn."

He takes forever to choose a name, and I'm not good at waiting. "C'mon, just grab a fekking name, Dick!"

He's frantic. His little brow is getting sweaty.

"What's wrong with you? Do it or I will!"

He gropes around in the bag some more, mumbling, "Oh shit, oh shit, oh...ta-dum!" and pulls, finally, Dora Tipplee. Her questionnaire says her age is fifty and that she's a hemiplegic. Assistance required—unsure.

"What's this?" I say, pointing out the word hemiplegic.

"Half-paralyzed."

"Half? I thought that was paraplegic."

"Para is more the bottom half, like waist down. Hemi is one side of the body or the other. For this woman, it's her right."

"Oh, kind of like where I'm headed," I say.

"You have a ways to go," he reminds me.

"It doesn't say right side here. How do you know?"

Dick seems flustered, but recovers. "My memory's better than yours."

"Weird. I don't remember her at all." This sends me back to her application. "What does this mean? 'Unsure?'" I ask.

"She's still adjusting. To her new...uh...injury. I told you, I had a chat with her...in the lineup."

"I thought nobody could hear you but me."

"Yes. No. I mean that's right. I must have just imagined that... having an actual conversation, I mean. I just listened...overheard her talking to the driver. When she was filling out the form."

"What if she needs too much help? Do we want someone who's new at this disability game? I mean it's a pretty emotional time..."

"Really? I can't even believe her eligibility would be in question." Dick is clearly disgusted. "She's too *new* for you?"

"Well..."

"Well, what?" he demands.

"I need easy clients."

"You *want* easy clients."

"What's wrong with that?"

He snaps, "What about stewardship? Support? Their well-being?"

"What about *my* well-being?" He gives me a scathing stare. I change tactics. "I have another business to run, too. The phone sex-thing doesn't run itself. What if I'm in over my head?"

"Wouldn't be the first time..."

"What if I have more seizures?"

"What if you don't?"

I grumble under my breath, "And I wouldn't mind some kind of *personal* life..."

"Look," says sensible Dick, ignoring my whining, "we need three clients and now we have three—Randy Paul, Dawn Barrington and Dora Tipplee—all high-functioning. What was that Leo quote about wanting what you have? Use what you've got?"

"Something like that."

Neither of the women stands out in my memory of the mostly desperate home seekers in the lineup, but Dick assures me that they're perfect. It does feel good to have come to a decision even if it wasn't totally mine.

"Okay. We have our three," I say.

Dick and I fist-bump, a good sign that we're on the same side.

m——

On day minus 10 John and the boys put the finishing touches on #1 for Randy. If Jackie does her super-clean, he can move in tomorrow.

When I call Randy, he's stutteringly exuberant.

"Just to be clear, you'll be on your own for all things Xmas. And the others won't be here until New Year's Eve."

"New Year's! Celebrate!"

I tell him no. "It's going to be incredibly busy around here. Maybe next year."

Randy sounds disappointed. "Maybe spring?"

"Sure, yes, maybe in the spring when the weather's nicer."

"For Christmas...I go...to my cousin's place for...turkey and prezzies."

"Perfect. See you soon. And Randy, I'm happy you'll be joining us."

"Yeah, me...too...I think."

We both have a little laugh and I say goodbye to Randy on an up note, then make calls to the other chosen two—calls to say yes, that they can move in on New Year's Eve, once the paperwork's out of the way—Dora into #4 on the north end next to me and Dawn in #2 closest to Randy, who's on the south end in #1.

Dora sounds pleasant but somewhat reserved. Her answers are brief, but she makes it clear in a deep melodious voice how relieved she is and thank you so very much, Miss Melanie. I can't peg her as interesting but she doesn't sound like she'll be a problem either. Phew, I think as I hang up. Dick smiles smugly.

My conversation with Dawn is definitely interesting but kind of confusing. She has a provocative voice that spouts nonsense. When I tell her who I am she responds with, "No shit. It is what it is." When I give her the good news that unit #2 is all hers, she says, "No shit. Karma's a bitch," and when I ask her if she's changed her mind, she says, "Well, aren't you a hottie!" When I ask if there's someone else there with her that I might talk to, she says, "Not my circus, not my monkeys. Have a nice day." I'm ready to hang up, draw another random name from the paper bag when Dick interrupts, reminding me about Dawn's jargon aphasia. Right. Now I get it. Patience required. And that thing called respect.

I ask her if she's sure she wants the place. She replies with, "Please and thank you," which is a pretty straight answer. So I maneuver cautiously into my spiel about moving in on the thirty-first and papers to sign and she interrupts me several times, excitedly even, but with the same banalities in random order. I say goodbye and she says, "Karma's a bitch! No shit! Have a nice day!"

I hang up wondering if I've heard her entire array of platitudes in one phone call.

Dick and I make post-task eye contact. Our situation is sobering.

"It is totally our circus, Dick."

He looks a bit shell-shocked. "And we are the monkeys."

We burst out laughing, suddenly hysterical. My phone rings. I sit on Dick, pin him down so he can't make me laugh when I answer. It might be Dawn or Dora or even Randy with a question. Hope nobody's changed their mind.

m—

On day minus 9, December 24, John and I do a proud walk and roll-through of unit #1. The interior is impressive—simple, practical and modestly attractive. Jackie's stocked the kitchen with basics and added a few homey touches—new towels are hanging in the shiny tiled bathroom, there are sheets and a quilt on the Murphy bed, a little houseplant on the table.

Later, standing in my doorway, we survey the whole site. Although the units themselves look fabulous—painted olive green with white awnings and trim—there's still a lot to be desired. The driveway and muddy ground need gravel and time to recover, the surrounding decks need to be finished, and I'm determined to rebuild the butterfly garden before spring—before John heads north and I'm left to my own disabled devices.

He's talking about lighting up the burn pile of construction debris when Randy arrives, delivered in an old red pickup. Randy's blue-haired buddy hauls his motorized chair out of the truck box and then retrieves him from the cab and settles him into his chair. Randy's smile lights up the whole day. I motion to them to go ahead.

"The door's open!" I call. "It's all yours!"

Randy waves an envelope. "Got rent!"

"I'll be down in a minute!"

John's ready to step in and help with the rest of Randy's belongings.

I hold him back. "John, wait. Randy gave me an idea the other day." Optimism breeds optimism. "Don't light the fire today, okay?"

"You sure? It'd really clean up the place before everyone gets here. And I won't be around for a few days. Family stuff...Christmas. You want to come over? Mum's turkey dinner maybe?"

"No. Thanks though. Listen, I need a little quiet time..." I know that with the holiday blues running between Xmas and the new year, the phone-sex business will be booming, and I need to be available.

"You okay, Mel? Christmas can be..."

"C'mon," I say, "you know I don't do Xmas." I watch Randy and his chum navigate the mud with enthusiasm. "But I was thinking I'd like to have a little party on New Year's Eve. Just hot dogs...I can afford that with Randy's rent money...and a big bonfire. Char and Glen are on the Island, and you, and Jackie and her Cameron...and the new inmates."

"Yeah, sure Mel. I'll get the boys to level out some space around the burn pile, give it a rake so everybody can get around."

"Not too much gravel, okay? Don't want anyone getting stuck."

"Right."

"Rain in the forecast?"

"Nope. It's supposed to stay cold."

"If we're lucky, it'll freeze. Nice hard surface."

"And, hey, I'll man the fire for you. Set up the barbecue. Sounds kinda nice."

"Nice? You know *me*."

"Okay, fun."

"That sounds better." I reach up from Adele and pull John down for a hug. "A million gazillion thank-yous, my friend. Money soon to follow."

"Sorry about going over budget, Mel."

"I'll sort it out," I say, almost believing it.

"I'm sure you will," John says, and I think he almost believes it, too. "Well, you have a merry—"

"Don't say it!"

"Ho-ho to you, Mel." He squeezes me again and sets me loose.

"Fine. Same," I say. "I want to give Randy some space, but let him *and* his friend know about the fire, eh...5:00 p.m. New Year's Eve. And bring your own booze."

John gives me a thumbs-up and a smile as he walks away. A ridiculous feeling of generosity washes over me.

"And tell your crew! But don't forget it's BYOB!" I call after him. "And tell anybody else you feel like! No, tell everybody!"

17
Coming Together

It's been a relative bonanza of a phone-sex week. Between four new customers and my regulars, I, Ginger, have been pounded, kerponked and boofed. I've also buffed a record seventeen pickles and referred one client to the suicide line.

I turned off my train-whistle ring tone this morning but covered my Ginger-ass by leaving an appropriately husky message on my answering app. "Hello there, darlin'…Ginger speaking. So-o-o sorry I missed you. The Do Not Disturb sign is up tonight, but call me tomorrow for a free ten-minute session. I can't wait! Oh, and Happy Naughty New Year!" There, I've done my sex-positive bit.

Day minus 2 has had only one glitch. A flat tire interrupted my shopping trip with Jackie for the New Year's Eve party, so John had to check in the new tenants, Dora and Dawn. He assured me that it went well. The table is set, so to speak.

n⌣

A few solitary snowflakes are falling from the black winter sky. Sparks fly up to meet them. The container units look cozy and warm. The darkness between their lit windows and the blaze of the fire obscures the mess of frozen mud and unfinished deck and walkways.

I'm warm too, outside and in. I'm appropriately bundled up and wearing my striped mittens to keep Dick from acting out. I don't even need rose-coloured glasses to see everything and everybody in their best light. By everybody I mean the forty or so people clustered around the bright fire for warmth—a few sitting on tailgates attached to pickups, one overflowing with upbeat tunes.

Randy, whose five hot dog-devouring cousins left earlier, is freed up now to ask me, "Is Ginger coming?"

John chimes in, "Yeah, where's this Ginger?"

Jackie and Char look confused and mouth, "Who?"

I don't even have to lie. "Ginger? Haven't seen her."

m⁓

I scoot around and about. There's John and his date; and Char and hubby Glen, looking a little more world-weary but surviving; and Jackie and Cameron, busy with hotdogs and condiments; and John's two-man crew, who are ecstatic and relieved to have received postdated paycheques; and Char's hubby's stepbrother's cousin's ex, who owns the crane-truck company, smiling despite not yet being paid in full. And there's the crane-truck operator and three of the staff from the Build-All Depot, including Char's uncle's golf buddy's son-in-law. There's Bert the lawyer and his twin janitor-brother and some people I don't even know but who seem to know somebody, and if they don't know somebody who knows somebody, it doesn't matter anyway because everybody's happy.

I flit around on my scooter, chatting here and receiving hugs there, riding the wave of positivity. I feel like a bit of a miracle, more hopeful and successful than I have in years. Meanwhile, I keep an eye on the newbies across the flames. To get a feel for the future in our little compound. Randy's so close to the fire that his tires start to smoke a little. Before I call out to warn him, Char and Glen roll him out of harm's way. Dora has talked Dawn into moving back from the heat and flying embers, too. I see or sense the beginning of a good dynamic: the four of us in wheelchairs living well and together, rather than alone. Happy and functioning—with a little help. I'm aware of our obvious physical disparities but our differences make us...interesting.

Randy holds his own, being our only male and the youngest.

Dawn and Dora—the Double Ds—are as different as sparks and snowflakes.

Dawn's attractive in a tough-girl way—her pleasant round face surrounded by soft brown curls under the peak of a Canucks ball cap, her ample breasts pushing out of her half-zipped puffy silver jacket, her tight jeans tucked into worn purple cowboy boots. When she bends forward in her chair to retrieve a gooey toasted marshmallow, I spot her turquoise thong.

She's funny. At least folks think she is. With her limited reper-toire—*No shit. Karma's a bitch. Have a nice day! Not my circus, not my monkeys. Well, aren't you a hottie! It is what it is. Please and thank you!*—she manages to charm people and/or confuse them into laughter. Everybody likes her, which makes me a bit suspicious, but I can over-look that for tonight at least. And, unlike Dora or Randy, Dawn smokes, which makes us minority allies.

Dora, on the other hand, is built like a squat bear, ugly as sin, badly put together, heavily made up and nervous—which makes most people steer clear. I make an effort but it's hard to see past the poufy blond hairdo—is it real? Is that glitter?—to look her in the eye. She keeps her head down mostly, avoids my eyes anyway, which also makes me suspicious.

I need a closer reading on these two, so I join them.

"So what do you think?" I ask, after scooting up between them and faux-staring into the fire for a small eternity. "About the place... about living here..."

"Oh, it could be worse," Dora replies, just as Randy rolls in next to Dawn, who sounds nonplussed—"It is what it is"—but she's smiling ear to ear, especially at Randy.

"All...good!" he sings.

What a crew! I feel empathy for each of them, but I don't want to feel more for one over the other. Or more for them than me.

Dick seems partial to Dora, on my left, because, despite the mit-ten, he keeps patting her paralyzed right hand and eventually just holds it. I have a freaky realization sitting like this—that Dora's good left side plus my good right side would make a whole able-bodied person. Or, at least, an entity capable of able-bodied accomplishments.

I grab the bottle of Fireball between my feet, asking Dora, "Would you mind opening this?"

She doesn't hesitate, unscrewing the lid while I grasp the bot-tle. Simple mission accomplished. This bodes well for cooperation. Especially as she doesn't seem to mind Dick holding her lifeless hand. Nor does she mind taking the bottle for a stiff swig. She's hanging on to it.

My right hand wrestles the bottle from Dora's left. She's strong. I offer it to Dawn. "Like some?"

Dawn jiggles her erupting breasts, grins at Randy and, ignoring my question, exclaims to him, "Aren't you a hottie!" She pops a marshmallow into his mouth, causing him to splutter, blush and jerk furiously.

Good grief. I hadn't taken tenant attractions into consideration.

The four of us look into the mesmerizing fire like it'll reveal something crucial to each of us. I think back over the last couple of years. It's been quite the herky-jerky ride. I'm way past ready for some smooth sailing.

I'm starting to stiffen up from both the chill and the lack of movement. My sociability hat's slipping, and I just wish everybody would go home. But first I have to make my speech. John and Randy help get everyone's attention. Somebody mutes the music.

"Well," I begin, letting the word hang in the air. "You folks...have been *ab-so-lute-ly* amazing! I don't know where to begin, how to thank you...aside from settling up accounts...all accounts, every penny!"

This gets some laughs and clapping and woo-hoos.

"So I'll just say a massive heartfelt thank-you to each and every one of you. Especially you, John...and Jackie, over there...and Char, even though you were freezing your butt off in Winterpeg. Thank you for your patience, your hard work, and for believing in this project! For seeing my vision from its weird beginning through to completion. You kept me going." I hear some aws. "There's also a very special person...who can't be here today..." This is harder than I thought...I have to blink back tears. "A person who gave me the beginning of this new home. His name was Leo Moss—a kind, funny, practical, incredibly generous guy—who had a way of seeing things differently. A guy who would appreciate what we've built here. It's a beautiful thing, these compact, accessible, totally cool homes for the four of us." I gesture to Randy, Dora and Dawn before wiping my eyes. "Okay, enough speechifying. Thank you, everybody! And thank you, Leo, most of all!"

John interrupts the clapping and hoots. "We have a little something for you, Mel. The boys put it together."

They carry a big tarp-covered object from the darkness into the firelight. It must be six feet across—big as a door. The boys are sweetly embarrassed, one explaining apologetically that they didn't have time to finish it properly. The other says he's just learning to weld.

"Ohhh," I exclaim, curious. "What is it?"

They draw off the tarp, unveiling a heavy wrought-iron sign. I see why they're both proud and embarrassed. It's a really big sign.

I scoot over—amid heartfelt clapping and shoulder slapping—to have a closer look. I could almost cry...again.

Everyone seems to have taken this as a cue to pack up and bid adieu. Char and her hubby say their goodbyes. Jackie makes a final trip to my unit with the last of the food. John and Cam throw the last scraps of wood on the fire. Jackie asks, as an afterthought, if any of *us* need help. Randy, Dawn, Dora and I all communicate "no" in one way or another. We each ride the fine line of ease versus independence but seem emboldened by our gimp fellowship. Dora says good night and wheels off to her new home. I holler more thank-yous and we wave to the departing vehicles before Randy and Dawn tootle off toward their units.

ᴍ⁓

Suddenly there's a gunshot blast. I mean *kaboom*! Windows rattling. There's an acrid smell. Smoke?

"The old...lady!" Randy yells, heading fearlessly for Dora's #4, where an orange glow lights up her window.

"Not my circus, not my monkeys!" shouts Dawn, in contradiction to her hot pursuit.

"Oh shit, oh shit, oh shit," I mutter, trying not to spastically plank from fear and dread. "Nine one one!" I call out as I fumble for the phone, and they disappear into Dora's unit. I want to disappear too, like, to another planet, but I'm fucking responsible! And my phone...my phone is fucking dead! All I can do is follow, trying to cram my scooter into the already crowded narrow unit amid a drift of smoke and whirling glitter and a curtain-fed lick of flame.

"Extinguisher!" Dawn commands.

Dawn? Commands? Questions later.

I'm the closest to the fire extinguisher near the front door. I manage to haul that heavy mother out of its harness with my one good hand and pass it forward to Dawn.

"Let 'er...rip!" Randy screams. "Hurry!"

Dawn pulls the safety pin on the extinguisher. She aims it wobbly and vaguely toward the flame.

Whitish powder shoots everywhere. Mostly onto Randy. Luckily, it reaches the burning curtain, too. Then envelops us all in a floury cloud.

"Fuck," says Randy, once the flame's died out.

"Dawn, enough! Shut it off!" I yell, pulling my scarf up over half my face.

"No shit!" says Dawn, between coughs.

"Where's Dora?" I sputter as the powder swirls and settles. Her wheelchair sits empty in the corner.

"Here," says Randy, reaching down from his chair to shake something. It's Dora, lying on the floor.

"Is she alive?" I ask, trying to crane my head around Dawn to see Dora's condition for myself.

"It is what it is," says Dawn, complacently, as she attempts to wave away the dust cloud.

I want to slap Dawn into next year. "Which is what?" I scream at the back of her head.

"Calm...down," Randy stutters. "Look."

Dora's tattered suitcase lies smoking—under a layer of white—near the baseboard heater. There's a mangled hairspray can embedded in the ceiling above. Randy pulls the suitcase away from the heater and Dawn gives it another good shot from the extinguisher.

A raspy cough erupts from the lump on the floor. I snap back to reality. "We have to call nine one one!"

"Please and thank you," Dawn chimes in.

"Who's got a phone?" I ask. "Mine's dead."

"Karma's a bitch," says Dawn.

Dora's voice rises weakly from below, "Wait!" She attempts to sit up. "Let's not," she wheezes, "and say we did."

Dawn and I cram our wheelies in tighter. I can't get close enough to assist, but I'm compelled to give advice—higher, lower, on the right, no, the left, under, not over! Dora is finally sitting upright, but despite Randy's efforts and a great deal of grunting, she can't get up into her chair.

"You're all right though?" I ask her. What's left of her glittery wig is askew above her smudged face, but her winter clothing is mostly intact.

She looks stunned but responds. "I've been better but I've also been worse."

We breathe a collective sigh of relief before Dora is overcome by a fit of coughing.

"We have to get you out of here," Randy points out, waving his hand through the acrid glittery air. "We need help."

"No, no, please...I'll be fine. I feel so foolish," Dora says. "And, to be honest, I'd rather not involve the authorities. And, Miss Melanie, you might prefer that too."

I consider the implications for my unlicensed facility. I consider dragging John or Jackie out of bed. *Do not call Jackie. Think, Mel, think!* "We'll take her to my place."

"How?" Randy asks.

"No shit," adds Dawn.

"You'll see." If Jackie could move me, then we can move Dora. "Think furniture moving. Grab that blanket, Randy. Now double it."

We attempt to organize ourselves in the small space in order to tow her out.

I send Dawn ahead to open my door and instruct Randy to roll Dora onto the blanket and to put his chair into neutral so that I can back out, pulling him along with my scooter power while he has both hands free to grasp the blanket-caboose. It takes a fair bit of adjusting and modification—like tying Randy into his chair for added leverage.

It's not pretty, but eventually it works. Dora whimpers a bit when we drag her through a pothole and then through my door. She's in! Being the reverse engine, I have to back right into the bathroom to get her into position by the bed. With Randy's help and my experienced tutelage, Dora grasps the taut sheet to hoist herself—one-handed—up onto the bed and finally into a sitting position. We're all winded and hot and bothered. We look like a bunch of ghouls, pale and dusty.

"Are you sure you're okay?" I ask, unbuttoning Dora's coat and peeling it off.

Dawn bamboozles Dora's chair in and manages to get her a cool glass of water. But when she attempts to straighten her wig, Dora waves her away. She says, "Better now, thank you," after catching her breath.

We all have questions, I'm sure, and admonitions and warnings. But later for all that.

"I don't want any trouble, Miss Melanie," Dora says.

That "Miss Melanie" triggers a sad sweet flashback. I shake it off. "Neither do I. So it only makes sense for you to stay here with me, Dora."

She shakes her head. "No. No, I can't..."

"Of course you can. It's no trouble."

"Just until we get your place cleaned up. It'll be okay," I reassure her. "It'll be fine."

"Okay then," Randy declares, with a sigh of relief. Dawn nods enthusiastically in agreement.

"Thanks, you two," I tell them. "You were great. Now get some sleep. We'll sort it out tomorrow."

They don't hesitate. Dawn calls, "Have a nice day!" as they roll out the door.

When I turn back to Dora, she has her right hand over her face.

"Dora, it's okay. You've had a shock. Let's get you to bed. I'll just find you something to wear."

"No, I'll just stay in my chair," she sobs. "My clothes are fine. Until tomorrow."

"Don't be silly. It's a big bed, and I'm sure I have a T-shirt or something you can wear."

"No! Just no!"

I ignore her protests, dig through a drawer for my Hawaiian GET LEID T-shirt. I smile, tossing her the shirt. "C'mon. It's two in the morning, and I'm exhausted. You must be too. I don't bite, you know."

My smile is wasted. She goes from sad upset sniffing to mad sniffing. Transferring to her chair, she motors into the bathroom.

"Clean towels on your right," I tell her before she closes the sliding door. "Anything else you need, just..."

Maybe she's shy about her body or maybe it's about her body's new defects. I listen to her putter around in there for half an hour. When I get tired of waiting, I change, turn down the lights and slide under the covers, keeping my back to the centre, making sure I take up less than half the bed. I ask if she's okay.

"Fine," she says through the wall.

"Okay. Goodnight then."

She mumbles something. I don't even care enough to ask what. Gawd, I'm tired. Dick must be too. He's been clenched and silent in his striped mitten. What a day, what a year, what a life.

Much later, I feel her weight on the bed. She gets in, turns away. Then neither of us moves a muscle.

🙥

Morning is a bit of a shock—that stranger-snoring-in-your-bed surprise until the brain sorts it out for you. I turn to check, to see if last night's fiasco really happened. Dora's wiggy head rests on the pillow.

I prepare to sneak out of bed to go quietly about my business while Dora snores. But the snoring abruptly stops. So does the breathing. I nudge her. Nothing. I shake her. Nothing. "Dora?" Nothing. I pull her over onto her back. "You're not fucking dying before you move in, Dora!" I push away the covers so I can get at her chest. Poor thing, there's a bruise on her chest, just below her collarbone. Her breathing quietly resumes— phew! I pull the neck of the T-shirt down to see the mark better.

"What the..." It's all I can say.

Her eyes fly open as she lurches to sitting, clutching the T-shirt to cover herself.

Dick has a sudden fit, shaking his mitten right off. He nudges the covers up to Dora's chin but it's too late.

I know what I saw, but I can't wrap my head around it—the tip of a tattoo. A tattoo of a butterfly wing. Dora sits stock-still when I move Dick out of the way to look further. It's a swallowtail, its defining spots staring back at me.

Dick backs away as I remove the sad blond wig. There's a terrible silence.

I breathe life into his name: "Leo." My heart fills with hope but also a terrible confusion.

"I can explain," wigless Dora/Leo says.

"Listen," Dick whispers in my ear.

"What the fuck, Leo? You're not *dead*? You were *never* dead?"

"Almost dead," whispers Dick.

"I don't know where to start," says Leo.

"How about at the beginning!"

Dick positions himself against Leo's tattoo, facing me. "Be friends," he tells me. "Everybody just be—"

"Friends?" I say. His guilty little eyes get bigger and rounder. "You two are friends?"

Leo's clearly confused.

"He can't hear me!" Dick explains. "It was just emails."

I grab Dick ready to throttle him. "You little shit! It was a conspiracy! You set me up!"

Leo recoils.

"Not at the beginning," Dick splutters, darting in next to my ear. "It started out as a rescue! Then it just kind of spiralled..."

"Mel, please," Leo begs, oblivious to Dick. "Just..."

"Listen. Listen to Leo. He doesn't want much."

Looking Leo straight in the eye, I realize what this means. "This is all yours."

Leo tries to hold my hand. "Melanie, no. No, it's yours. It has to stay yours. Leo is dead. Legally dead. And he has to stay that way."

I refuse to listen. "I'll stay at Jackie's tonight," I say, trying to head for the door, but Leo won't let go of Dick. "You must think I'm the stupidest cripple around. That you could just manipulate me! And not even just me but the other two out there, Randy Paul and Dawn!"

"Whoa!" says Leo and he gestures to his own wheelchair. "I'm in the same boat." He keeps his voice steady. "Will you let me explain?"

"It better be good."

"Oh, it's good," whispers Dick.

So I give in, finally, and listen. And quite a story it is. A long complicated story that I'm supposed to keep mum about until one or the other of us dies. A story that involves a man chasing rare South American butterflies, a man being in the wrong place at the wrong time with the wrong million-and-a-half-dollar suitcase, a nightmare bus getaway that ended in loss of life for twenty-seven other passengers, and waking up to the renewed terror of being found—now half-paralyzed—in a Bolivian hospital. Lucky he was resourceful! He survived! The man—feigning memory loss—stole clothing, the wig and wheelchair before vanishing from the hospital and acquiring a new identity and documentation in the La Paz market. Some Dick guy made the final arrangements to get the man back to Canada, and to find a safe place to live as the new Dora Tipplee...like a safe place with some disabled chick that you trust and that you left money to even though she's already spent it...but in a good way.

Like I said, it's complicated. A lot to take in. But I don't have a lot of choice. I mean Leo gave me his all, his everything and all he needs now is a safe and decent place to live. This place. I don't expect to ever forgive Leo for dying...and then not dying.

"Buck up or fuck up," I tell myself, worried about so many more things—different things—than when I got up this morning.

Leo slips the wig back on. "None of us can really go it alone. Remember that the key to life—"

"I know, I know. It's wanting what you have, not having what you want."

Acknowledgements

Imagine the following with all the hearts and exclamation points!

Thank you, Canada Council for the Arts, for your existence and your funding assistance with this book.

Much gratitude once again to publisher Vici Johnstone of Caitlin Press, repeat editor Meg Taylor and publicist Michael Despotovic.

Massive thank-yous to longtime mentor Betty Keller, as well as Kathy Page, Marilyn Bowering, Rebecca Hendry, Erin Whalen, Diane Foley, Richard Till and James Ingram.

Sara McIntyre, thank you so much for stimulating conversations and inspiration.

Darryl Knowles, did I ever tell you? You deserve the biggest thank-yous for being you, for accepting me being me, for making me laugh, for being my legs and for doing more than your share of the heavy lifting.

Family and friends who have (sometimes unknowingly) helped along the way, thank you.

Gratitude in memorium to Ellen Frank and Donna DeLorme, two MSers who chose medically-assisted dying.

The non-fiction excerpt from chapter two, "Chicken in Mourning", was published in *Body Breakdowns: Tales of Illness and Recovery*, edited by Janis Harper, Anvil Press, 2007, and republished in the short story collection *Attemptations*, Caitlin Press, 2011.

A One-Handed Novel is based on a short story called, "Six Degrees of Altered Sensation", originally published in *Attemptations*, Caitlin Press, 2011.

PHOTO CHRIS HANCOCK DONALDSON

Kim Clark is an author, poet and playwright, and gimp who lives in Nanaimo, BC. Clark has published short fiction: *Attemptations*, Caitlin Press, 2011 and poetry: *Middle Child of Summer*, Leaf Press, 2013, *Sit You Waiting*, Caitlin Press, 2012, and *Dis ease and De sire, The M anu s cript*, Lipstick Press, 2011, as well as co-editing the red-head anthology, *Canadian Ginger*, Oolichan Books, 2017. She's also been a finalist in Theatre BC's Playwriting Competition and has a novella under option for a feature-length film. Kim is currently working on a sequel to *A One-Handed Novel*.